Seducing
the Moon

Seducing the Moon

SHERRILL QUINN

BRAVA

KENSINGTON PUBLISHING CORP.
www.kensingtonbooks.com

Prologue

Declan O'Connell paused next to a large tree. Bending slightly, he braced himself with one palm on the rough bark and tried to catch his breath. He'd been at a full-out run for half an hour, testing the limits of his new metabolism.

His new *werewolf* metabolism.

In seconds his breathing was back to normal. He straightened. At times it hardly seemed possible that it had been four months since he'd been bitten, since his life had been turned upside down. Other times it seemed like he'd been this way all his life.

He didn't know why his friend Ryder kicked up such a fuss about it. Ryder Merrick had been a werewolf for nearly twenty years now. He'd been adamant that Declan learn how to control the beast within, stressing that the urge to shift could come upon him quite unexpectedly, especially at times of high emotion.

Declan frowned. He hadn't been so sure about that when Ryder had first said it, and he wasn't so sure about it now. He'd always been able to keep a cap on his emotions, especially during crises. Even with only having lived with this—

condition for four months—he'd been able to control when he shifted. But he hadn't been able to stop the shift part-way, becoming something not quite wolf but not fully man, either.

Ryder, as someone who had become a werewolf due to his bloodlines, was incapable of becoming a wolfman. When he shifted, he went from human to wolf almost faster than the eye could follow.

Declan, being a werewolf through the bite of another, would eventually be able to turn into a wolfman, though he hadn't yet mastered the ability.

Concentrating, he stared at his right hand and tried to make just his hand morph into that of a wolfman. His finger-tips tingled, sharp pain throbbed in the joints as if with the onset of arthritis, but nothing else happened.

At least, nothing worth much—his nails darkened and, perhaps, looked a little longer, but his hands were still human looking.

So, no luck with a partial shift.

Yet.

He knew with enough determination he would eventually figure it out. It would just take more practice.

He was certain he had achieved the restraint needed to control the shift to his wolf form. Except for the three nights of the full moon. During those nights it was impossible to resist the metamorphosis into wolf, and equally impossible to shift back to human until the morning sun forced the moon to give up its hold in the heavens.

He glanced up at the robin's egg blue sky. Toward the east he could see the half moon, clearly visible in daylight. Just one more week until the full moon. . . .

He could hear the lap of the ocean and jogged down the path, leaving the wooded area and venturing onto the rocky shore. He focused his attention westward and, with the enhanced vision of his inner wolf, could make out the larger island of St. Mary's in the distance.

St. Mary's, the biggest island in the Isles of Scilly off the coast of Cornwall. St. Mary's, where Pelicia was.

Where his heart was.

It was time to go get it back and claim his mate.

Pelicia wouldn't know what hit her.

Chapter 1

"**O**'Connell, you had better be all right, because if you've broken your worthless neck on my property I'm bloody well going to kill you."

Declan raised his head from the steering wheel, rubbing the sore spot on his forehead where he'd connected with the unforgiving plastic. Already he could feel the slight bump caused by the impact was lessening. Being a werewolf did have its advantages. And from what he'd experienced in the last four months, not that many disadvantages.

He focused on the woman stomping toward him. The deep red T-shirt she wore set off her creamy skin to perfection, and her jeans hugged curves that he hadn't touched in much, much too long. The morning sunlight glinted on her honey blond hair and reflected off the anger glittering in her ocean-blue eyes.

Stripping off her gardening gloves, Pelicia Cobb stopped beside his vehicle and looked at the corner of the historic bed and breakfast that had seconds before become an unplanned hood ornament on Declan's rental car. "Oh, my God. Look what you've done!" She planted her hands on her hips and glared at him. "Where did you get a car?"

"They've set up a small 'cars for hire' booth near the ferry office, darlin', you know that," he said through the open window.

"Like we need more cars on our tiny stretch of roadways." Her scowl deepened. "And don't call me darlin'. I got over that charming Irish brogue a long time ago." Her gaze went back to the corner of the house. Something like a growl came from her throat. When she looked at him again, her eyes were hard with anger. "Just when exactly did your mission in life become one of making *my* life a bloody impossible mess? Tourist season just got underway and now you've demolished my house."

Thinking to tell her she was overreacting—as a former commando and demolitions expert in the Royal Marines he damned well knew how to properly destroy something, and this wasn't anywhere near what he *could* have done— he opened his mouth to respond.

She forestalled him with a sharp downward slash of one slender hand. "Never mind," she growled. "I already know the answer. It was two years ago, the last time you deigned to grace me with your presence."

Even with the deep frown on her face, Pelicia was still the most beautiful woman he'd ever seen.

"You'd damned well better have insurance, because I can't afford to fix this." She gestured toward the corner of the granite house where several large blocks were clearly askew. "Even with an occasional guest, it's been a hard off-season, as usual."

"It's not like I did it on purpose," he responded, doing his best not to sound like a teenager making excuses to his mum. Although she certainly was doing a bang-up job of making him feel like he was about fourteen again.

He pushed open the car door. The crumpled metal protested with a loud grinding groan, and he had to exert pressure to get it all the way open. He climbed out from behind the wheel. "Besides, you know I'm not anythin' if not responsible."

Her lips twisted. "Ah. Right. How could I forget? The great Declan O'Connell, commando *extraordinaire*, responsible for eradicating villains from the world one innocent at a time."

Declan gritted his teeth at her sarcasm. Forget fourteen years old. Try five. Though as unfair as her words were, he couldn't fault her for her feelings.

Two years ago, the firm he'd worked for at the time had sent him to London to assist with an investigation into an international document-forging organization—primarily because of his friendship with Pelicia and his knowledge of the Isles of Scilly. In the course of his investigation, he'd been instrumental in getting her arrested. Even though she'd been cleared of all involvement, in the end she'd lost her job and her reputation had suffered. She'd returned to St. Mary's to take over this bed and breakfast after her grandfather—the real talent behind the forgery ring—had been sent to prison.

"Listen, Pel—"

"Oh, forget it." She sighed and crossed her arms.

She looked so fragile and defenseless that he had to fight to keep from pulling her into a comforting embrace. He knew the second he did he'd have a snarling wildcat on his hands that would quickly dissuade him from thinking she was either fragile or defenseless.

"Just give me your insurance information. Then you can contact them and file a claim."

Without a word he pulled out his wallet. He retrieved the card he carried that had his insurance company information on it. Replacing his wallet in the back pocket of his jeans, he asked, "You have paper and pen?"

"Wait here." She turned and started back toward the two-story house.

Declan found himself unable to look away from her pert derrière. God, but she had the most beautiful ass. It had fit him as if it had been specially made for him.

"Stop staring at my bum," Pelicia called without looking around.

"Can't blame a man for admirin' the view, darlin'."

"Oh, yes I bloody well can." She went inside, slamming the door shut behind her.

He sighed and shoved the card into the front pocket of his jeans. She'd used the word "bloody" three times in as many minutes. Other than a "damn" now and then, it was as close as she got to really cursing, and that she had used it so often spoke to her anger with him. It seemed two years had done little to diminish it.

He heaved another sigh and looked at the car. Circling it, he checked for additional damage. Thankfully he hadn't been going that fast when the tire had blown. Otherwise, he'd have done a hell of a lot more damage. Mostly to the car. Pelicia's bed and breakfast, the Nola—named after her maternal grandmother—was one of those three-hundred-year-old granite cottages that could stand up to a lot more than a car barreling into it. Still . . .

Declan assessed the destruction to the stone building. From the outside there didn't appear to be too much structural damage, but he was no expert and couldn't tell what kind of repair might be needed on the inside.

Looking down, he inspected the front of the car, wincing at the thought of what he'd tell the insurance company. Let alone the folks at the rental company. He'd been driving along with no problem and then, all of a sudden, the tire had blown, and he'd lost control of the vehicle. He hadn't had time enough—or room enough—to regain control before he'd slammed into Pelicia's place.

Which was where he'd been headed anyway, giving another go at getting her to talk to him, but this latest wrinkle was *not* going to aid his quest to get back on her good side.

He hunkered down to look at the tire. He had no idea what he'd run over, but it had ruined the tire—damn thing was completely shredded. A glint of metal caught his attention and he reached down. His fingers closed around a small fragment. As he lifted it, his gut tightened. He stared at the flattened metal slug.

It was a bullet, the type fired from a high-powered rifle. *What the hell!*

Still crouched, he twisted around and scanned the surrounding area. If someone had been aiming for him, they'd had plenty of time to take another shot. Hell, another several shots. The sniper had either gotten scared off or . . .

Holy shit. Could he have been aiming for Pelicia? With his heart beating a staccato rhythm against his ribs, Declan got to his feet and gazed over the roof of the car. She'd been kneeling by the flowerbed, bent over pulling weeds, when the shot had been fired. If Declan hadn't driven by when he had . . .

. . . that bullet would have struck her.

He headed toward the house. The front door opened and Pelicia came out onto the small portico. Before she could start down the cobbled pathway, Declan grabbed her by one arm, turned her around, and hustled her back into the house. He pushed the door shut behind them.

"What the . . ." She yanked away from him and scowled.

"What the bloody hell is wrong with you, O'Connell?" She rubbed her arm where he'd gripped her.

He tamped down the annoyance he always felt whenever she referred to him by his last name. He knew she did it to try to keep things more impersonal between them but now wasn't the time to get into it with her. "Sorry." He raked a hand through his hair. "I didn't mean to hurt you. But you need to stay inside."

She blinked. "I need to stay inside," she repeated. Her fine brows lifted. "For any particular length of time? Five minutes, an hour, the rest of my bloody life?" Her lips thinned. "How about if I just cloister myself? That way I wouldn't be any kind of threat to anyone. At all. That should make you happy."

Declan hid a wince. She was angry again. Or still. Probably still. He sighed and scrubbed the back of his neck with his hand. He always seemed to muck it up with Pel when all he wanted to do was to set things right. "My back tire was shot out," he said, twisting around to peek out the window. Nothing seemed out of the ordinary, but then he probably wouldn't be able to see a camouflaged sniper without a scope of his own. Even with his exceptional werewolf vision. He turned to look at Pelicia. "I don't know if someone was taking a shot at me or at you."

"Me? Why on earth would someone be shooting at me?" She propped her hands on her hips.

"You tell me." Declan folded his arms over his chest. "Maybe someone who's upset with your granddad?"

Her face went blank as she shut down on him. He should have known better than to bring it up. But it was a real possibility he couldn't ignore. His emotional comfort—and hers—was secondary to her safety.

"Pel, it's entirely possible—maybe even probable—that

someone's life got majorly screwed up when your grand-dad got caught and sent to prison." When she shot him a glare, he muttered, "Don't look at me like that." *Jaysus.* He was amazed his eyebrows weren't singed.

"He's in prison because of you," she spat out. Her hands fisted. "*I* almost went to prison because of you."

"Your granddad's in prison because he broke the law." Declan reined in his anger with difficulty. He felt guilty enough over what happened without her embellishing the facts and heaping even more blame on him. "And I think you're exaggeratin' a wee bit, darlin'." He let his hands drop to his sides. "You weren't anywhere near bein' sent to prison. You were arrested and released, no charges filed."

He fought back the remorse he felt over the way he'd used her in the investigation. What had started out as a means to get closer to her grandfather had ended up with them falling in love—an emotion she had quickly fallen out of once Declan's perfidy had been discovered.

But once the wheels had been set in motion it had been out of his hands. He'd thought—hoped—that once the dust had settled they could go back to the way things were.

That hadn't happened. Yet. But past experience had taught him that persistence paid off, so he kept pressing on.

A muscle twitched in her jaw. "You are unbelievable." Pelicia shook her head. "Arrogant, patronizing . . ." Al-most to herself she muttered, "I must have been out of my mind, thinking I was in love with you."

A spark of warmth hit his gut at her admission but was quickly extinguished by her use of the past tense. *Was* in love. Not *am* in love.

"Whatever else I am, you know I don't worry without cause. There's somethin' wrong here, Pel. You need to stay inside. Until," he added when she opened her mouth, probably to blast him again, "I check the perimeter and determine it's safe. All right?"

She gave an abrupt nod. "I think you're making an elephant out of a mosquito, but if it'll appease you and get you out of my hair faster, I'll stay inside while you look around."

Damn. Hand him a rifle and tell him to take out an enemy, and he knew what to do, didn't hesitate to carry out the mission. Faced with this hostility, he was flummoxed. He had no idea how to overcome her resistance.

Except through unrelenting perseverance.

When he stood there and stared at her, one slender foot started tapping on the floor and those eyebrows climbed up again. "Anytime you're ready, O'Connell."

Shock and awe, he heard in his head. There was that little devil inside him, pushing him to do something unexpected, something that would push her off-balance. Though it had always driven his sainted mother to distraction, it had yet to lead him wrong. *Shock and awe.*

Declan walked the few steps it took to bring him close to Pelicia and cupped her face in his hands. He stared down into wide blue eyes a few seconds and then slanted his mouth over hers.

He'd meant to be gentle, to take it slow, but when she gasped, her lips parting under his, thoughts of tenderness fled right out of his head. So did all the blood, rushing away to his cock.

Her lips were like silk under his. He deepened the kiss, sliding his tongue into the hot recess of her mouth. Her lashes fluttered then her eyes closed, and she leaned into him slightly, her hands gripping his waist.

Christ, it had been too long. Too long since he'd held her in his arms, since he'd tasted her lips, since he'd slid his cock through the slick cream of her arousal and into her sweet pussy. But going at her like a battering ram wasn't going to aid his cause. He had to slow down or he'd end up pushing her even further away.

He pulled back and rested his forehead against hers. "We have to talk about what happened two years ago," he murmured. Before she could say anything he drew away. "You know we can't keep avoidin' it, darlin'."

Pelicia clamped her lips together and shook her head.

Stubborn little cuss.

Declan stepped back. "Once I make sure it's safe outside, you and I will have that talk, Pel." He walked to the front door and cautiously opened it, peering around the edge. There was no movement other than a couple of tourists dressed in shorts and floppy hats lingering outside the pub a few doors down. He looked over his shoulder and added, "Count on it."

He started to go outside. Remembering he needed to give her his insurance information, he stopped. He pulled the card out of his pocket and held out his hand, the card between two fingers. "Here. Call the insurance company and see if you can't get the ball rollin'. They'll want to talk to me, but tell them I've asked you to give them your particulars."

She walked toward him but stopped far enough away that she had to lean forward and stretch to take the card.

He shook his head. "Coward." He cocked an eyebrow.

A scowl covered her face. "Piss off, O'Connell."

He *tsked* her, knowing even as he did so that it would raise her ire. But treading lightly and trying not to upset her hadn't gotten him anywhere in the last four months. Perhaps getting her a little emotional and slightly off her stride would work in his favor. As she began to sputter some sort of indignant response, he pulled the door open wider. After checking the area, he glanced back at her and muttered, "Stay away from the windows," and went onto the portico, closing the door softly behind him.

Let her stew for a while. If there was one thing that would make Pelicia act contrary, it was telling her she was something that she wasn't. Calling her a coward should make her face her fears—and then, perhaps, him.

Pelicia ignored his damned order—really, no one would be shooting at her, but at stubborn, macho, infuriating Declan Joseph O'Connell? She'd believe *that* in a second. She wrapped her arms around herself and paced by the windows, her gaze fixed on Declan as he prowled around the front garden. The Nola perched on the edge of Hugh Town so there weren't many people moving around nearby. For now, Declan was the only human in her sight.

Watching him as he bent to look at something, she sighed. His jeans pulled taut over the muscles of his ass. He was a sight worth seeing, she couldn't deny that.

She sighed again. What had she been thinking, to let him kiss her like that? After all her posturing, all it took was hearing that sexy Irish brogue of his and one touch of his mouth against hers, and she'd melted like soft butter in a hot skillet.

One kiss and the folds of her pussy were slick and swollen, ready for sex. Her nipples were diamond-hard points that ached. God, she felt like it would take only the briefest, lightest of touches against her pulsing clit for her to splinter in an orgasm.

Declan had always been able to do that to her. Get her revved up in a millisecond, so on fire for him she would do about anything for his touch.

She wouldn't go there again. She *couldn't*. She had loved him with a depth she'd never before experienced, and he had torn her heart out. When she'd discovered that he had gotten close to her, that he'd made love to her as a means to complete his investigation, just as a way to get to her grandfather . . . that had been bad enough.

But when the police had come, handcuffing her in front of her boss, her friends, and hauled her off to jail to be booked and fingerprinted, tossed into a holding cell with prostitutes and drug addicts. . . . Her cheeks burned at the remembered humiliation. In the end it hadn't mattered that she'd been an unwitting dupe, used by her own grandfather to transport forged documents to his clients who stayed as guests at the upscale hotel where she'd worked.

Pictures of her being shoved into the back of a police car had been plastered all over the front pages of the newspapers—legitimate ones and the tabloids as well. When the authorities had finally acknowledged her innocence—after two days behind bars—the damage to her reputation had been done. Senior management at the hotel didn't want any notoriety associated with their good name, so within a matter of hours upon her release from jail she'd found herself released from employment as well.

She'd been made redundant.

She'd not had the emotional energy to fight it. She'd been heartsick at Declan's duplicity—which had somehow seemed so much worse than the betrayal by her grandfather. For the first few days following her release from jail and the termination from her job, she'd lain in bed and slept. And cried. Slept some more and cried some more.

Eventually her growling tummy had roused her, and she'd realized that she had to find work—she didn't have the financial wherewithal to lie around feeling sorry for herself.

And so in the two months following her redundancy she'd tried to find work at other hotels but had hardly been able to secure any interviews. When she had, they'd gotten one look at her infamous face, conducted what was obviously a five-minute courtesy interview, and let her leave with a polite "We'll be in touch."

None of them ever had gotten "in touch" with her. Without a job she couldn't afford her London flat. And without a place to stay—it was amazing how many of her so-called friends couldn't afford to put her up on their sofa for a while—she couldn't continue to look for work in the city.

She could have asked her father for help, or even his employer, Ryder Merrick, who owned a private island here in the Isles of Scilly. But she hadn't wanted her dad to know how completely suckered in she'd been by Declan, how devastated she'd been by his betrayal. And she'd felt the need to hole up by herself and try to come to terms with what had happened.

But of course William Cobb had seen through her forced gaiety right away, and the story had come tumbling out. She'd never seen her father so angry, so ready to do battle.

A smile flitted across her lips. Her father stood barely five and a half feet tall, but he'd have taken on Declan in a heartbeat. She hadn't wanted anything more to do with the man—her bruised and battered heart couldn't take it—so she'd told her dad to drop it.

Now here she was, home on St. Mary's, the largest of the Isles of Scilly, running her grandfather's bed and breakfast. She did know the hotel business, after all, and with her grandfather in prison the Nola would otherwise be sitting empty. Thankfully the scandal in London was far enough removed from the Isles of Scilly that tourists had no idea about her past. And the locals—most of them, anyway—didn't care, though there were a few who looked at her as if she had some sort of contagious disease.

To them she smiled and waved, following something her clever dad had drilled into her from the time she'd been little—be kind to your friends and even kinder to your enemies.

For it will drive them insane.

She sighed. It had been hard work, getting the Nola ready for business. And lonely. She had a few friends still on the island, but most of them were gone—it was much easier to establish a career off-island. Most young people found that here on the islands they could have steady low-wage jobs that barely put food on the table. Establishing careers they could put their hearts and souls into was pretty much unheard of.

Which was what had sent Pelicia to London to begin with. Now here she was, back on the island, full circle. This was her second season to run the bed and breakfast. She tried to stay optimistic, but last season hadn't gone so well. She'd had to tap into some of what remained of her savings just to put food on the table for her guests and pay the utilities. By the end of this season she had to be operating in the black or she wasn't sure she could open up for guests next year.

Luckily over the last two years she'd had a sporadic guest year-round—a photojournalist who was working on a coffee table book and preferred taking his pictures without a lot of tourists getting in the way. Neal White had insisted on paying her the full rate throughout the year instead of the off-season rate she had offered, and with the state of her current finances she hadn't been able to decline his generosity.

He would book a week or two at a time and then be

gone for three months or so—working to support his project, she supposed. He'd just checked in for another two-week stay yesterday, plus she had another man who had arrived just this morning. She stopped pacing and stared out at the car still jammed into the corner of her house. It was a good thing both of them were out now, or they'd have had as big a surprise as she when the car had hit.

She'd thought the entire building was coming down.

It was the same feeling she'd had just now when Declan kissed her.

Aaaargh! Enough already. Pelicia started pacing again. Four months ago Declan had approached her, wanting to talk about what had happened between them, and she'd had the strength to ignore him then, to turn the other way before he'd had a chance to get close enough to touch her. Why hadn't she done that this time?

"Because he ran a bloody car into your house, you bloody idiot," she muttered. She'd been so shocked, so disbelieving that she'd been thrown off balance.

She chewed on her thumbnail as she continued to stride back and forth in front of the windows. Absently she noticed that the sky had clouded over and was getting darker by the minute. She huffed a sigh.

Now even the weather suited her mood.

She couldn't believe she'd let him kiss her. That could never happen again. She might still have feelings for the man—she really couldn't deny it—but that didn't mean she trusted him.

The front door opened, and she whirled to face her sexy bogeyman.

Declan closed the door behind him. "It seems clear outside." His lips tightened. "I thought I told you to stay away from the windows."

"They weren't shooting at me."

His gaze snagged hers, holding it for several seconds before she looked away. He sighed and said, "Well, no one took any pot shots at me, and I couldn't see where anyone was hiding."

"Well, then, I guess you can be on your way." Pelicia hurriedly scribbled down the phone number of his insurance company and then put the card on a small telephone stand near the door. "There you go."

"It still doesn't mean you're safe." He frowned. "We need to call the police."

Her eyes widened. "No!" God, that was all she needed—the local constable poking around, his vehicle and its flashing lights outside her bed and breakfast, driving away any additional tourists who might be thinking to stay at the Nola. Or scaring off the two guests she *did* have. "I can't afford that kind of publicity." Not again. Never again. She shook her head. "Besides, no one was shooting at *me*," she said again. "I'm a nobody."

His frown deepened. "No, you're not, darlin'. You're certainly somebody to me."

And just that quickly her anger and hurt returned. Declan had ruined her past and now here he was, crashing his car into her remaining source of livelihood, trying to destroy her future as well.

She had no problem looking into his eyes now, and she did so with a glare. Her heart pounded fast and hard in her throat, making it difficult to speak. "And just how am I 'somebody' to you, O'Connell? Somebody you can use? Somebody you can betray?" She clenched her fists to keep him from seeing how badly her hands shook.

"Goddamnit!" Declan raked one big hand through his

dark hair and returned her glower, shifting his stance so that the sunlight from the window lit his face.

For just a second she thought she saw his eyes lighten, but when she looked closer they were the same deep brown they'd always been. It must have been a trick of the light shining in his eyes that had given them that amber glow.

"If you'd just let me explain—"

"Explain what?" Pelicia threw up her hands. "Fine. Enlighten me as to how you thought seducing me, making me fall in love with you—having sex with me—was the best way you had to get close to my grandfather." Her eyes burned with tears she refused to shed. She was bloody well done with crying because of him. "Well? Go on. Explain it to me."

His jaw clamped down, a look of frustration spreading over his face.

She raised her eyebrows in an exaggerated lift, waiting for him. When he didn't say anything, she muttered, "Oh, just go away, O'Connell. You've done enough damage for one day. For an entire lifetime." Without waiting for his response, she turned and went down the hallway to the kitchen, closing the door behind her.

She collapsed on a chair and propped her elbows on the small country-style table, resting her forehead against her fists. God, dealing with him was exhausting. She wanted to curl up and sleep. At least then she wouldn't have to think. Wouldn't have to remember.

Remember what his callused hands felt like against her skin. Remember the look of love in his eyes, the same love she'd felt for him. Remember the horribly blank look on his face—such an utter lack of expression she'd gone cold—when the police put her in handcuffs and read her her rights.

"It's over," Pelicia whispered and made herself get up. She went to the counter. She filled her copper teakettle with water and placed it on the hot plate. As she flipped the on switch, she sniffed back threatening tears. She'd done all the crying she was going to do over him. It was over, and she'd do well enough to get on with her life.

No matter how much Declan O'Connell tried to derail it.

Chapter 2

Declan stared at the closed kitchen door, fighting the urge to follow Pelicia and make her talk to him. But he knew he'd only upset her more, and they'd get nowhere. So instead he turned and left the Nola, closing the door behind him. Thrusting his hands into his pockets, he stared up the street, trying to determine from where the shot had come. His eyes lit on a small knoll roughly eight hundred feet to the north that he'd noticed earlier.

An ideal spot for a sniper to lie in wait. He started up the street, keeping to the side to let vehicles and giggling tourists pass. Even though St. Mary's was the largest of the Isles of Scilly, it was still a tiny island with only ten miles of roadway.

Ten miles of roads with about sixty times that many vehicles. He grinned. People back in Arizona thought having the winter visitors made traffic a nightmare—they should come here when tourist season was in full swing.

As he made his way up the incline, a steady rain began to fall. He paused, tilting his face up, letting the cool water hit his skin. Then realization dawned, and he muttered a curse.

The rain would wash away any scents and possibly evidence as well. He jogged the rest of the way up and crouched at an area where the grass was matted down. With his sensitive sense of smell he tried to filter through the various odors but the rain blurred the scents until the only thing he could smell was wet dirt.

But, wait . . . There was something more, something out of place. He drew in a deep breath and held it, trying to pick out the faint smell that was fading even as he tried to categorize it.

Gunpowder.

As he'd suspected, this was the spot from which the sniper had fired.

Looking down toward the Nola, Declan's eyes burned.

The bastard. If he came near Pelicia again, he was a dead man. Even as he watched, he saw her hurrying toward the house, an umbrella protecting her from the rain but not hiding her blond hair from his sight.

He swore and got to his feet. She must have snuck out when his back was turned. By God, he was going to paddle her sweet bottom. What the hell was she doing out of the house?

Another woman stopped her, her head and shoulders hidden from his view by the large umbrella she carried. Her legs were bare beneath the thigh-length skirt she wore. He focused, his enhanced vision zeroing in on a tattoo on her left ankle—a red heart surrounded by thorns.

Interesting.

Before he could take more than a few steps, Pelicia moved away from the woman and went the last few feet up to the Nola. She stepped onto the small portico and collapsed the umbrella, propping it against the house beside the front door. As she did so, she partially turned her head, giving him a better view of her face.

His muscles eased. It wasn't Pelicia—it was her friend Brenna Brown. And when Brenna Brown came for a visit, it lasted for hours. That made him feel better—at least Pelicia wouldn't be alone. When the front door opened and Brenna went inside, he turned his attention back to the task at hand.

He palmed through the tamped down grass until something smooth hit his skin. He stopped and rooted it out of the wet grass. A spent shell casing. He brought it to his nose and sniffed, but the overriding scent was gunpowder. No human odor remained for him to suss out the identity of the sniper.

Straightening, he pocketed the casing and looked again toward Pelicia's bed and breakfast. The car had been towed away, and her place looked worse than it had with the car hiding the damage. A few rather sizable chunks of granite rested on the ground and those that remained intact in the building remained slightly skewed.

Since Brenna was there, he'd go back to Phelan's Keep—the private island his friend Ryder Merrick's family had owned for generations—and gather his things. Then he'd come back and sit a stakeout on the Nola to make sure Pelicia stayed safe.

After he made a call. It was time to get the police involved—and not the locals. No, he'd call his good friend DCI Rory Sullivan and see if he could interest the other man in an early vacation.

An hour later, Declan slouched on the leather sofa in the study of Ryder's house. It seemed odd that such a short amount of time had passed since he'd come here with a friend, seeking Ryder's help, and Declan had been bitten by a werewolf for his troubles.

On the other hand, four months sometimes felt like a lifetime. Four months of learning what being a werewolf was all about. Four months of Pelicia avoiding him.

Four months of fighting back a sense of hopelessness that he'd never be able to win her back.

"She hates me." Resting his head against the plump back of the couch, he stared at the floor-to-ceiling bookshelves across the room. Reference books mostly, though one shelf was dedicated to Ryder's published books. Declan briefly closed his eyes on a sigh. He was no closer to mending things with Pelicia than he'd been months ago when he'd made his first attempt to see her.

Since then he'd been concentrating on learning just what being a werewolf involved. For one thing, he had an even greater appetite for red meat—the rarer, the better, though whatever he ate seemed to taste better now. His taste buds had grown more acute in sensing the differences between sweet and bitter, smooth and tart. His gut tightened.

God, he wondered what Pelicia's sweet pussy would taste like. He couldn't wait to get between her thighs and drive her to distraction with lips and tongue. His cock jumped in agreement, and Declan shifted on the sofa, trying to make his suddenly too-tight jeans a bit more comfortable.

"So, what're you saying?" Ryder asked, drawing Declan's attention back to the conversation.

"Everythin' I try to do just makes it worse." Declan looked over in time to see the smirk on his friend's face.

"Oh, so I presume barreling into the corner of her house was supposed to be a good thing? Hmm. I wonder why she didn't see it that way?" Ryder swiveled back and forth in the chair behind his massive desk and raised one dark eyebrow.

Declan raised a lone finger in return.

Ryder grinned and leaned forward, resting his elbows on the desk. His cobalt blue eyes twinkled with merriment that hadn't been there when Declan had first arrived all those months ago. "You should be so lucky," Ryder said. "But I don't swing that way." Sobering, he added, "You knew it wasn't going to be easy, Declan. And it's much more complicated now that you're . . ." He trailed off with a shrug.

Declan sighed. "Now that my ass turns furry once a month?" He rolled his head against the back of the sofa. "Maybe she wouldn't have to know," he muttered almost to himself. "I could always take a business trip at the time of the full moon."

Even as he said it he knew it would never work. First, because Pelicia wasn't that dense and, second, because he couldn't build a life with her based upon a foundation of deceit.

Ryder snorted. "And you think Pelicia would settle for that? Or that she wouldn't eventually start adding things up? She's not stupid." He tapped two fingers on his desk. "She *did* spend a lot of time here on the Keep when she was young, so she knows all about werewolves. She'd recognize the signs—eventually. She might not be looking for them at first, but she's not slow by any means." He leaned back in his chair and crossed one leg over the other. "Anyway, dishonesty is what got you into this mess to begin with, my friend. Remember? Failure to give full disclosure will only impede your mission."

"You sound like my old commander." Declan shot to

his feet and began to pace from the sofa to the bookshelves and back again. He sent a scowl his friend's way. "Anyway, it's not a mission."

It was his *life*.

"No?" Ryder lifted his eyebrows. "Seems to me that's the way you've approached it. Target acquired. Damn the torpedoes and full steam ahead." He rocked back in his chair.

His serious gaze made Declan squirm just a bit.

"Or is that 'damn the consequences'?" Ryder went on, his tone musing.

Declan stood still. Ryder was wrong. Wasn't he? Declan stared with unseeing eyes at the rows of books in front of him. What would happen if he did tell Pelicia what had transpired four months ago? Just because she knew about werewolves didn't necessarily mean she *liked* them. It sure as hell didn't mean she wanted one as a lover. Though he'd never heard her speak ill of Ryder or his family, she and Declan hadn't really talked about them. It might simply be that the subject had never come up.

He frowned. They hadn't really done a lot of talking about anything, really. Other than what he needed to learn about her grandfather and the goings on at the hotel, he'd been too busy loving her to waste time in speech.

It wasn't in his nature to share information that wasn't on a need-to-know basis. It was part of who he was, beyond his Special Ops training. And as far as he was concerned, Pelicia—at this particular moment—didn't need to know he was much more of a monster than she already thought he was.

He had to have time to convince her that his love two years ago had been real, that their relationship had been more to him than just a means to an end. If she knew he was a werewolf, he might not get that chance.

He was much more comfortable with taking action than having conversations. And sitting still, unable to do anything at all, was worst of all.

Declan looked at Ryder and shook his head. "The timin' has to be right. I can't tell her yet." He threw Ryder a hard look. "And don't you tell her, either."

Ryder's new wife Taite, Declan's good friend, walked into the room and asked, "Tell who what?" Her American accent gave more of an international flavor to the conversation—not that Declan needed more people wading in to tell him what a putz he'd been.

She went to Ryder and leaned over him, planting a kiss on his lips. He put both feet on the floor and pulled her down onto his lap, making her laugh. She wrapped one arm around his shoulder and looked at Declan. "Tell who what?" she asked again. Without waiting for a response from either man, she went on, "Oh, you're talking about Cobb's daughter, aren't you? I gotcha." As she stared at Declan, her eyebrows drew down. "What did you do now?"

He propped his hands on his hips. "An' just what makes you think *I* did somethin'?"

She knew him too well, of course. Almost six years of friendship and trial-by-werewolf brought people together like nothing else.

With her head tipped to one side, she pursed her lips for a moment. "You barrel people over, Declan. You're charming—too charming for your own good sometimes, if you wanna know the truth—but in the end your absolute focus on the goal can be a bit . . . one-track." She gave a shrug. "You don't always look at both sides of the picture."

He scowled. "Just whose side are you on here, darlin'?"

"Yours, of course." She wiggled a bit on Ryder's lap, apparently trying to get comfortable, which had the opposite effect on her husband if his darkening expression was anything to go by.

Declan had a feeling it wouldn't be too much longer before the two of them excused themselves to their bedroom. His scowl deepened. They should have been able to spend their first few months as a married couple alone, not babysitting a fledgling werewolf. As soon as this was all over, he'd head back to the States—providing he could get Pelicia to join him—and let the newlyweds be newlyweds.

"Besides," Taite went on, "if your friends can't be honest with you, who can? I know you're a man who appreciates honesty."

Ryder let out a snort of laughter that he tried to pass off as a cough.

"That's right, furball," Declan muttered. "Laugh it up." He rubbed his forehead with his middle finger and ignored the laugh Ryder didn't bother to hide this time. "Just remember, not all that long ago it was *you* who wasn't exactly bein' forthcomin' about things."

"That was different." Ryder shifted in his chair, his expression showing his emotional discomfort with the direction the conversation had taken. His fingers linked together around Taite's waist. "I didn't think either of you would be around that long, and you didn't need to know . . ." When Taite and Declan both looked at him in disbelief, he trailed off with a sheepish shrug.

"Aye. Exactly." Declan went back to the sofa and plopped down with a sigh. He stretched out his legs and crossed his ankles. "You didn't think we needed to know. Even after we *did* need to know you were reluctant to tell us, so don't be preachin' to me about how important it is that I tell Pel what I am."

"Point taken." Ryder stroked one hand up Taite's arm, settling his broad palm against her nape. "What about the car?"

Taite looked at Declan, curiosity swirling in her eyes. "What about what car? Dang, I hate coming into the middle of a conversation."

Ryder gave her a little shake, grinning like a love-sotted fool. Declan couldn't help but smile as well. His two best friends in the world—that they had found each other because of a werewolf, and that Taite had been able to love Ryder despite his own tendencies to howl at the moon—gave Declan hope for *his* future.

"Declan ran his car into Pelicia's bed and breakfast this morning, after someone shot out the back tire." Ryder sifted his fingers through her dark hair.

She twisted around to stare at her husband. "No! Really?" She shifted on Ryder's lap to look back at Declan. "Someone shot at you? Are you all right?"

"Sweetheart, would you please be still?"

Declan could see a muscle in Ryder's jaw flex as his friend struggled against the arousal he knew Taite's squirming caused. He pressed his lips together against a grin.

Ryder glanced at him and scowled. "Yeah, laugh it up, furball," he muttered, tossing Declan's earlier words back at him.

"Sorry," he said at the same time that Taite did. They grinned at each other, but Taite quickly sobered and asked again, "You're all right, though?" Her gaze danced over Declan, obviously seeking signs of injury. "The bullet didn't hit you? You didn't get hurt when you crashed?"

"I'm fine, darlin'. Had a wee bump on my forehead that

was gone in less than a minute." He grimaced. "Can't say the same for the Nola. Poor ol' girl has some structural damage, though I don't know how much." He met her gaze and tried not to let his misery show. "Pel isn't very happy with me."

"No, I imagine not. What did the police say?"

He shrugged. "Didn't call 'em."

"Why not?" Taite's brows drew down in a frown.

"Pel didn't want me to—said it would be bad for business." Declan shrugged again. "Besides, I did some, ah, sniffin' around after I left the Nola. I wasn't able to get the scent of the shooter"—he tapped his nose— "because of the rain, but now I know he's out there. If I do get a whiff of someone with gunpowder residue on him, the bastard's mine." He glanced at Ryder. "And I know someone at Scotland Yard. I'm thinkin' maybe I'll call him."

Ryder's brows rose. "You want to call Sully?"

"Why not? He owes me one." Declan shifted on the sofa, settling deeper into the plump cushions. "Anyway, he's due to leave for his annual holiday soon enough. I think they'll let him take time off early. And he'll get to stay at a charmin' bed and breakfast in the beautiful Isles of Scilly." He met Taite's gaze. "Whether Pel likes it or not."

Taite rose from Ryder's lap and walked over to the sofa. Sitting down beside Declan, she put her arm around his shoulders and hugged him. "I'm sorry this is so hard, Declan. I know how much you love her. Tell me how I can help."

Not the "Can I do anything?" that most people would have asked with the hopeful undertone that there was nothing to be done. Just a simple statement of her readiness to support him.

He returned the hug, raising an eyebrow when he heard

a low rumble from Ryder. Declan looked at the other man. "Ease off there, boyo. I'm not poachin' on your territory."

Taite removed her arm from around his shoulders and sat back, crossing her legs Indian style. "He doesn't like other men touching me," she whispered in a voice just loud enough for her husband's sensitive werewolf ears to hear. "He about chewed poor Cobb's arm off the other day when he gave me a hug."

"What?" Declan straightened and pasted a look of exaggerated shock on his face. "Cobb hugged you?" He looked at Ryder and caught the pained expression on his face. "What's this world comin' to?"

"Smartass." Ryder leaned back in his chair, hands clasped over his stomach. "You've been here the last four months, too. The house has been much brighter of late. As have those in it." He glanced at his wife as he said that, his dark blue eyes sparkling with love.

They shared a look that filled Declan with envy. That was what he wanted with Pelicia. A look that had no need for words.

It had to work out between them. It *had* to. He'd accept nothing less than success.

As much to lighten his own mood as to turn the conversation, he said, "Aye. I'd hoped you'd noticed what a positive influence I was havin' on you."

Ryder groaned and rolled his eyes. "I was talking about Taite."

Declan just grinned.

"Back to this car thing," Taite said, as usual drawing them back on topic when they drifted off. "You don't think . . ." She glanced at her husband. "Could it have been Miles?"

Miles Edward Hampston, Ryder's cousin and the man

ultimately responsible for Declan becoming a werewolf. Oh, he hadn't delivered the fateful bite himself, but the werewolf he'd sent to do his dirty work had. Taite had been terrorized and Ryder and Declan both injured, but in the end only the bad guy—someone whose help Miles had enlisted—had bit the dust.

"I suppose, but it seems a bit too indirect for him." Declan crossed his legs, resting one ankle on the opposite knee. Hunching forward, he scrubbed his hands over his face. He raked hair off his forehead and said, "If it were Miles—or even another one of his little minion bastards—I don't think they'd have gone for the tire. I think they'd have been shootin' at *me*." He shook his head. "No, actually, they'd have come after me in their werewolf form." He drew in a deep breath and slowly let it out. "I'm afraid it was directed at Pel, though the bloke's aim was off. Maybe he was startled by somethin' and jerked."

"Why on earth would someone be shooting at Pelicia?" Taite stretched one arm out along the back of the sofa. "And aren't ordinary people prohibited from having guns here?"

"If you want one badly enough, you can put your hands on a gun." Declan sighed. "The shootin' could have somethin' to do with the case from two years ago." He stood and stretched, then rotated his head, trying to work the kinks out of his neck. "Forged passports, birth certificates, and the like just might have stranded some of her granddad's clients. They wouldn't be too happy about it."

Taite frowned. "But Pelicia didn't have anything to do with that. The charges were dropped." Her frown deepened. "Weren't they?"

"Aye." Declan ignored the sense of guilt that always flared

whenever he thought about Pelicia's arrest. "But someone might not know that. Or care."

Ryder stood and came around his desk to rest his buttocks against the front edge. "You think someone would be mean enough to try to kill her because of something her grandfather may or may not have done? That doesn't make much sense."

Declan blew out a sigh. "I know," he agreed. "Now that I've thought on it more—and said it out loud—it doesn't make a lot of sense. But it doesn't track that it was Miles, either."

"Maybe it was just an errant shot," Taite offered, standing and crossing the room to be enfolded in her husband's embrace. "A duck hunter or something."

"A duck hunter?" Declan raised his brows.

She scowled. "You know what I mean."

"The slug was fired from a high-powered rifle. The kind a sniper uses." He shook his head. "Not somethin' an ordinary hunter would have." He clenched his jaw. "Unless he's huntin' humans."

Pelicia set the platter of lamb and roasted vegetables on the heavy oak table in the formal dining room and took her seat at the head of the table. Her guests had opted to pay extra in order to be served an evening meal, and she was happy to provide it because it meant a nice increase in revenue.

Though truth be told, she was also glad of the company. It grew tiresome always eating alone. "Thank you for staying, Neal. Although I'm not sure it's the most prudent thing to do."

Neal White looked up from the notebook he'd been perusing. "I should leave this lovely house just because some drunken tourist stupidly fired off a gun?" At her raised eyebrows he gave a shrug. "Or whoever it was. I can't believe someone was actually aiming for you. I *won't* believe it."

She smiled. "Well, thank you for that. And, truly, thank you for staying."

He returned her smile, showing off his white, straight teeth.

Must have cost him a fortune in cosmetic dentistry came the unbidden and quite unkind thought. Pelicia reprimanded herself and paid attention to what he was saying.

"I know how much you need this season to be a success. I'm happy to stay. And Andrew had much the same response as me, you know."

She nodded. She had only Neal's word on that—she hadn't had a chance to speak to Andrew herself, as he was proving to be quite elusive. "Well, I'm happy to have the company." She glanced at the empty place setting. "I'm sorry we had to start without Andrew. I wonder where he is."

Neal gave an unconcerned grunt and looked back down at his notebook, apparently re-engrossed in his work.

Obviously he didn't know and didn't care. It was entirely possible that Andrew had stopped off at one of the pubs for a bite—many tourists wanted as much to sample the local ambience as they did the local food. But if he didn't come back tonight to sleep, she'd start to worry.

Changing the subject, she asked her photojournalist guest, "Were you able to take some good pictures today?" She passed him a bowl of salad.

"Mmm?" He looked up with a start, then took the bowl from her with his right hand. As the bowl wobbled, he placed his left hand beneath it to steady it. "Oh, aye. I was. Thank you." His accent was difficult to place—a blur between Scottish and something one might hear in the East End of London. She'd asked him once where he was from, and he'd given a rather vague response that hadn't really answered the question. But she wasn't a prying person by nature and decided that if he didn't want to talk about his past, she'd respect that.

God knew she had no desire to talk about *her* past.

He served himself, sprinkling oil and vinegar on the salad, and topped it off with some fresh lemon juice. "I finally had to stop when I lost the light."

"Not too many tourists blundered into your shots, then?" Pelicia forked up some of her salad and munched away, curious for his answer. He'd made a point, when he'd first arrived two years ago, of saying that he wanted to be on the island during the off-season so he wouldn't have his photos mucked up by a lot of people. Tourist season was now in full swing, which made his recent stay rather surprising. But not unwelcome.

He gave a shrug. "The publisher who's expressed an interest actually wants some photos with people in them, so . . ." Another shrug. "I'm not going to quibble about it, not when I get to stay on this beautiful island with such a charming and gorgeous woman." He smiled and lifted his wineglass, giving her a small toast.

She clicked her glass against his then took a sip of wine. She and Neal spent a few minutes in comfortable silence, eating their meal. "Where are you planning to go tomorrow?" she asked once she'd taken the edge off her hunger. It had been a long time since breakfast. Between being on the phone with insurance people and worrying about the damage to her house—and trying to shake off the low hum of arousal she always felt whenever Declan was around—she hadn't gotten around to eating lunch.

"I thought I'd rent a boat and motor around some of the uninhabited islands. You know, get a real picture of the wild beauty here." He stabbed up his last bite of potato. "Any specific place you'd recommend?"

She shook her head. "They're all equally beautiful." However, not all of them were open to tourists. Especially the one with a resident werewolf. "But be careful—a couple of them have private owners who don't take kindly to trespassers."

Neal pulled a map out of his notebook and put it on the table between them. "Why don't you show me which ones those are, and I'll be sure to steer clear."

"Sure." Pelicia scooted her chair a little closer and pointed to Phelan's Keep. It would be best to make sure the photojournalist stayed away from werewolf central. "This one is privately owned, as is this one." She pointed to another small island. "Other than that, as far as I know, they're all uninhabited and open for exploring."

"Excellent." Putting down his fork, he brought out a nub of a pencil and circled the two islands. She noticed for the first time that he was left handed. He then put both pencil and map away. "I'll get started at first light so I can have the entire day. Must take advantage of natural light." He smiled, showing off the deep dimples in his cheeks.

He was a handsome man. Tall, blond, built like an American football player—all big, hard muscles. And those dimples. . . .He was someone any woman would love to date.

It really was too bad she preferred the dark-haired, bad-assed lean and mean former commando type. No matter how much she tried not to.

Feeling more charitable than she could afford, Pelicia

offered, "I can put together some sandwiches for you to take. No charge." She wiped her mouth. As she stood she scooped up her plate. "Are you finished?" she asked. At his nod, she picked up his plate and went into the adjoining kitchen.

Neal followed her, carrying the platter that held the leftover meal. "I don't want to put you to any trouble."

She gave him a smile over one shoulder. "It's no trouble, really. I don't want my favorite guest to be overcome by hunger."

He sighed and leaned one hip against the counter, watching her put the leftovers into containers. "I don't want to sound callous, but I'm usually your *only* guest, luv. How do you stay in business like this?"

She stifled a sigh. He was a good guest and had become a friend, but she still didn't really know him all that well and wasn't ready to discuss her financial difficulties with him. "I have a married couple who are supposed to check in tomorrow." She smiled. "I'm confident I'll have more guests as the season progresses. It takes time to build up a reputation."

And to tear down the old one.

Pelicia crossed her fingers behind her back. She wouldn't admit to a guest—and probably not to very many other people, either—but running this bed and breakfast wasn't turning out to be as much fun as she'd hoped. While she loved getting to meet people and enjoyed making them feel pampered, there were too many ghosts here. Too many people who knew her life story. That was one of the things she'd enjoyed about London—the anonymity of a big city.

Sometimes, in the quiet of the middle of the night, she wished she could go somewhere and start over. Begin anew in a place where no one would care about what happened in London and who didn't know anything about her grandfather.

But that took money and contacts and, right now, she didn't have enough of either.

"Well, I won't keep you." Neal turned to leave but paused. "Unless you want help cleaning up?"

She frowned at him and made a shooing motion. "Guests don't help clean up. Go on with you."

He grinned and left the room. Pelicia watched him until he turned the corner to go up the stairs to the second floor and wondered again why she couldn't be more attracted to him. He was easygoing, charming, and intelligent.

While Declan was certainly also charming and intelligent, he was not easygoing. Not by a long shot. He was intense, obstinate, and so wickedly sensual she got wet just thinking about him. Her mind played back over his kiss from that morning, and she pressed her thighs together to try to stem the flood of arousal.

"Stop it," she muttered. She didn't want to think about Declan, because thinking about him only made her desire him. And she didn't want to desire him because that was what had gotten her into trouble to begin with.

She busied herself with cleaning up the kitchen, purposefully making her mind go blank. Better not to think. At least about *that*.

She had lots of things to keep her mind occupied. Tomorrow morning she had to deal with the insurance adjuster and make arrangements for stonemasons and other workmen to begin repairs on the house. And she had to figure out an inexpensive way to get at least one more boarder. Once the married couple registered, she would still have a vacant room. One more person would give her a full house and would also provide the additional income she needed.

Pelicia inhaled and held her breath a moment, then slowly exhaled. Turning, she opened the refrigerator and pulled out the ingredients she'd need to put together a picnic lunch for Neal. If she kept her hands busy, her mind would hopefully not wander.

It was something her father had impressed upon her early on. "Idle hands are the devil's playground," he used to say. And he was right. If she didn't keep busy she'd just stand around and fret about things over which she had no control.

She'd worry about tomorrow . . . tomorrow.

Chapter 3

The next morning, Declan paused in front of the Nola. The big two-story house with its heavy stone blocks and dormers could have looked intimidating but for the cheery flowers Pelicia had planted in the narrow front garden. Bright yellows and blues drew the eye and made the gray granite seem not so dismal.

He stepped onto the small portico and drew in a breath, then knocked on the white door. Hopefully Pelicia had had a good night's sleep and would be more amenable to seeing him this morning. He glanced at the side of the house where he'd tried—accidentally—to make her bed and breakfast a drive-through. He winced.

His hope for a warm greeting would probably not be realized.

The door swung open and there she was, blond hair pulled back into a simple ponytail, looking fresh and so lovely his cock burgeoned to life. Even the unwelcoming scowl that curled her lips downward didn't detract from his erection.

"Come to finish what you started yesterday?" she asked with a gesture toward the damaged part of the house. She leaned one shoulder against the doorway.

He started to reply but stopped when a piece of the lintel near her head suddenly splintered, exploding toward her face. She screamed at the same time the sound of a gunshot echoed in the calm morning air.

Declan was already moving. He curled one arm around Pelicia and swung her back inside, dropping them both to the floor, his body curved over hers, his hands covering her head. He rolled them once, twice, then twice more until he was sure they were out of the open doorway. Another shot sounded. Then silence.

He waited another minute, ignoring Pelicia as she struggled beneath him. That is, he *tried* to ignore her, though her wriggling was having an obvious effect on his body even in the midst of danger. His flesh thickened, pressing against the zipper of his jeans. He bit back a groan and fought the urge to shove his erection against the soft V of her thighs.

A musky scent wafted from her, and he lifted his head to stare down at her. She was aroused. She fought it, but there was no mistaking that aroma. It was all that was needed to send his cock into full-blown rigidity.

He grimaced at his thoughts. *Full-blown* made him think of having her mouth wrapped around his shaft, taking him deep as he fucked between those luscious lips.

"Get off me," she muttered, bucking against him, driving her softness into his hardness. She obviously wasn't having the same fantasy as he was. "And stop that."

"Sorry, darlin'." He didn't budge at first, but after she managed to poke him in the ribs with her elbow, he decided now was really not the time to follow through on this interesting development. *Damn it.* He rolled off her onto his knees. "Stay down," he cautioned.

In a low crouch he made his way to the door, making

sure to stay to one side. He cautiously peered through the open doorway. As before, he could see nothing out of the ordinary. After several more minutes he stood, still searching the area for whoever it was that had shot at them.

At Pelicia.

Various locals and tourists alike were starting to gather, heads turning this way and that, trying to figure out what was going on. Someone gestured and the words "call the police" came clearly to him.

Didn't look like this time they'd get out of talking to the cops.

He heard movement from behind him and turned his head to see Pelicia walking toward him. "Goddamnit." He shoved the door closed. Grabbing her by one hand, he dragged her deeper into the house. Once they got to the kitchen he muttered, "I told you to stay down."

She jerked away from him. "I highly doubt I'm the one he's shooting at." She pressed her lips together for a moment. "If it is a he. With you, I wouldn't be surprised if it's a she." She looked him up and down. "God knows *I've* been tempted."

He clenched his jaw. Christ, she was stubborn. A trait she'd inherited from her father. "Just . . . stay inside, all right? I'm going to take a look around outside."

She scowled. "And if the guy was shooting at you?"

"Then he'll get another chance to put me out of your misery, won't he?" He grinned at her gasp and the widening of her eyes.

Keep her off balance. That was the only way he'd win her back. Give her too much time to think and she'd keep coming up with excuses.

"I'll be back in a few minutes."

As he had the morning before, Declan scouted around

the house and found nothing. The local police constable arrived just as Declan was heading back into the Nola.

Declan pulled the door closed behind him and met the man on the walkway. "Constable."

"PC Charles Tremwith," he said by way of introduction. "I was told there's been a shooting." He glanced at the damaged corner of the building then looked back at Declan. "You're O'Connell, right? You do that?" He jerked his head toward the site of the accident.

If he was asking, then he already damn well knew Declan had been the one to cause the damage. "Aye. My back tire blew."

"Hmm." The constable looked at the Nola. "And the shooting?" He brought his sharp green gaze back to Declan's face.

Declan gave a nonchalant shrug. He had nothing against the local constabulary, but he was more than capable of looking after Pelicia. Besides, with his newly acquired werewolf senses, there wasn't anything the constable could learn that Declan couldn't. "Just happened. Maybe a tourist?"

Tremwith's thin, dark moustache twitched with his frown. "Not too many tourists bring guns with them." His eyes narrowed. "Actually, I can't imagine why any of them would. And the number of residents with firearms is limited to those of us wearing police uniforms. Which is a total of three."

"That you know of." Declan didn't want the man poking around. Were his condition to be discovered, it would lead right back to Ryder, and *that* wasn't his secret to tell.

A slight lifting of his eyebrows was the constable's only response. He pulled out a small notebook and jotted down a few words then looked toward the Nola again. "I need to speak with Ms. Cobb."

"She's a bit shaken up," Declan said. "As you can imagine. Bein' shot at—even if it was a stray bullet—isn't somethin' she has a lot of experience with."

"But you do, don't you?" The other man lifted his chin. "Are you so sure the shooter wasn't aiming at you?"

There was no reason to prevaricate here. Obviously the man knew Declan's background. "No, I'm not sure. And, as a matter of fact, he probably *was* shootin' at me rather than Pel. Unless you know somethin' about her that I don't, PC Tremwith?"

Tremwith shook his head. In a hard voice he said, "Pelicia Cobb is as straight-arrow as they come, regardless of her ne'er do well grandfather." His gaze bored into Declan. "But of course you know that, right?"

"Aye, I do." Declan held onto the irritated response he itched to give. So the constable wanted to take a dig or two at him—that was his prerogative. He tucked his hands into the front pockets of his jeans and shrugged. "But I can't tell you anythin' except that someone took a shot at us. Or me. And Pel can tell you the same thing, if you still want to talk to her. Tomorrow."

Tremwith studied him then nodded. "Fine. I'll stop by first thing in the morning."

Declan watched the constable walk back to his vehicle. Once the man had climbed behind the wheel and driven off, Declan went through the front door of the Nola, closing it behind him. He stopped still. As focused on protecting Pelicia as he'd been earlier, scents he hadn't noticed before wafted to his nostrils.

The clovelike smell of hatred. He tilted his head. A sugary aroma of fondness.

The faint odor of spent gunpowder.

The mixed signals confused him, but one thing was clear.

The sniper had been in Pelicia's house after he'd fired the gun and gotten gun powder residue on his clothes. As recently as this morning, since the scents were still fresh to Declan's enhanced sense of smell. Yet she was obviously unhurt, so it seemed likely that Declan *was* the target.

Or the bastard was having some fun before settling down to business.

Damn, which was it? Declan hated the uncertainty—and the thought that Pelicia was the intended victim for any reason. If the bastard was after him, fine. But Declan just wasn't sure, and he couldn't very well tell Pelicia that he smelled the sniper in her house—she'd want to know how, and he wasn't prepared to tell her that. Not yet. So for now he'd keep that bit of information to himself.

Scowling, he walked down the hallway and entered the kitchen. The scents were here, too, telling him the sniper had had the run of the downstairs. He wondered briefly about the upstairs, but the sight of Pelicia stopped him short.

She stood beside the sink, her slender arms wrapped around herself, looking heartbreakingly young and forlorn. Worried despite her obvious effort not to be. "Did you find anything?" she asked.

He shook his head and continued into the kitchen. "No. Either the bastard's a lousy shot or . . ."

"Or what?" she asked when he trailed off.

"Or he's playing with me." He stared at her. "Or you." He wasn't entirely ready to give up the idea that this had something to do with her grandfather.

She made an aggravated noise deep in her throat. Worry changed to irritation and darkened her blue eyes. "How many times do I have to say this? He's not shooting at me."

"Are you so sure of that?" Declan stared at her, trying

to keep calm. God, but she drove him crazy faster than any other woman ever had. "Your granddad—"

"My grandfather," she interrupted, "is in prison. His clients would have come looking for their belongings a long time ago. Or if they'd wanted revenge, don't you think they would have done so two years ago?"

"Not if they've been in prison for the last two years." Declan paused, turning his earlier thought over in his mind.

What if it didn't have anything to do with Pelicia's past? What if it had everything to do with *his* present? Perhaps Miles was doing to Declan what he'd tried to do to Ryder— do damage to Declan through someone he loved.

He went cold and stared hard at Pelicia. God. He couldn't let anything happen to her because of him.

"What?" She rubbed one cheek with her fingers. "Do I have something on my face?"

He walked up to her and cupped her face. "No. And it's the most beautiful face I've ever seen."

She shrugged away from him with a frown. "Don't start that again, O'Connell. I'm not falling for your shit this time."

Declan grimaced. Her language was getting bluer— she'd progressed from using bloody. It was only a matter of time before she ended up telling him to fuck off.

He'd rather fuck *her*. He was a firm believer that if he wanted something badly enough, if he worked hard enough to get it, eventually he would. So he would proceed with that in mind.

He cleared his throat. "Listen to me. For just a minute," he added when she seemed about to interrupt. "There is a possibility that someone might be tryin' to get to me through you."

She crossed her arms. "What the bloody hell are you talking about? You and I aren't together." He could almost hear her added *Thank God.* "Why should anyone think you'd even care?"

"No, we aren't together." He stared at her, willing her to believe him. "But you are important to me."

"Oh, I don't believe this," Pelicia muttered under her breath. "You use me, get me arrested, then ignore me for two years, and have the gall to tell me I'm important to you?" She threw up her hands. "Are you deliberately trying to make me insane?"

"No." Declan clenched his fists to keep from reaching out for her. He knew she wouldn't want him touching her right now, not in the mood she was in. And he didn't blame her—he blamed himself. But . . . "I didn't have a lot of choices two years ago, Pel. You have to know that. But whatever else happened durin' the investigation, what happened between us was real."

"Was it? Was it really?" She shook her head. "I didn't see you going to any effort to keep me from getting arrested. You *knew* I didn't know he was using me for something illegal." She turned away from him. "But I guess that's beside the point."

"Pel—"

She whirled around. "Why would someone be trying to hurt you, O'Connell? Someone besides me, I mean." She gave him a patently false smile.

He grimaced. She was *not* going to make this easy. Fine. He could do things the hard way when necessary. He usually preferred not to.

Although sometimes there was nothing quite like a good fight to work off tension.

"It's complicated."

She gave an inelegant snort. "You'd better do better than that."

He still wasn't ready to tell her about his tendency to go furry once a month. "It's really that someone's after Ryder."

Pelicia scowled. "Would you make up your mind? Is someone after you or are they after Ryder?" She shook her head. "And why would someone be after Ryder, anyway?"

"You've no doubt heard him or your dad talk about Ryder's cousin?" Declan watched her, saw the confusion in her eyes. "Miles Hampston," he prompted.

She shrugged. "I may have heard mention of him before, but I honestly don't remember." She stared at him, lines furrowing her brow. "You're saying he wants to hurt Ryder? His own cousin."

"Aye." Declan chose his words carefully. "He wants what Ryder has and has already sent someone after me."

Her eyes widened. "But he failed, right? I mean, you look fine."

"I am fine," he responded evenly. *If you discount the fangs, claws, and fur that sprout once a month.* "He . . . hired someone to do his dirty work. The bastard turned his sights on a friend of mine instead, with the primary purpose of gettin' her and me to Phelan's Keep so he could show Ryder how powerful he was." He couldn't help but grin at the outcome. "Instead Ryder and Taite fell in love, and the bad guy lost all the way 'round."

"Yes, I know. Well, at least the part about Ryder and Taite falling in love." She gave a small frown. "I was at the wedding, remember?"

How could he forget? She'd stood in as maid of honor for Taite, who'd been so far from home, and Declan had been Ryder's best man. It had made Declan think about his and Pelicia's own wedding, though that future might never play out.

He clenched his jaw. He refused to believe that, refused to accept that he wouldn't be able to turn Pelicia around. Win her back. Any other outcome was inconceivable.

Unacceptable.

"I never asked her, but I assume she knows that Ryder's a . . ." Pelicia trailed off. Uncertainty clouded her eyes as she must have realized that it was possible Declan didn't know the full story about Ryder, even if Ryder's new wife did.

"We both found out about Ryder's . . . condition," he said. "Neither of us was particularly happy about it."

"No, I imagine not." She pulled one of the chairs away from the small kitchen table and sat down. She clasped her hands, resting them on the table, and said, "Although from what I remember, Ryder was never very happy about being a werewolf, either."

At least she wasn't running away from him. Declan pulled out the chair at the end of the table—the one closest to her—and sat down. "No, he wasn't," he agreed quietly. "But he's come to finally accept that the wolf is part of who he is."

She looked up at him. "He has?" A genuine smile tilted her lips. "Dad said he had, but it's nice to hear it confirmed. I'm glad. It hurt to see him so unhappy."

Her compassionate nature was one of the things that had made Declan fall in love with her. But while she seemed to be able to feel sympathy for Ryder, it was apparent her quota of compassion was used up where Declan was concerned.

Yet another reason to hold off on telling her that he'd joined the ranks of the fanged and furry. He needed to score some major points with her first.

"So he is happy, then? With Taite?" She propped her chin on one fist. "I've only talked to her a few times." Pelicia tilted her head to one side. "She seems nice. Dad really likes her and tells me all the time how glad he is that she's there."

Declan raised his brows. While he agreed with Cobb, he was surprised that the little man would speak so highly of Taite—he always seemed to keep his opinions about people to himself.

Well, except for where Declan was concerned. Cobb had no qualms at all about letting Declan know what he thought of *him*.

"Aye," he said in answer to her question. "In the last four months I think I've seen Ryder laugh more than I have in the last twenty years." He grinned. "Well, except for the six weeks Taite was back in the States wrapping up her life there. Then he was a real . . ." His grin widened. "Well, I was goin' to say bear, but maybe 'rabid wolf' would be a more apt description."

Her brows knit in a frown. "Just why have you been staying with them the last four months, anyway? I mean, they are newlyweds. I'd think they'd want some privacy instead of a . . . houseguest."

His lips twisted. She'd obviously been about to use another word, maybe something along the lines of "leech" or "hanger-on" instead of "houseguest." And if he hadn't needed Ryder's guidance on being a werewolf, he *would* have left them alone.

But, there it was. Declan had made the transition three

times already, not pushing his luck by trying to transform at will but rather waiting until the rising of the full moon triggered the change. And always Ryder had been at his side, helping him, guiding him.

Declan had never felt an urge to hurt anyone on the island, though some of the indigenous animals hadn't fared so well. But Ryder had told him there might come a time, under the influence of heightened emotions, when Declan might have less control of the wolf inside.

Declan couldn't see that happening. If there was one thing he *could* control, it was his emotions.

Seeing that she waited for his answer, he said, "While Miles is up to his tricks, I'm stayin' to help protect both Ryder and Taite." Which wasn't a lie. It just wasn't the entire truth.

Pelicia nodded. She stared at him a moment, then stood and walked to the counter, turning on a hot plate beneath the teakettle. He heard her sigh before she turned to look at him. "Would you like a cup of tea?"

At last. An olive branch.

"Aye. Thank you."

She gave a brief nod and turned back to the counter, putting cups and a sugar bowl on a small tray. After she placed a ceramic teapot on the tray, she pulled a canister from the cupboard in front of her.

"How did you fare with the insurance adjuster?" Declan asked, as much from curiosity as to fill the silence. "He came today, I assume?"

"Yes." She took the kettle off the hot plate, tipped some water into the teapot, and placed the kettle on a nearby iron trivet. "It's not as bad as I thought it would be."

He heard the note of grudging admission in her voice, as

well as a spark of embarrassment. No doubt she was remembering how she'd acted toward him and was regret-
ting it.

Sweet Pel. Even when she'd been wronged, she still tried
to act the lady.

She finished putting the tea things together and carried
the tray over to the table. Once seated, she poured him a
cup and passed it to him, taking care, he noticed, to make
sure their fingers didn't touch. Then she poured herself a
cup, stirred in two teaspoons of sugar, and lifted the cup to
her lips.

Pelicia took a sip of her tea and mentally kicked herself
for softening toward Declan. She wanted nothing more to
do with him, right? Yet here she sat, having a polite cup of
tea and acting like they were friends.

It had been his concern for Ryder, his genuine—or what
appeared to be genuine—satisfaction over Ryder's happi-
ness that had lowered her defenses. That and his desire to
protect his friend.

Of course, she'd never doubted Declan's ability or will-
ingness to safeguard the physical well-being of those he
cared about. Her fingers began to tremble, and she set her
cup down onto the table with a thunk.

They'd been so much more than friends once upon a
time. Earlier, when he'd forced her to the floor and covered her with his body to protect her from bullets, she'd
felt every solid muscle where he rested against her. And
she'd felt the hard ridge of his erection pressed between
her thighs. Her sex had immediately swelled, the folds becoming slick with desire.

He'd known. Somehow he'd known she'd gotten aroused.
She'd felt him go absolutely still above her, not unlike a

predator that's spotted its prey and doesn't want to do anything to scare it. He'd moved off her without comment, other than to order her to stay where she was.

But she'd seen the knowledge in his eyes.

Now, watching him handle the teacup—a cup that looked tiny in his broad hand—Pelicia found herself wishing things were different. She wanted those hands on her again, wanted to feel him on top of her, inside her.

Yet, she didn't trust him. Couldn't trust him. But she still wanted him.

She swallowed and traced the rim of her cup with one finger. *Say something.* Thinking it would be a safe subject, she glanced up at him and asked, "So, how is it you know Ryder's new wife?"

"Taite and I met just over five years ago when we crossed paths on a case I was workin' on. She used to be an investigator for a county attorney's office in Arizona." His fondness for the other woman was reflected in his eyes. "Taite the Terrier, they called her. And it's a true enough nickname—she's downright tenacious." He grinned and shook his head.

She tried not to notice how cute he was when he smiled. He was handsome enough when his expression was sober, but when he smiled, his entire face lit up, his eyes sparkled, and he looked like a mischievous boy.

It was one of the things that had first attracted her to him.

Of course, looking at him sitting there with a navy polo shirt showcasing his biceps and the strong column of his neck, molding the hard muscles of his chest and showing dark chest hair at the base of his throat, she acknowledged there was nothing remotely boyish about him.

"As a matter of fact," he went on, "Taite's one of the

toughest women I know." He looked at her, his dark eyes glinting.

Pelicia stared down into her teacup. She knew what he was thinking. That she was tough, too.

But she wasn't. If she were, she would have stayed in London, muscled her way through finding a job. She wouldn't have been so devastated by his betrayal.

She was the farthest thing from tough one could get.

Picking up her cup, she curled her hands around it, trying to warm suddenly cold fingers. Ignoring what he'd implied, she looked up. "And Ryder's happy, you say?"

"Oh, aye. Taite's the best thing that could have happened to him." Declan tipped his cup to his lips.

Her gaze centered on his throat, the muscles flexing with his swallow. As he started to lower the cup, she dropped her gaze to the amber liquid in her own mug. She couldn't do this anymore—sit here drinking tea and pretending to be unaffected by his presence.

But she'd be damned if she gave in to her desire. He'd had his chance, and he'd blown it.

Pelicia pushed away from the table and stood. She put her cup on the tray and carried the tray over to the sink. Turning around, she went still, her breath hitching in her throat.

Declan stood less than an arm's length away, so close she could feel the heat emanating from his big body. He reached toward her, and she tensed, but all he did was place his cup on the counter behind her.

Except he remained in that position, resting his hand on the edge of the counter. He loomed over her, so close she could see amber flecks in the dark brown of his eyes. Even as she wondered about that—his eyes used to be so dark they were almost black—he leaned even closer.

With his mouth a breath away, he murmured, "Are you so sure you hate me, Pel?" He pressed a soft kiss against the corner of her mouth. "'Cause I have to tell you, darlin', this doesn't feel like hate to me."

Before she could form a response, his mouth covered hers and for the second time in two days her rational mind was overwhelmed by the reality of being in his arms again.

Chapter 4

The watcher stood at the corner of the window on the east side of the kitchen and peered carefully inside the house, taking care to remain hidden from both those inside as well as the work crew that had just pulled up in front.

He'd deliberately missed each time he'd shot at Pelicia, because he wanted to make O'Connell sweat. As far as that Irish bastard knew, twice now bullets had come close to striking her.

Or had they?

Let O'Connell worry about his lady, let him wonder if the bullets were truly meant for her or, perhaps, were they meant for him?

The watcher had decided to use a gun to throw O'Connell off the scent. When he made his move for real—when *he* decided it was time to fulfill his mission and not before—it would be up close and personal, not through the use of such an impersonal tool as a high-powered sniper's rifle.

The watcher had been too far away to hear the conversation O'Connell had had with the police constable, but it was interesting that he'd sent the man away without letting him speak to Pelicia. He wondered what had been going through the big man's head then.

Now he *knew* what O'Connell was thinking and with which head he was thinking it. The Irishman had his hands cupped on either side of Pelicia's face, holding her still as he plundered her mouth. Her hands at first rested against his chest but soon slid down to curl around his sides, then up his back to clutch handfuls of his shirt.

But suddenly she pushed him away, a look of dismay on her face. The watcher couldn't hear what she said, but O'Connell gave a response that must not have set well, because her lovely features darkened. She said something else and pointed toward the front of the house. O'Connell looked at her for a long moment and then turned and left the room.

The watcher stood still, listening. He heard the front door open and close and, after several minutes, heard O'Connell get into his car and start it up. He waited until O'Connell drove off before he left his hiding place from behind a large camellia bush.

He walked around the corner of the house and peered through the glass panes of the back door. Pelicia was sitting once again at the table, her hands pressed to her face. As he watched, she wiped her fingers under her eyes.

Swiping away tears?

He fought against feeling sympathy for her. She was a means to an end. Nothing more. Just because she was lovely and . . .

He scowled. *Stay focused*. A means to an end was what she was, and that was all.

A means to O'Connell's end.

Chapter 5

Declan strode down the cobbled path toward the back door of Ryder's house, his thoughts racing. The twenty-minute boat ride from St. Mary's had done little to calm him—if anything it had given him even more time to think.

Walking away from Pelicia had been difficult. She had responded so sweetly, her tongue meeting his, her lush curves resting against him. Then she'd seemed to remember she was supposed to be angry with him, and she'd pushed him away.

He'd protested, but she'd been adamant. And so, with an erection that could've drilled through stone, he'd left. He'd checked out the stonemasons getting ready to repair the Nola—it was a father and son team who lived on the island. Their scents were unfamiliar, telling Declan they hadn't been in the house. He'd felt secure leaving Pelicia alone for a short amount of time. Since the two men were there it seemed unlikely the sniper would try again.

Now, back on Phelan's Keep, Declan had a plan. Well, part of a plan, anyway, and one that should keep Pelicia safe until he could figure out what the hell was going on.

Declan keyed in his code on the newly installed alarm keypad and pushed open the back door. He went into the house, shoving the door closed with one foot. Force of habit had him toeing off his boots, leaving them on the rug beside the door.

Hearing movement, he looked up to see Cobb walk into the kitchen.

"Oh, good morning, Mr. O'Connell." Cobb glanced at the clock hanging above the refrigerator. "Almost good afternoon, I see."

"Aye." Declan padded across the room, his socks making him slip a little on the tiled floor.

"Will you be staying for lunch?" Cobb picked up a dish towel and began wiping down the already spotless counter.

"Ah, no." Declan paused in the doorway and looked back at the houseman. "But if you could put together somethin' I could take with me—maybe a couple of sandwiches?"

Cobb gave a nod.

"Thanks." Declan started to say more, thinking to fill Cobb in on what was happening to his daughter, but decided against it. Best not worry the little man until Declan had his facts straight.

Besides, Cobb, at least, seemed to have softened toward him—probably felt sorry for him now that he was a werewolf. Whatever the reason, Declan would take the change. He'd been getting tired of all the dirty looks Cobb sent his way when no one else was looking.

Not that they were completely undeserved or that Declan didn't understand where they were coming from. Cobb obviously knew the story of what happened between Declan and Pelicia, and he was bristling over the treatment his daughter had suffered at Declan's hands. But for the moment, at least, he seemed to be giving Declan a bit of a break.

He'd take it.

Declan went on through the house, taking the stairs to the next floor two at a time. The next set, leading to the third story, he took four at a time.

Not something he could have done before he'd become a werewolf.

He paused on the landing, amazed to find that he wasn't out of breath and his heart rate remained normal. This werewolf metabolism was something he surely didn't begrudge. He honestly didn't understand why Ryder had had such a hard time with it.

Declan went on to his room and packed a few things in a small duffel bag—another pair of jeans and a black T-shirt, a pair of underwear and socks, and his can of spray deodorant. Sitting on a stakeout wouldn't give him an opportunity to bathe, but he could at least spray on more deodorant if the need arose. With duffel in hand he went downstairs once again and down the back hallway to the gun cabinet.

He pulled out a handgun, popped out the clip to check the rounds, and then pushed it back into place. He made sure the safety was on and tossed the gun into the duffel bag. He added extra ammunition and, dropping the bag on the floor, went down on one knee and zipped it closed.

Declan stood and pushed the bag to one side with his foot. He walked down the hallway and across the foyer, stopping at Ryder's study door to rap on the wood with his knuckles.

He heard Ryder's irritated "What!" and opened the door. "Sorry, Ry," he said, knowing he'd interrupted his writer friend's train of thought as he was hard at work on a new novel. "Just wanted to use the phone."

Ryder motioned toward the satellite phone on his desk and put his attention back onto his laptop. As soon as Declan placed his call, however, Ryder stopped what he was doing. "So you're going ahead with a call to Sully?" he asked.

"Aye." Declan listened to the phone ring on the other end and looked at Ryder. "I want him to come and help me keep an eye on Pel."

Ryder frowned. "Why? Has something else happened?"

"You could say that." When Sully's voice mail came on, Declan held up one finger, signaling Ryder to wait. He left a message with explicit instructions and his cell phone number as well as Ryder's number, then hung up. He raked his fingers through his hair. "Someone took a couple of shots at us again this mornin'." He sighed. "Probably at me, but I can't take the chance that someone—like your bleedin' cousin—is after her because of me."

"You mean because of *me*." Ryder leaned back in his chair and scrubbed one hand over his jaw.

"No, that's *not* what I mean. None of this is your fault, boyo." Declan leaned one hip against the desk. "I'm still havin' to tell Taite every now and again that what happened to me isn't her fault. I don't need to be tellin' you the same thing." He shrugged. "It was my idea to come here in the first place. My idea, my fault."

Ryder inclined his head. "I appreciate that you feel that way, but let's face it—if you weren't my friend, Miles wouldn't be after you."

"Aye. I suppose that's true enough. It's also true that if I weren't your friend you'd probably have never met Taite.

So, all things considered, we're good." Declan lifted a brow and waited for his friend's response.

Ryder's lips pursed. A small smile twitched one corner of his mouth. "Well, of course I can't say I'm disappointed at the outcome." He met Declan's gaze. "She's the best thing that's ever happened to me."

Declan grinned. "Just what I said to Pel this mornin'." He straightened. "I'm goin' to head back to her place and camp nearby, just to keep an eye on her until Sully can get here, which hopefully will only be a couple of days." He turned. As he walked out of the room, he said, "If I don't hear from him in a couple of hours, I'll check in with you later to see if he's called, just in case he can't get through on my cell."

Ryder nodded and turned back to his laptop, his mind already delving back into the world he was creating.

Declan grinned and left the study, closing the door quietly behind him. On his way to the kitchen he grabbed his duffel bag. He went into the kitchen in time to see Cobb wrapping up a second sandwich. Declan put the duffel bag on one of the chairs in the small breakfast nook and unzipped it. He grabbed a couple of apples off the counter and put them in the duffel. After adding four bottles of water, he accepted the sandwiches Cobb handed him.

Declan took a handful of power bars from the pantry and, with a lift of one brow, a packet of gum. He wouldn't have an opportunity to brush his teeth, either, so he'd make do with chewing gum. He dumped the pilfered goods into the duffel.

"You'll be gone only a short time, I take it?"

Declan nodded. "A day or two at the most, I hope." Especially considering the first night of the full moon was due in just a few days, it would probably be best if he was back on Phelan's Keep at that time.

Just in case.

Less than forty-eight hours later, Declan sat slouched in the front seat of his new rental car—where he'd been for the last day and a half except for the few times he'd had to use the facilities—and watched a tall, broad-shouldered man enter the Nola.

Rory Sullivan had arrived.

Already Declan could feel his gut relaxing. Between the two of them, they should be able to keep harm from Pelicia.

A few minutes later, his friend came out of the bed and breakfast and, after a casual glance around, walked down the street toward Declan's car. He went around to the passenger side and got in, twisting sideways in his seat to look at Declan. "Dec."

"Sully. Thanks for comin'." Declan glanced at his friend and went straight to the point. "I don't know if someone's after her or after me, but in either case she's in danger."

Sully nodded. "Don't worry, mate. She'll be safe with me." His deep voice was calm, the crisp accent a reflection of his cultured upbringing. Rory Sullivan could have sat back and lived on the considerable investment income his family had built over the years, but he'd chosen to do something with his life that would benefit others. Poor Lady Sullivan continually fretted over the safety of her son and had yet to come to terms with her son's choice of occupation, regardless that she felt no small amount of pride over his accomplishments on the force.

Declan let his friend's relaxing tones soothe his anxiety. Sully was the best there was, and Declan would do well to

remember that. "Don't let her know that you know me."
He sighed. Here he was, once again dealing with Pelicia
with secrecy. But he knew she'd be livid if she found out
he'd planted someone close to her, and until he found out
what was going on and neutralized the threat, the less she
knew, the better. He shook his head and stared at the
Nola. "What name did you use?"

"Sullivan O'Rourke." When Declan looked at him, he
shrugged. "I reckoned that way if anyone who knows me
sees me here and calls me Sully, it won't cause any suspicion on her part." When Declan gave a nod of approval,
Sully sent him a slight scowl, his green eyes lit with mock
irritation. "It's not like I'm an amateur at this sort of thing,
you know."

"Oh, I know, Detective Chief Inspector Sullivan of Scotland Yard." Declan grinned at Sully's grimace.

"Yes, well." Sully stared toward the Nola. "What's the
story with your girl?"

Declan couldn't tell Sully about him being a werewolf
without exposing Ryder as well. So, keeping with the story
he'd told Pelicia, he explained to Sully about Miles.

Without any reference to fur.

When he was finished, Sully sat there shaking his head.
"Man, I knew Ryder's cousin was twisted, but this . . ."
He rubbed the bridge of his nose with two fingers and stared
out through the windshield. "This is fucked up."

"Aye. It is." Declan turned his head toward the Nola.
Whatever the reason, his woman was in danger, and he
would do everything in his power to protect her.

Whether she liked it or not.

"I need you to stay as close to her as possible *without*
arousin' her suspicion." He shot a quick look at Sully.
"Think you can do that?"

Sully scowled at him. This time the irritation was real. "Probably better than you on your best day, O'Connell."

Declan grinned and looked again at the Nola. The front door opened, and Pelicia walked out onto the front portico. He and Sully both scrunched further down into their seats and watched as she shook the small rug that normally lay just inside the front door. God, she was so lovely it hurt his heart to look at her.

She waved at a dark-haired woman in jeans who walked down the sidewalk in front of the bed and breakfast. The woman stopped and they carried on a conversation. But just as Declan cracked his window to try to hear what they were saying, the woman walked away.

"I don't think that's going to help you, Dec. You're too far away." Sully's voice was amused.

Not too far away for alert werewolf hearing, but he couldn't tell Sully that. Instead, he watched Pelicia while he said, "I appreciate you taking your holiday early to help me."

"I remember how you used to talk about her even when we were at university together. You were smitten then."

Declan turned his head to stare at his friend. "She was a teenager."

"She was fifteen—blossoming into womanhood. You were nineteen. Not that big of a gap." Sully met Declan's gaze. "And two years ago, when the two of you finally hooked up, the few times you and I talked on the phone you seemed happy."

"I was. We were." Declan rubbed one hand along the outer seam of his jeans. "Until she found out I had used our friendship to get close enough to her and her grandfather to gather evidence against him." He sighed. "I tried to tell the powers that be that she wasn't involved, that even though she had been transporting forged documents from St. Mary's to London, she had to be unaware of it."

"They didn't listen, obviously."

"No, not at first, and later neither would she." Declan shook his head and looked back at the Nola. Pelicia stood in the sun, eyes closed, face tipped up to soak in the warm spring rays. She always had been something of a sun worshiper.

An unwilling grin crossed his face. Better to be a werewolf than a vampire—he wasn't so sure she'd make the sacrifice of giving up her time in the sun to be with him. He frowned. That was if vampires existed, which he rather hoped they didn't. Dealing with being a creature of legend come to life was enough for him, but he'd have to ask Ryder about vampires just the same.

Declan watched Pelicia's chest lift with her deep breath. Then she turned and went back inside, closing the door behind her. He looked at Sully again. "In the end, what matters is she was arrested because of me. She lost her job because of me. Her reputation was shattered because of me." He heaved a sigh. "And now her life is in danger. Because of me."

"She lost her job and her reputation because of her grandfather, Dec. Not because of you." Sully's dark brows dipped. "And I don't think you're right about now, either. It's because of Miles that she's in danger, not you."

Declan shrugged. At this point, trying to fix blame was moot. She was in danger, and he had to take care of it. Period.

"Don't worry. I'll protect her like she was my own." Sully put one hand on Declan's shoulder and gave a squeeze, then opened his door and got out of the car. He pushed the door shut and sauntered up the street, crossing the road in a casual, leisurely manner.

Declan stayed where he was until Sully went inside. Then he started the car and drove off. He'd park the vehicle out of sight of the Nola and do some more sniffing around.

Literally.

He was constantly astounded at how acute his sense of smell and hearing were now. His distance vision had improved as well. All pluses, as far as he was concerned. So far, he'd not really experienced any of the negatives that Ryder kept talking about. Perhaps because of his military training he'd been able to deal with the transition easier than Ryder.

But with Pelicia in danger, being a werewolf seemed like a good thing. He was faster and stronger than before. Anyone who messed with him—or those close to him—might just find themselves with their faces ripped off.

As Sully walked down the hallway toward the kitchen of the bed and breakfast, he glanced toward the drawing room. The small room was bright from sunlight streaming in through the two large front windows. A burgundy and gold area rug covered most of the hardwood floor, and plump armchairs in matching hues complemented the color scheme. The room was empty, but a gray backpack leaned against the leg of a small end table. It hadn't been there when he'd gone outside to talk to Declan.

He paused, listening. He didn't hear any voices or movement in the house. With a sense of alarm tightening his gut, he made his way to the kitchen and stopped. The room was empty, though the kettle boiled away on the hot plate. Wherever she was, Pelicia hadn't been gone long.

He clenched his jaw. Had something happened to her in the ten minutes or so he'd been talking with Declan? If it had, some hotshot protector he'd turned out to be.

The back door opened. He whirled around, one hand reaching beneath his jacket to clasp the butt of the gun holstered at the small of his back.

"Oh, God, Sully. You scared me!" Pelicia closed the door behind her and walked over to the counter. She held an armful of flowers, freshly picked, which she laid on the counter.

The only blooms he recognized were the ones from the camellia bush at the corner of the house. Everything else was completely foreign to him, though he thought a few of the flowers looked like tulips. Or were they daffodils?

She glanced at him as she bent, reaching into the cupboard beneath the sink. "Are you all right?"

Her denims pulled taut across her ass. Sully felt a tightening of his jeans as his body reacted to her. *Down boy*, he cautioned his unruly prick. *She can't be yours*. He wouldn't come between his best friend and the woman he loved.

Sully eased his hand away from his weapon and let it fall to his side. Willing himself to settle down, he gave a nonchalant shrug. "You startled me."

"Well, I guess we scared each other." She smiled and lifted out a large glass vase. Once she'd filled it with water, she put the flowers in it, taking a few moments to haphazardly arrange them. She placed the vase on the kitchen table. The result was a riotous collection of colorful blooms that lent cheer to the room.

"You said earlier you have other guests." Sully leaned one hip against the table. "Are they around?"

She shook her head. Taking the kettle off the hot plate, she flipped the power switch off. "Neal's working. He's a photojournalist, off somewhere taking pictures. Andrew's here on holiday. I was expecting a married couple to check in this morning, but they phoned late last night to say they had to cancel their trip." She glanced over her shoulder at him. "So I'm glad you decided to spend your holiday here in the Fortunate Isles."

They shared a grin.

"Would you like a cup of tea?"

"Love one." He walked over and stood beside Pelicia. "May I help?"

She smiled again and shook her head. "You and Neal, both of you here as guests but wanting to help the hostess. Just sit down." She put together the tea tray and brought it over to the table. As she poured him a cup, she asked, "Black or white?"

"Black." He accepted the cup she held out to him and took a sip. "Perfect. Thank you."

She nodded. "My pleasure. It's nice to have an almost full house."

He shifted on the chair, stretching his legs out beneath the table. "Do you normally live alone?" At her nod he said, "It must get lonely during the off-season, being here by yourself."

A ready smile curved her lips but he saw a shadow in her eyes. "Oh, I'm good company. And there's plenty to do that can't be done when guests are here, so I don't get bored."

Sully studied her a moment then looked down into his cup. "Even with tourists, though, it must be pretty quiet around here." He glanced up at her.

She shrugged. "We don't have the kind of night life that London has, if that's what you mean."

"Nor the crime," he said quietly, wondering if she'd say anything about being shot at not once, but twice.

"That's a definite plus." Her voice was equally soft. She took a sip from her cup and stood. "Feel free to help yourself to anything in the kitchen," she said with another smile that didn't quite reach her eyes. "I need to get started on laundry." She seemed to push her sadness away and smiled again, and this time it sparkled in her gaze. "It's good to have you here, Sully. I hope you enjoy your stay."

So she wasn't going to be forthcoming about her own difficulties. He gave a nod and watched her leave the room, her shapely bottom swaying as she walked away.

No wonder Declan was so smitten. Not only did she have a lovely body, she had an equally lovely personality to go with it.

Declan had been an idiot two years ago. Sully thought perhaps he'd deserved to lose Pelicia. He frowned at his uncharitable thought, but there it was.

Shaking his head, he stood and carried his cup to the sink. He dumped the remaining tea and rinsed out the cup, placing it on the counter. Then he went out into the drawing room, where he could sit and pretend to read but in reality watch over Pelicia.

Chapter 6

Three hours later, Pelicia had finished the laundry, made the beds with fresh linen and was in the drawing room with Sully, laughing over a rather risqué joke he'd just told. She didn't know what she'd done right, but it was a nice change to have three handsome men as guests, even though Andrew was gone most mornings by the time she got up and didn't come back until very late. But his bed was slept in every night, so she knew he was around.

She gave a mental shrug. Andrew was apparently doing what he wanted to do on his holiday, whatever that was. Pushing away worries about her absent guest, she looked at Sully. He was as humorous as Andrew and every bit as charming as Neal, but with his dark hair and lean build he reminded her more of Declan.

She refused to follow that line of thought. Declan O'Connell was the last man she wanted to be thinking of right now. For the first time in two years she was with a man who flirted with her, just being friendly with no ulterior motives—at least none that she could sense. Sully had a way about him that put her at ease. She didn't want to start thinking about Declan and get all hot and bothered again.

She'd just opened her mouth to start telling Sully a joke when the front door opened, and the man she was trying so hard to *not* think about walked in.

Sully got to his feet. "Is this one of your other guests?" he asked with a glance down at her. "Neal, was it? Or is it Andrew?" He looked at Declan and held out his hand in greeting. "Sullivan O'Rourke."

A scowl crossed Declan's face though he shook Sully's hand civilly enough. "Declan O'Connell."

"Oh, not Neal."

"No. Not Neal."

"Or Andrew either." Sully's lips pressed together as if he were fighting a grin.

"Not Andrew, either." Declan's brows drew down even farther as he looked at Pelicia. "Who the hell are Neal and Andrew?"

"My other guests," she said slowly, exaggerating her enunciation. Sully had just asked if Declan was one of her other guests. Declan wasn't obtuse—but he was certainly acting that way. What was his problem? She turned toward Sully with a polite smile, though she was beginning to seethe at Declan's gruffness. Her smile turned to a grimace at Sully's raised eyebrows over Declan's rude behavior. "Declan's an old . . . acquaintance of mine."

She glanced at Declan in time to see his eyes flare with irritation. "I need to talk to you," he muttered. He turned and walked away, heading down the hallway toward the kitchen, his booted heels clomping on the hardwood floor.

Pelicia watched him go, hard pressed not to admire the taut curve of his ass and strong lines of his back. Determined to stand her ground, she stayed where she was. Just because he barked a command didn't mean she had to obey.

She caught the look Sully sent her way and shrugged. "Sorry about that," she said. "He's not housebroken. I usually just ignore him and eventually he goes away." Although she had a feeling he wasn't going to go away any time soon.

Sully grinned. "No need to apologize for him, love. It's not a reflection on *your* manners."

She nodded. Then, partly because she really did need to finish her chores and partly because she wasn't going to let Declan order her around—and she knew he'd be right back out here as soon as he realized she wasn't following him like a lemming rushing over the edge of a cliff—she stood. "I do have a few more things to take care of upstairs." She smiled. "But I've enjoyed spending time with you."

"Me, too."

She gave him a slight nod and left the room. She went upstairs, out of habit skipping the third step that squeaked, and fetched towels from the linen cupboard to place in each of the guest bathrooms. She refreshed the potpourri she had in small bowls on the backs of the toilets, the fresh scent of lavender tickling her nostrils, then went to her room and closed the door behind her.

Pelicia walked over to the window and stood there, staring out at nothing in particular, and tried not to think. But her mind kept rolling in circles, images of her and Declan together—laughing over a silly movie, strolling around Piccadilly Circus hand-in-hand, alone in her flat with their legs tangled on cool sheets. . . .

She clenched her fists and tried to direct her mind elsewhere. The very last thing she wanted to do was think about Declan and what she'd lost when he'd betrayed her trust.

Especially since he wanted to talk to her and didn't seem in all that good of a mood.

And him being cantankerous usually brought out her own irritation. Even as she thought that, she realized by not following him into the kitchen she was egging him on, precipitating a fight.

Bring it on.

Her bedroom door opened and without turning she knew it was Declan. Even as she wondered what had taken him so long to follow her upstairs, she asked, "What do you want?" Her tone was unwelcoming, and she didn't give a flying fig how he took it.

"I told you I wanted to talk to you." There was little inflection in his low tones, though she caught a note of annoyance.

She heard the quiet snick of the door closing. She also thought she heard him sniffing, like he had the beginnings of a cold, but when she glanced over her shoulder he stopped doing it. She turned back to the window and crossed her arms, clasping her hands around her elbows.

He moved closer, stopping just behind her. "Why'd you run?" His voice was still quiet.

Pelicia whipped around to face him. "I didn't run." As a matter of fact, she had walked. Rather quickly, but it had been a walk nonetheless. "I . . . have work to do. A bed and breakfast to run." She forced a shrug, trying to appear more at ease than her twisting insides allowed. "Besides, I don't have to jump just because you tell me to, O'Connell."

Declan closed his eyes. With a sigh, he dipped his head and scrubbed the back of his neck with one big hand. Lifting his head, he stared down at her. Pain swirled deep in his eyes. "I never wanted to hurt you, Pel. If you won't believe anythin' else, please believe that."

For the first time since she'd known him, he wasn't hiding behind his boyish charm. His sincerity was unmistakable. But . . . "It doesn't change anything, Declan."

He clasped her shoulders. "You're right. I can't go back and change what happened." A muscle in his jaw flexed. "To be honest, I don't know that I'd change much if I could—your grandfather was guilty, Pel." She tried to jerk away from him. His fingers tightened briefly.

"And he's paying his debt to society." She lifted her chin. "I've forgiven him and put that behind me."

"Have you?" he asked. "Have you really? Because you haven't forgiven *me*, and I wouldn't have been involved if it hadn't been for your grandfather's betrayal of your trust. *He's* the one who used you as an unwitting courier to deliver his forged documents to his clients, not me." He gave her a little shake. "Maybe the reason you're so angry with me is because of him."

"I don't need armchair psychology from you, O'Connell." Her anger flared anew. "*You're* the one who fucked me over, in more ways than one." This time she jerked hard enough to dislodge his hands. She moved away, putting several meters of space between them. "And you yourself admitted you wouldn't do anything differently—"

"I would try to do things differently so you wouldn't have been arrested," he interrupted, his voice harsh. "If I could change that one thing, darlin', I would."

She stilled. He'd never before said that to her. He'd only ever said he was sorry about what had happened, but he'd said it in such a way that she'd thought he would have done pretty much the same thing all over again if he had to.

Even when she'd known him when he was younger, he'd been driven by determination. Driven to prove . . . something, whether to himself or to others, she'd never known.

But he'd always hidden behind a casual, carefree attitude toward life, never letting her get too close.

Not even when they'd become lovers.

She searched his gaze. His candor was impossible to reject.

He must have seen something in her soften, because he slowly came forward. "I would turn back time if I could, Pel. I never wanted you to get hurt. If you don't believe anythin' else, believe that."

And she did. Heaven help her, she believed him. But it was hard to let go of the hurt and anger she'd been holding onto for the past two years. She wasn't entirely sure she could—or wanted to—trust him again, but she couldn't deny any longer that she'd missed him.

Missed touching him. Kissing him. Making love with him. She'd even missed arguing with him. But still . . .

"I don't think I can trust you." Her voice trembled. She cleared her throat. "I'm afraid you'll hurt me again."

"I won't, I swear." Declan brought his hands up to cup her face. Callused thumbs swept slowly back and forth across her cheeks. "I know I fucked up, Pel. I've had two years to decide what was important in my life, to set some priorities." He brushed the hair away from her face, letting one broad palm curl around the curve of her skull. "I don't work for the security company anymore. I'm strictly a one-man operation—my own boss. I promise you I won't let my job come between us again."

Even as Pelicia mentally accepted the olive branch he offered, she knew it wasn't enough. She drew in a deep breath and let it out slowly. "Well, since I'm not doing anything that would make your job come between us," she responded while she eased away from him once again, "that's not much of a promise."

He frowned, his forehead lined with confusion. "What the hell do you want from me, then?"

She sighed. "I don't know." She didn't. Her feelings were in such turmoil that she didn't think she could articulate what she wanted from herself, let alone what she wanted from him.

His eyes sparked once more with irritation. "Well, when you figure it out, call me."

So much for the peace offering. He hadn't changed, not one bit. "You're a real tosser, you know that? You act like you're throwing me a bone yet you still want things on your terms." She poked him in the chest and tried to ignore how very firm and warm he felt. "Not this time, sweet cheeks." She quashed the urge to reach around and give one of those sweet cheeks a quick, hard pat. It would irritate the bejesus out of him and . . .

On second thought, maybe a smack on the bum was just what the man needed. Before she could follow through, though, Declan stepped back and raked both hands through his hair.

"How the hell am I supposed to fix things if you can't even tell me what you want?" His deep voice rasped with frustration.

Pelicia narrowed her eyes. "Don't put this on me. I wasn't the one who mucked things up." Her voice rose with indignation and the flare of remembered hurt.

He sighed and turned away from her. "We're obviously not gettin' anywhere. I'm goin' to let you cool down. I'll come back later when you're calmer."

"Typical." Scorn lay heavy in her voice. Faced with something he couldn't immediately fix, he was going to make a strategic retreat and plan his next move. Instead of staying to talk things out now, he would leave to regroup and come back later to try and bulldoze her into his way of thinking.

His shoulders went back. He stopped and pivoted to face her. "And just what the hell is that supposed to mean?"

"Just what you think it means, O'Connell." His scowl deepened at her use of his last name. She knew he hated it when she did it—it was much less intimate than using his first name, which of course was why she did it. "You've discovered you can't sweet-talk me into falling into bed with you again, so you're going to tuck your tail between your legs and run away."

A growl rumbled from his chest. With a muscle in his jaw flexing, he slowly announced, "The only thing that's goin' to get tucked, darlin', is my cock into your sweet pussy." The Irish brogue was very much in evidence, attesting to his growing aggravation.

There was the Declan she remembered. Arrogant and so confident in her surrender that she wanted to smack him. Again.

"You should be so lucky." Pent-up anger flared. He'd been everything to her and had turned her world upside down when he'd betrayed her. She'd survived, had become stronger for it, and knew she could live the rest of her life without him.

But she missed him, the cocky smartass, and *that* made her angry, too. And more turned on than she'd been in two years. "Your randy prick isn't coming near me any time soon, you can bet on that."

She'd feel better if she could believe what she'd just said, but her body felt like one big throb of arousal. Hopefully Declan wouldn't call her bluff.

His eyes glinted. "Do I detect a challenge?" Lustful anticipation flicked over his face.

Pelicia went very still. Even her breath seemed suspended. Why not? She gazed at him and wondered why she was holding back. Sex with Declan had never been the problem. As long as she kept her emotions out of it, why not do the horizontal mambo with him?

"If you think you're man enough," she drawled, holding her hands out in front of her and crooking her fingers at him, "come and get me."

A slow smile curved his mouth. Lust rolled off him in waves, making her shiver in anticipation. As he began stalking toward her, she wondered if she hadn't perhaps wakened a beast that she should have left well enough alone.

But what a sexy beast he was.

She backed up until she hit the door. Palms flat against the wood behind her, she stared at him, her pulse pounding madly in her throat.

This was what had been missing in her life in the last two years—that sensation of being alive. Only Declan had ever made her feel quite like this.

Like she was standing on the edge of a cliff without a parachute, ready to jump, trusting he'd be there at the bottom ready to catch her.

Only he hadn't.

She shook her head, dislodging that thought. Right here, right now, this was about sex. Pure and simple. Nothing more.

When he stopped a few feet away, she wondered if he'd changed his mind. "What's the matter, O'Connell?" she taunted. "Can't get it up?"

Declan quirked an eyebrow. Pelicia was spoiling for a fight, and after the last four months of trying to get near her only to have her continually push him away, he was primed to give it to her. All she had to do was glance below his beltline, and she'd see *getting it up* wasn't a problem for him.

If she wanted to do the old bone dance, he was more than happy to oblige. Arousal throbbed deep in his gut, danced along his veins to pulse behind his eyes.

He trapped a snarl in his throat. Desire had awoken the beast within, startling him with its intensity. But he welcomed it—he could see so much more acutely, could smell how aroused Pelicia was. Her heartbeat pounded against her ribs, fluttered in her throat.

It wasn't fear—he'd have been able to sense that, too. Smell it, even. No, she was nervous and even a little apprehensive, but she wasn't afraid. Which was good—he didn't want her to be frightened of him.

Mindless with passion was another thing.

This certainly wasn't the way he'd planned to get back in her bed. He'd had more wooing in mind, thinking flowers and some expensive wine would be involved. But he'd take whatever she was willing to give.

And if she wanted it this way, well, she'd always been able to make him hot, aching and hard with little effort on her part. He was more than ready to accommodate her.

He took the next few steps necessary to bring them face to face. Leaning one forearm against the door jam, he bent until his lips were a breath away from hers. "You sure *you're* up for this, darlin'?"

Her tongue swept across her lips, leaving them wet and inviting. "I'm sure," she whispered. Her gaze locked with his, the blue of her irises almost swallowed up by the pupils. "But if you've doubts . . ."

Declan pressed his hips against hers, letting her feel just how many doubts he *didn't* have. Her lips parted on a gasp. He took her mouth with his, hard, unable to summon gentleness through the wild arousal beating at him.

He brought his hands up, cupping her face between his palms, and tilted her head for a better angle. God, she tasted better than anything he could remember. Sweet like honey with a hint of something tart. He licked across her lips then dove back into her mouth.

Her tongue twisted around his, surging into his mouth when he retreated only to tempt him back to her when she withdrew. He forged inside her mouth. She suckled his tongue, drawing him deeper, making him groan as his cock hardened even further.

Her scent made him crazy with need and her touch—soft and hungry and searching—made him ravenous. Leaving her mouth, he worked his way down her throat, stopping at the pulse pounding under her soft skin. He rested his lips there for a moment before touching the tip of his tongue to the spot. Life thrummed beneath his tongue, awakening a different sort of hunger.

He closed his eyes and fought back the wolf, fought back the instinct that told him to fit his teeth into her soft skin, to irrevocably mark her as his.

He'd had no choice in becoming a werewolf—he wouldn't force the same fate upon Pelicia.

And that thought gentled his response. Declan placed a kiss on the corner of her lips and drew her to the bed. He eased off her clothing, his eyes narrowing at the sultry picture she made. Pink-tipped breasts billowed above a narrow waist and generous hips. With economical movements he took off his clothes and then came down on top of her again. He kissed her, his tongue sweeping into her mouth to mate with hers.

Her hands came around him, fingers flexing into his back muscles. She moved her legs restlessly. He slid between them, his cock stiff against her belly.

He kissed his way down her throat, closing his eyes at the softness of her skin. Scattering kisses across her chest, he tongued each stiff nipple before kissing his way down her flat stomach.

His hands parted her thighs just a little wider, his fingers stroking a long caress in the moist folds between her legs. She jumped when he touched her, jerked against his hand, a sharp cry of pleasure escaping her.

He pushed a finger slowly inside her tight, hot sheath. At once her muscles clenched around him, velvet soft yet firm and moist. His own body throbbed and swelled in response.

Her hips pressed forward wantonly, in her rising passion all inhibitions gone. Declan thrust another finger into her, stretching her, preparing her. More than anything, her pleasure mattered to him. Her velvet folds pulsed for him, wanting, *demanding*, and he fed that hunger, pushing deep, retreating, thrusting again so that her hips followed his lead.

"That's it, darlin'," he breathed against her stomach. "Just like that. I want you ready for me."

"I am ready for you," she panted, her slender hands grasping his hair, trying to pull his face up to hers.

"No, you're not. Not yet." His mouth found the triangle of damp curls at the juncture of her thighs. Her breath hissed out as his tongue tasted her, his name a whispered plea. He lifted his head to look at her. "Open your legs wider. Let me have you."

To his surprise, she clamped her thighs together. Her

grip on his hair tightened. "I don't want you playing nice, O'Connell. I want you inside me. Now."

Who was he to argue? Declan reared up, bracing himself with palms against the mattress on either side of her arms. "Condoms?"

"Are you contagious?" she purred, stroking one finger down the middle of his chest.

"You should know me better than that." His voice came from a throat tight with need. She circled her finger around his navel. His eyes widened as sensation jumped straight to his straining cock.

"I do," she answered with a grin. "You're nothing if not careful." A slight dip lined her brow for a moment and then it was gone. "I'm safe, too." Her hand curled around his erection. "I want you inside me. Naked. Nothing between us."

Her thumb swept over the tip of his cock, spreading the bead of pre-cum over the fat head. With a gasp, Declan pulled her hand away and knelt between her legs to guide his throbbing shaft to the entrance of her body. She was unbelievably wet, her cream trickling down her thighs. Any worry he'd had that he would hurt her if she was unprepared was pushed away.

He punched his hips forward, saw the moist tip of his cock slide past the slick folds of her sex, and felt her, tight and hot, close around him. The sensation shook his control even further.

"Pel!" Her name burst from between his clenched teeth. He grabbed her firm ass and lifted her as he slid in another inch. "Tell me you're okay, darlin'."

"I'm fine. I'd be better if you'd just hurry up." She gasped, her eyes bright, her hands sliding around him to clutch at his back.

He laughed, a short, sharp burst of sound from a throat tight with need. With a hard flex of his hips, he buried his cock deeper. It had been a long time since he'd felt such ecstasy—two years, in fact. It was all he could do to keep from ravaging her, so great was his need. Lowering his head, his tongue flicked the taut peaks of her breasts. The action tightened her body around him even more.

"I feel full, like you're part of me," she whispered. "But I want more, Declan. I want all of you." She slid her hands from his back down to grasp his buttocks.

"Me, too," he gritted his teeth and surged forward. Her sheath was slick and hot and velvet soft, and so tight it was just about to kill him. He buried himself deep, withdrew, thrust hard again. He watched her face for signs of discomfort, but her expression held only a look of passion, her eyes glazed, her breath coming in pants.

Satisfied she felt the same pleasure as he, Declan began to move, gliding in and out of her, deeper with each stroke. He tilted her hips so he could thrust even deeper, wanting her to accept every last inch of him, as if by her body accepting his she could see past the monster in him and love him.

He buried himself to the hilt, shoving so deep he felt her womb, felt the spasms of her climax beginning. "I've never felt like this, *mo chroi*. Never." He needed her to know how he felt, what she meant to him.

His rhythm became faster, harder, his hips surging forward, beyond any pretense of control. Pelicia cried out as her body splintered and Declan felt the strength of her inner muscles gripping him in the intensity of her orgasm. He pumped into her frantically, the explosion ripping through him from his balls through the top of his head.

When he could make his mind work rationally again, he eased out of her, groaning as her inner muscles clung to his sated cock. He tucked her against his side and blew out a sigh. Finally he had her where he wanted her—in his arms again, limp and soft. Before he could get comfortable, though, she stirred, pushing away from him to sit on the edge of the bed.

"What's wrong?" he asked, sitting up and pressing a kiss on her shoulder.

She shook her head. "I . . . I can't do this."

"Can't do what?"

"This." She made a vague gesture at him, at the bed. "Sex is one thing, but this . . ."

He frowned. "What're you sayin', Pel? I'm good enough for sex but that's it?" With some chagrin he realized he sounded like a wronged woman, but damn it! That was how he felt.

"Now that the shoe's on the other foot, it's not so pleasant, is it?" She glanced at him and shook her head. "And before you get angry, that wasn't what I had in mind when I started . . . this. I wanted you. I still do." She sighed and looked away. "I just don't think I—I don't want to snuggle. It was just sex."

And that was the hell of it. This reticence of hers to let him close again was what he'd been trying—unsuccessfully it seemed—to overcome. What in God's name was he to do now?

He drew in a slow breath and released it just as carefully. Sliding an arm around her, he drew her back against him. She remained stiff. And he was damned if he knew what to do.

Pelicia held herself still. Declan always had been a great

cuddler after sex—something not many men seemed to be comfortable doing. But for him it came as naturally as the intercourse part did.

But now, to lay in his arms in the aftermath, to hear the thump of his heart beneath her ear, the warmth of his skin against hers . . . that level of intimacy with him scared her. She was too vulnerable, too emotionally fragile where he was concerned. She couldn't—*wouldn't*—open herself up like that to him. Not now.

Maybe not ever again.

With a shake of her head, she moved away from him and climbed off the bed. She began to dress in silence. She heard the squeak of bedsprings as Declan shifted behind her. She glanced over her shoulder to see him sitting on the edge of the bed, dark eyes slightly narrowed, brow furrowed with puzzlement.

"Talk to me, Pel."

"I can't do this." She sat on the bedside chair and pulled on her sandals. "Please get dressed."

To his credit, he didn't argue but stood and grabbed his underwear. As he pulled the boxer briefs up his muscled legs, he said, "I don't understand. Darlin', what's goin' on inside that head of yours?"

She got to her feet and crossed her arms. "This is exactly how things started out between us two years ago, O'Connell. A little flirting, some heavy petting, hot, raw sex and then . . ." She shook her head and clamped down on tears that burned her eyes. "I'm not going down that road again."

He yanked on his jeans, zipping them but leaving the top tab undone. His heavy sigh bespoke his confusion. His dark gaze held hers. "Tell me what I can say that'll make you believe me. Tell me what to *do*."

She shook her head. "I'm not sure there is anything you *can* do."

A gruff sound left him, and he reached for her.

Pelicia held out one hand. "Please, Declan. Don't. Don't push."

"I'm not even allowed to hold you?" He shoved his hands in his front pockets, thumbs hooked over the edge. "That's not bloody fair, Pel."

She searched his face. "I'm sorry. I just . . . If you touch me, we'll end up on that bed again." Deciding a strategic retreat was in order, she walked toward the bedroom door. "Give me time."

"If you keep pullin' away from me, we'll never be able to talk about what happened. About us."

A pulse throbbed madly in her throat. She lifted her hand, pressing her fingers against the fluttering vein. She partly turned and met his gaze. "I'm afraid of you," she admitted quietly.

Pain and regret flared in his eyes. "I realize that." A muscle twitched in his strong jaw. "You trusted me and I betrayed you. That's goin' to take a lot of forgettin'. A lot of forgivin'." He drew in a breath. "But you have to let me close enough to give me a chance, darlin'."

She pressed her lips together. "Just . . . give me time," she repeated.

He let her go without another word. Declan had always been such a persistent suitor—for him to let her walk away from him now meant a lot. Yet it made her sad that he seemed to give up so easily.

She was being so contrary. *You can't have it both ways, you nit.*

Pelicia went downstairs, and as she reached the bottom of the stairs, she saw Sully back on the small sofa in the drawing room, his nose in a book. He lifted his head briefly and cocked an eyebrow in greeting, then went back to his reading.

She frowned. Sitting indoors reading a book wasn't the way she'd spend her holiday, but maybe this was how he unwound. When he'd first checked in she'd learned he was from London and that his family was "in investments," whatever that meant. If he was a high-powered broker, she guessed just sitting around and reading for the pleasure of it might be the only time during the year he had the chance to do something so inactive.

A bracing cup of tea was what she needed. And maybe a day away from this place. She'd call Brenna and see if she'd come tomorrow to watch over the guests. If she could, then Pelicia was heading to London for a day trip. Not that she could really afford it. Not financially. But emotionally she needed the break.

From the Nola.

From Declan.

And, perhaps, even from herself.

Chapter 7

Sully stood at the window in the drawing room and watched Pelicia get into the front seat of a taxi. He'd heard her on the phone earlier, making arrangements to meet someone for an early dinner, and that was when he'd realized she was leaving for a trip to London.

He could hardly tag along without raising suspicion. He'd tried to reach Declan, but couldn't get through. He'd sure as hell keep trying. But in the meantime he had reached a friend of his at Scotland Yard who'd promised to be waiting at Heathrow and would follow Pelicia, watch over her, just in case. Sully had snapped a picture of a photo of her with her grandparents and sent it by e-mail so his friend would know what she looked like.

He pinned his hopes for her safety on the fact that this was unplanned. Whoever had been taking shots at her wouldn't have a heads-up about this trip and so would be less likely to be in a position to pursue her.

"Hallo, luv."

At the sultry tone, Sully turned toward the doorway. A curvaceous blonde walked into the room. She wore a flowered skirt that bounced around her knees when she moved, and a blouse the color of a robin's egg made her clear blue eyes all that more startling.

When she reached him, she held out her hand. "Brenna Brown. I'm a friend of Pel's. I'll be your hostess for the day." She gave him a flirtatious smile. "And you are . . ."

He shook her hand, noticing with a small grin that she held onto it longer than necessary. "Sullivan O'Rourke." As she let go of his hand she trailed a finger along his palm. His grin widened. He did like a woman who wasn't afraid to let her feelings be known. "My friends call me Sully."

"Well, Sully." Another smile and a slow wink. "I have a feeling we could become very good friends." She looked at him from beneath long lashes. "Unless you're already spoken for?"

He glanced at her left hand and saw a narrow gold band on her ring finger. Looking back at her face, he raised one brow. Flirtation was one thing, but he wouldn't get mixed up with a woman who wasn't free to enjoy the carnal side of life with him. "I'm not, but it looks as if you are."

She twisted the ring around her finger and shook her head. "My husband died three years ago." She brushed her bangs away from her forehead. "I just . . . haven't been able to take it off. Not yet."

Sully inclined his head. "I'm sorry."

She smiled, though the sadness didn't leave her eyes. "He was a good man and I miss him. But I know it's time to get on with my life." She started to say more, but broke off when the front door opened. Walking out into the foyer, she greeted the big blond man walking into the house like a long-lost friend, giving him a hug and kiss on the cheek. "Neal! You didn't let me know you were back, you naughty boy."

The man returned her hug and smiled. "I thought I'd surprise you."

She drew back and looked over Neal's shoulder toward the door. "Are you by yourself? Isn't there one more guest? An . . . Andrew something-or-other, I think?"

"He's never around." Neal glanced at Sully. "You never did say this morning at breakfast what it is you do for a living."

Sully cocked his head to one side, wondering why it mattered. But he'd sized up this bloke at breakfast—he knew the type. Big, brawny, full of testosterone but insecure around other men, needing to point out their shortcomings to bolster his own. Not that most women seemed to mind that. Sully gave a nonchalant shrug and stared straight into Neal's eyes. "My family is into investments."

Which wasn't a lie.

Neal gave a nod. "Good for you. With as much as I enjoy photography, I don't think I could make a living any other way. Well," he grinned, "not completely. It'd be nice to have a cushion, though."

Brenna tucked her hand in the crook of Neal's arm. "I've always wanted to learn how to take really good photos." One lid slid down in a slow wink. Her smile was wide and eager and full of lust. "Perhaps I could train under you."

"Perhaps you could," Neal said, looking down at her. "You wouldn't be the first woman that's trained . . . under me." His grin was equally lustful. "My portfolio is in my room, if you'd care to see it."

Sully fought to keep from rolling his eyes. The man might as well have said *Why don't you come up and see my etchings?* It was obvious these two already knew each other and were just playing now.

Brenna glanced at Sully. "You'll excuse us, I'm sure."

She didn't wait for his nod, but turned toward the stair-case, grabbing Neal's hand and dragging him along behind her. Neal looked at Sully with a grin and obediently trot-ted up the stairs.

Sully went to the bottom of the steps and watched them. They went straight to Neal's room and closed the door. He heard them laughing, and then there was silence. In only a minute or so the bedsprings squeaked and a low male groan filtered through the door.

He shook his head and went back into the drawing room. To each his own.

His phone vibrated in its holder against his side. He pulled it out and answered with a terse, "Sullivan."

"I've been tryin' to reach you for over an hour." Declan's voice was a low growl of frustration. "Damned phones."

A high, feminine wail came from upstairs. Sully grimaced and got straight to the point. "Pelicia's off to London for the day. And before you yell at me," he said in a hard tone, "I've asked one of my inspectors to wait for her at Heathrow and follow her. And since she didn't give anyone advance notice, the chances of your sniper following her—let alone finding her—are slim."

Declan gave a snort. "An' you think she won't notice a police officer trailin' her through the streets of London?"

"He's plainclothes, O'Connell." Sully understood his friend's frustration, but he didn't appreciate it being taken out on him. He walked over to the window and glanced outside. Other than a few camera-toting tourists, there wasn't much going on. He turned back toward the room. "And he's good—one of my best men. Just how much of a muck-up do you think I am?"

"Sorry." Declan's heavy sigh echoed across the line. "Damn it. What the hell did she go to London for?"

"She said on a shopping trip." Sully walked over to one of the plump burgundy-on-gold striped armchairs and sat down, crossing one leg to rest his ankle on the opposite knee. "But she looked a little . . . fragile." When Declan didn't respond, Sully prompted, "Dec? You still there?"

"Aye." Declan's voice was harsh and deep. "What does that mean? Fragile?" His voice dropped even lower, the tones coming through in a guttural rasp. "What the fuck does that mean?"

"Just what I said. She looked like she was ready to break. Emotionally. I imagine she felt the need to put some space between her and . . . this place." More likely between her and Declan, but Sully wasn't going to go there. He rubbed his fingers across his ankle. "She'll be back in the morning, Dec."

"She'd better be." There was a pause then Declan asked, "Have you seen anything unusual? Anything odd about her guests?"

"How about odd friends?" Sully stood. Going to the doorway of the drawing room, he looked up the stairs. It was quiet now. Thank God.

"What do you mean?"

Sully sighed. "Oh, nothing. It's just one of Pelicia's friends is here supposedly to watch over things until Pelicia gets back, but right now she's upstairs shagging one of the guests."

"You're joking." Declan's voice held amusement mixed with incredulity.

"No, I'm not. Unfortunately." Sully went back into the drawing room. "She took one look at Neal and pretty much dragged him upstairs. I think they've, ah, been together before."

"What did you think of him?"

"Neal?" Sully shrugged. He transferred his mobile phone to the other ear. "First impression is . . . not much. We ate breakfast together this morning and he seemed rather interested in me, what I do for a living, and so on. He claimed his curiosity stems from his being a photographer and so is naturally inquisitive about his surroundings and the people in it. But I don't buy it."

"Why not?"

"There's just a bit something . . . off about the man. I can't put my finger on it just yet. And don't even get me started on the ever-absent Andrew." He heard footsteps on the stairs. "Hang on a minute." He dropped his hand to his side, still holding the phone, and went back to the drawing room doorway.

Neal came down the last few stairs, tucking his shirt into his pants, camera hanging around his neck. Whistling off-key, he looked up. A grin widened his mouth. "Never turn it down when it's free, you know what I mean?"

Sully gave a nod. As Neal continued toward the front door, Sully asked, "You're heading out again?"

"I just came back to pick this up." Neal hefted the camera. "And so . . . here I go again." He opened the front door and left, pulling the door closed behind him.

Sully glanced toward the stairs again. The door at the top of the stairs opened and Brenna stepped out. He ducked into the drawing room and brought his mobile phone to his ear. "Wait a sec."

"Sully!" Declan muttered something too indistinct for Sully to catch. "What about the other guy—Andrew What's-His-Name?"

"Haven't seen him yet." Sully glanced up as Brenna stopped in the doorway. He gave her a smile and a small wave. "Hold on," he said to Declan. He raised his eyebrows. "Is there something I can do for you?" He fought back a grimace at the opening he'd just handed her.

She grinned. "No, luv. I'm good. For now." She gave a waggle of her fingers and walked away, heading down the hallway toward the kitchen.

Sully exhaled and brought the phone back to his ear. "All right. I'm back."

"What the hell is going on over there?"

Sully shook his head. "Never mind. Look, I'll let you know as soon as she gets home, all right? And in the meantime, I'll see what else I can find out about her two other guests. Especially Andrew, since he seems to be something of a phantom."

"All right. Good." Declan paused then said, "The second she gets back—"

"I'll call you." Sully said good-bye and disconnected the call, replacing the phone back in its holder. He poked his head through the drawing room doorway, looking toward the kitchen, and saw Brenna bustling back and forth, towel tucked into her waistband in the front. Looked like she was busy. Time to go snooping.

Pelicia sat at a corner table in one of her favorite restaurants on High Street and idly sipped her coffee. She'd placed one call to Brenna and had been assured that the Nola was still standing and the guests were happy. And, no, Declan hadn't been by.

Which struck her as odd. That was one of the reasons she'd gone ahead with this shopping trip she couldn't afford—she hadn't wanted to deal with Declan today. But now it seemed she wouldn't have had to anyway.

She shook her head. That seemed to be the way her luck had run the last couple of years—things she braced herself for never materialized, and things she'd never expected to happen smacked her in the face.

"Pelicia?"

She looked up to see her dinner date, a friend and former coworker from the hotel. "Hallo, Lizzie." She put down her cup and stood.

The tall brunette leaned down a bit and enfolded her in a hug. "It's so good to see you," Liz said with a smile as she pulled back. From behind small oval-shaped glasses, her hazel eyes were alight with pleasure. "I'm glad you called me this morning."

"I'm glad you were able to meet me on such short notice." Pelicia sat back down and stared at her friend. Liz had been the one person who'd kept in touch with her after she'd been made redundant, had been the only one willing to put her up if she'd had the space. But she lived in a tiny one-bedroom flat that she already shared with a roommate, and it just hadn't been feasible.

The two of them had kept in touch for about six months after Pelicia had returned to the islands, but then life had gotten in the way and they'd stopped corresponding. Pelicia felt badly about that, which was the main reason she'd contacted Liz this morning. Catching up with her friend—and staying caught up—was something she was determined to do.

Life was too short and sometimes friendships too fleeting to let one go without a fight.

"So, what brings you to town?" Liz looked up as the server approached the table. After ordering a coffee, she turned her attention back to Pelicia. "Looking for work here?"

Pelicia raised her eyebrows. "God, no." Just a little respite from a very determined Irishman. "Anyway, I doubt anyone would hire me. Remember my . . . troubles?" she asked in a dryly sarcastic tone.

Liz dismissed that with an airy wave. "People forget. Management changes. You might be surprised what kind of offers you could get now."

"You're joking, right?" Pelicia picked up her cup and took a sip of tepid coffee. "There toward the end, I couldn't even get people to take my phone call, let alone schedule interviews."

"No, I'm not joking." Liz leaned forward, resting her elbows on the table. Slender fingers gripped her cup. "You were the best sous chef we had, Pel. Howard was an idiot to make you redundant." She grinned. "Now that *he's* been made redundant, there just may be a place for you back at the Cardiff."

Pelicia turned that over in her mind. Was it really possible that she could come back to London and pick up where she left off?

The bigger question was—did she want to?

She had made a home for herself on St. Mary's, and the B-and-B could be salvageable if this season turned out well. But there—as here in London—the specter of her grandfather's crime shadowed her. There were people who would believe she was involved regardless of what the final outcome had proved.

She still had the feeling deep inside that she wanted to start over somewhere new, some place where people didn't know anything about her background.

But the idea of sliding back into familiarity and the

anonymity a large city like London afforded was equally appealing.

"I'm in a better position to help you now, and even have a spare room I can put you up in whilst you look for your own place. And you are spending the night with me tonight. We have a lot to catch up on." Liz sat back and took another sip of coffee. "But think about coming back to the hotel, all right?"

Pelicia started to respond but stopped at the approach of the waiter. She and Liz both ordered a Caesar salad. Waiting until the waiter moved off, Pelicia looked at her friend. "I can't help but think about it, Liz."

The other woman smiled. "That's all I ask." She picked up her water glass and stroked a finger through the condensation. "So, have you seen Declan since . . . Well, you know."

"Funny you should ask." Pelicia leaned back in her chair. "He came to the islands about four months ago. He's been staying with Ryder—you remember I've mentioned him?"

Liz nodded. "He's your father's employer, right?"

"Mmm. And friend." Pelicia shook her head. "I'm not quite sure why Declan's stayed so long. Well—" She gave a snort. "Except to torment me."

"And did you enjoy the, ah, torment?" Liz waggled her eyebrows. When Pelicia sat there and stared at her, she went on in a seemingly casual tone, "I can always tell when someone's been laid, m'dear. The residual glow is good for up to seventy-two hours."

"You're making that up."

"Uh-uh." Liz paused, one finger tapping against the side of her nose. "I know these things."

Pelicia briefly closed her eyes and shook her head. When

she looked at Liz again, the other woman was grinning. "You *are* making it up."

"Maybe, but you answered the question without having to give me an actual 'yes' or 'no.' " She laughed, drawing the attention of nearby diners. Leaning forward, she clasped her hands around her water glass.

Pelicia sighed. "I suppose so."

"You don't seem happy about it, though." Liz reached over and put her hand over Pelicia's, giving her fingers a squeeze. "You still haven't forgiven him, have you?"

"You think I should have?" Pelicia sat back and crossed her arms. "He *used* me."

"He loved you." Liz tapped on the table. "He didn't use the best judgment in starting up a relationship with you during an investigation, but that just means he's human."

"But . . ."

"No buts, sweetie." Liz sat back so the waiter could place her salad in front of her. "He made a mistake," she went on as the young man served Pelicia. "Granted, it was a big one. Huge." As the waiter left, she stabbed into her meal. "Can you really tell me you don't want to give him a chance to make it right?"

No, she couldn't. But she was scared to and she said as much to her friend.

Liz's eyebrows went up. "Since when have you been afraid of a challenge?"

"It's one thing to take risks with my career. I can always start over," Pelicia responded. "I risked my heart once with Declan, and he tore it apart. I don't want to go through that again."

"Who says you will?" Liz put down her fork. She was as serious as Pelicia had ever seen her. "Listen, Pel. If you don't at least try to work things out with Declan—because I *know* how much you love him—you will regret it for the rest of your life."

She was right.

And that scared Pelicia, too.

Chapter 8

The next morning, Pelicia waited on the side of the road in front of the Nola while the cabbie fetched her packages from the boot of the car. The flight from London with the layover in Newquay, Cornwall, had been uneventful. The trip had given her plenty of time to think about life—in the general sense as well as on a much more microlevel.

She'd not thought about returning to London to live and work before now—she'd really believed that too many people would remember her humiliation. Would hold it against her.

But if what Liz said was true . . . Her stomach leapt with excitement. She could go back to her old life. Go back to where she'd been happy.

B.D.O. Before Declan O'Connell.

She smoothed the flowered skirt of her sundress over her hips. Liz had insisted on giving the dress to her, saying that she hadn't worn it in a year and it was time for it to go. The bright yellow had cheered Pelicia, and it hadn't taken too much persuading to get her to put it on.

She gazed around her. Regardless of the hope she tried

to mute at the thought of going back to London, coming back to the Isles of Scilly—those fortunate isles—had filled her with a sense of familiarity, a sense of returning that had surprised her. And as the taxi made its way from the airport across the island to Hugh Town, she wondered if, after all, she had made a home for herself on St. Mary's.

The cabbie handed over her packages and took payment of her fare with a crooked grin. "I thought maybe you were heading back to London for good."

Now there was a thought. One she'd had rolling around in her head ever since dinner with Liz last night. For now, though, she smiled and shook her head. "No, Fred, I have a B-and-B to run here, didn't you know?"

His grin widened. "Well, it's good to have you back on the island, Pelicia. You were missed."

She warmed at that. Fred was a kind man, and she appreciated that quality now more than ever. He got into the cab. Pelicia waved good-bye with the couple of fingers she could spare. He pulled away and headed toward the center of town.

She turned toward the bed and breakfast. Struck anew by the realization that she was glad to be back, she stared a moment at the Nola. The granite house had been repaired, the damage whisked away as if it had never happened. The flowers in the front garden gave the bed and breakfast a bright, welcoming aspect.

But as happy as she was to be back, she realized that this was merely the place where she worked, the place that enabled her to earn a living. It *wasn't* home.

Nor was London. But London at least could be a place where she could be productive and feel satisfaction in her career.

She could *make* it feel like home again.

She sighed and trudged forward. She was being pitiful, whining to herself that she didn't have a home—she had a roof over her head, enough food to eat, friends, and a father who was small in stature but mighty in spirit.

As always, thoughts of her dad made her grin. She should get over to the Keep to see him more often, but lately, since Declan had been staying there, she'd kept her distance. She knew her dad understood, but she shouldn't have let her feelings of discomfort mean that she couldn't visit with her father. Besides, Phelan's Keep was where she'd spent her childhood—if anywhere was home, that was it.

Pausing at the front door, she chewed on her lower lip and admitted that the only other place she'd felt at home was when she'd been with Declan. As trite as it might sound, she'd found her home in his arms.

If she could admit that, perhaps it was time to give Declan another chance. To give *herself* another chance.

"Pel!"

She turned and saw Brenna walking toward her from the side of the house. Pelicia smiled and asked, "How'd things go while I was gone?"

"Oh, fine. We had an American stop by wanting to check in without a reservation, and of course I had to turn her away. Which is a nice change—means the business is going well." Brenna brushed a kiss in the air near Pelicia's right cheek. "And I'm happy to say that all your boys behaved themselves." She drew back, grinning, and brushed her fringe of blond bangs out of her eyes. "Especially Neal. Talk about *fiiiine*." She waggled her eyebrows.

Pelicia rolled her eyes. Trust Brenna to take advantage of an opportunity when one presented itself. She and Neal had become lovers after Neal's second stay at the Nola, and Brenna always made sure she was nearby whenever he came to visit. "And Sully and Andrew?"

Brenna shrugged. "Sully pretty much stayed in the drawing room, though he did sit on the stoop and get some sun for a bit yesterday afternoon." She shook her head. "Always with his nose in a book."

Pelicia frowned. "He didn't go see any of the sights? The Garrison or Old Town? Or what about the museum or the Heritage Center?"

"No." Brenna held her hands out, palms up, in an I-don't-get-it pose. "He stayed here the entire day."

"And Andrew?"

Another shrug. "Haven't seen him. But his bed's been slept in, so I know he came in at some point last night." She patted Pelicia's shoulder. "Look, since you're back, I'm going to head out. I might be able to catch up with Neal." Her grin was unrepentant.

"Wait." Pel dug around in one of the bags and pulled out a small box. "I got these for you."

At the sight of the picture of Belgian chocolates on the lid, Brenna gave a little squeal of delight and hugged Pelicia. "You're such a darling. Thank you!" She wiggled the box. "I know just what—or should I say who—these will go with. Bye."

Pelicia watched her go and then twisted the knob and pushed open the door. She was just about to put her packages down when she heard Sully's voice coming from the drawing room.

"Would you stop already? You sound like an old woman."

That certainly piqued her interest. Not feeling guilty at all for eavesdropping, Pelicia quietly set the paper bags on the floor and straightened, tipping her head to listen as Sully went on with his conversation.

"She's outside talking to Brenna right now. My man in London said her day was without incident. As far as he could tell, he was the only one tailing her."

She frowned. It sounded like he was talking about her. But why would he be? And to whom?

And just what did he mean, *he was the only one tailing her*?

"Just sit tight, Dec. She's fine."

Dec? He was talking to *Declan*?

What the bloody hell!

"I know you're worried, mate." Sully's sigh was loud. "But she's fine," he repeated. "She obviously needed this trip, so give her some time." There was a short pause then he snorted. "Well, maybe you should listen to her, then."

Pelicia waited until he ended the call then she walked over and stood in the open doorway. He looked up at the movement, his eyes widening slightly when he saw her standing there. She folded her arms over her breasts and tried to contain the anger roiling in her gut. "Just how long have you and Declan known each other?" The words came from between clenched teeth.

To his credit, he didn't bother to continue the fabrication, though he did let out a sigh and slumped back in the armchair. "Since university."

"This was his idea, I assume? Whatever *this* is."

Sully tucked his mobile into its holder on his belt. He stood and walked closer to her. "He's worried about you. About the shooter."

She pursed her lips. "Knowing Declan as you do, don't

you think it much more likely someone was shooting at him, not me?"

He raised his brows. "And they just happened to shoot at him—twice, I might add—when he was with you? Don't you think *that's* unlikely?"

She decided to ignore his question and asked one of her own. "And I suppose your family's not in investments, is it?"

"Actually, we are." He grimaced. "But I'm also a DCI at the Yard."

He was a detective at Scotland Yard. Declan had gone against her wishes—and behind her back, big surprise there—and involved the police. Never mind that Sully had no jurisdiction here. A cop was a cop was a cop.

A muscle at the outer corner of her left eye twitched. She brought her hand up to press a finger against the tic. "Is your name really Sullivan O'Rourke?"

He at least had the grace to look shamefaced. "Rory Sullivan. But my friends do call me Sully." He gave a grin that faded when she didn't return it.

Her stomach was churning and her heart was breaking. Declan hadn't changed. She'd been an idiot to think he would. "And you're here to . . . what, Detective Chief Inspector Sullivan? Protect me? Or spy on me?"

His jaw tightened. "Now, Pel, I understand why you're upset, but this was done with you in mind. Dec's trying to keep you safe."

"He just couldn't tell me about it, right? Because I'd get upset or go into histrionics?" She clenched her teeth, hard. Damn that O'Connell. She'd been thinking about opening up and trusting him again, and the whole time he'd conspired to plant a mole in her house. Going behind her back once again. Nothing had changed. "That does it." She whirled around toward the front door.

She brushed off Sully's attempts to appease her and yanked open the front door. It was a ten-minute walk to the wharf—less than that if she power walked—and she was just by-damn angry enough to cover the distance in half that time.

Declan O'Connell was going to get a piece of her mind. A bloody big piece. And maybe a foot up his arse while she was at it.

Realizing Sully was right behind her, she stopped so abruptly he ran into her. She turned and planted her palm in the middle of his chest. "You're not coming with me."

"Pel, I'm supposed to make sure you stay safe. Declan wants—"

"At the moment," she said, glaring at him, "using the excuse of what Declan wants is not—I repeat not—a good thing. You are *not* coming with me." Without waiting for his response, she walked out of the house. Slamming the door behind her, just mad enough to hope the mole almost got his fingers caught, Pelicia stalked off toward the wharf.

In the thirty minutes it took her to get from the Nola out to Phelan's Keep, her anger had not cooled at all. It hadn't cooled on the climb up the steps from the dock to the top of the bluff where the big house sat like a king holding court.

As a matter of fact, by the time she lifted the brass door knocker and let it fall against the heavy oaken front door, she was clenching her jaw so tightly her teeth hurt.

If it had been anyone other than her dad who opened the door, she would have pushed her way into the house and hunted down O'Connell like the hound dog he was. As it was, she forced a smile to her face and returned her father's delighted hug.

"Pelly!" William Cobb drew her inside and closed the

door. "Why didn't you phone and tell me you were coming? I'd have prepared something for you to eat."

Her pasted-on smile turned genuine. He was really such a darling. She could kick herself for letting her aversion to seeing Declan get in the way of visiting with her dad. "I'm fine, Dad. I ate in London."

A frown crossed his face. "You were in London this morning?"

She nodded. "I went yesterday and spent the night with Liz. You remember her?"

"Yes." Concern darkened his eyes. "Are you all right, darling? I could fix you a nice cuppa, if you'd like."

"No, no tea, thanks." She glanced around the foyer. "Where is everyone?"

He raised his eyebrows. "Ryder and Taite have gone for a stroll around the island, and I have the feeling you didn't come here to see your old *pater.*" He waved away her protests. "It's all right. With the way Mr. O'Connell has increased his forays to St. Mary's, I reckoned you'd be here sooner or later." He tipped his head toward the stairs. "He's in his room—second story, first room on the left."

"Why isn't he on the first story?"

"He, ah, wished to give the newlyweds as much privacy as possible."

Pelicia gave a nod of understanding and planted a quick kiss on her father's cheek before walking toward the lift.

"Do leave some skin on the boy, won't you?" Cobb called after her, a teasing lilt in his voice.

"*You* want me to be nice to him? I thought you didn't like him."

"He's . . . grown on me," came his dry response.

"Well, no promises," she responded, smiling at his laugh. Once the door slid closed, her smile faded. She pressed the button for the top floor. The lift started up, going much too slowly for her liking. She found herself tapping one foot impatiently.

God help him, Declan had better not try to weasel his way out of this one.

The lift came to a stop, and the door slid open. She strode down the hall and, not bothering to knock, twisted the knob to Declan's room.

When the door to his room pushed open, Declan looked up from the crossword puzzle he was working. Pelicia stood in the doorway, hands on hips, eyes flashing fire. God, she looked beautiful, wearing a sundress that flattered her lightly tanned skin. The skirt flirted with her trim thighs, the top with its square neckline showed off the plump slopes of her breasts.

He'd been expecting her—Sully had called to warn him as soon as she'd left the Nola. Declan slid a small piece of paper between the pages to mark his place and put the puzzle book facedown on the bed beside him, then swung his legs to the floor.

"Just stop right there." She held out one hand, index finger up. Red slashed across her cheekbones—he couldn't tell if it was anger or if she was just the teeniest bit turned on because all he had on was his boxer briefs. When her gaze didn't flicker from his face, he figured it was anger, not arousal, putting the color in her face.

"I want to know who the hell you think you are," she went on. "Planting a spy!"

He got to his feet. "Whoa, wait right there, darlin'. I didn't plant a spy. I asked a friend to help me keep an eye on you, to keep you safe."

"And you didn't feel it was necessary to ask me first? Or at the very least let me know what you were doing?" She crossed her arms and glared at him.

"No, I didn't." Her anger flared, and Declan was surprised her head didn't start twisting around on her neck like in that horror movie scene. "You didn't need to know."

"I'm not one of your bloody soldier boys!" Pelicia took the few steps it required to reach him and poked him in the chest. "This is my life we're talking about here—I need to know *everything* you do that might affect me. So cut the 'need to know' crap right now."

He clenched his jaws. He'd done nothing wrong, and he wasn't going to let her pile a load of guilt on him again. "I will continue to do what I believe is best to ensure your safety. With or without your knowledge and cooperation, if need be." When her mouth opened, he went on, his voice hard, "I'm not finished." He grasped her shoulders, tightening his grip when she tried to pull away. He gave her a little shake. "Now you listen to me, Pel. You've been in harm's way twice in the last few days. Regardless of who the bastard was shootin' at, those bullets could have hit you. So I'm not playin' around." This time when she tried to shrug away from him, he let her.

"Neither am I," she snarled. "You keep telling me you've changed, that you want to make things right between us. Keeping secrets and going behind my back is not the way to do that."

Declan tried to ignore the little fact that she was right about that. "Would you have agreed to let Sully stay had you known he was my friend? If you knew he was a cop?"

"Of course not."

He shrugged. "I rest my case."

Pelicia's slender hands clenched into fists at her sides. "You are the most . . . stubborn, hardheaded—"

"That's the same thing."

"—chauvinistic, arrogant bastard I've ever known," she went on as if he hadn't interrupted her.

"You forgot charmin' and irresistible." He didn't know why he was pushing her buttons, except that she was breathtaking when she was angry. That this mattered so much to her gave him hope that she still loved him.

At last her gaze roved over him, starting at the top and working its way down then back up again to pause at his groin. The heat of her interest generated a response. His cock swelled, pressing against the soft cotton of his boxer briefs.

"I can't argue with that," Pelicia said softly.

Declan thought, for a moment, that she was over her anger, though he could still smell the cayenne pepper scent of it. But when she lifted her gaze, the anger remained, though tempered somewhat by the stirrings of desire. And a heart-wrenching sadness that deflated his burgeoning arousal as well as a cold shower could have. Better than, even.

"But your arrogance overshadows everything else," she said, putting a pin to his small bubble of hope. "You just stay away from me, O'Connell."

His gut seized. "For how long?"

"Until I'm not mad at you anymore." She turned and left the room.

He listened to her footsteps grow faint as she went to the elevator. She wanted him to wait until she wasn't mad anymore? The last time he'd done that, it had been two years.

Hell. Who was he kidding? She was *still* mad about what happened two years ago. This could be a long wait.

And waiting wasn't something he did well.

Well, if she wanted him to wait, he might as well do it from outside the Nola. Whether she liked it or not, Sully would be on the inside, and she'd have a werewolf on the outside.

Chapter 9

She returned to the Nola less than two hours after she'd left. The watcher eyed her through his spotter scope, appreciating how pretty she was—this was the first time he'd seen her in a dress. Her legs were long and lean, feet arched in strappy mid-heeled sandals. She wore her blond hair in its usual ponytail, which left her shoulders bare except for the thin straps of the dress's bodice.

She was beautiful—she should wear dresses more often.

He pushed back guilt at the idea that she didn't have much longer to wear anything and steeled himself for the task at hand. He would follow the plan to make that Irish bastard suffer as much as possible—and that meant Pelicia Cobb had to die.

That hadn't been in his original plan, though, of course, he'd known about her. He and O'Connell shared a past, and O'Connell's talk of Pelicia was what had brought him to the Isles of Scilly to begin with. He'd decided that if he stayed around Pelicia long enough, eventually O'Connell would come sniffing around.

He'd been right. And now it was time to heat things up. By tomorrow afternoon, there would be no question in O'Connell's mind that his lady love was in danger. It would be too late for him to do a damn thing except mourn.

And prepare to join her.

Chapter 10

Pelicia came to wakefulness with a start. She glanced at her bedside table and read the muted readout on her clock radio. Two A.M. Sleep had come hard tonight. After she'd returned from Phelan's Keep this morning she'd busied herself around the Nola, spent time with Brenna, trying to keep her mind off of Declan and using whatever excuse she could to avoid Sully. She was still upset with him for being part of the subterfuge and, truth be told, a bit embarrassed that he was caught up in the middle of whatever was going on between her and Declan.

Her tummy rumbled. She'd elected not to have dinner with her guests—instead she'd had tea and biscuits in her room. Now she was paying for skipping dinner with a very unhappy stomach, which growled even louder.

With a soft curse, she threw back the covers and got out of bed. Might as well go down to the kitchen and get something to eat. At two A.M. it was unlikely anyone else would be about.

But, just in case, she shrugged on her light cotton robe to cover up her short nightshirt. She slid her feet into her open-toed slippers and quietly opened her bedroom door.

She walked as softly as possible down the hallway, then down the stairs. The small lamp she always left on in the drawing room lent a soft glow to the ground floor but not much light filtered past the foyer. Intent on getting down the dim staircase without falling, she didn't realize someone was coming up the stairs until she was almost on top of him.

Pelicia gasped and jerked her head up. Her eyes widened. The person standing two steps down, whoever it was, was dressed in dark clothing and wore a ski mask that covered all of his face except for his eyes and mouth.

His eyes widened briefly, too, then he lunged for her. She yelled and scrambled backward, losing her balance. She landed on her rear on the edge of a step and cracked her elbow on the step above it. Her eyes swam with tears of pain. She pushed his reaching hands away and was able to get one foot between them.

She shoved her slippered foot into his gut for all she was worth. A startled grunt escaped him as he went down the stairs, arms flailing for balance. Pelicia shot to her feet and turned to go back to her room, intending to lock herself in.

A hand wrapped around her ankle, yanking her off balance. She cried out. Putting out her hands, she broke her fall but could do nothing about the man pulling her the rest of the way down the stairs.

He straddled her. As his hands wrapped around her throat she heard Sully's shout from above, then the front door slammed open. Thinking it was someone coming to help her assailant, her stomach dropped with dread.

Her attacker turned his head at the same time that Declan ran in. He pulled the intruder off her and threw him across the foyer into the drawing room. Pelicia heard the smashing of glass and wood and tried not to care that it sounded like the man had just landed on—and demolished—her grandmother's favorite coffee table.

What was that compared to Declan saving her life? She coughed and waved him off. "I'm all right." She sat up and rubbed her throat.

He glanced up the stairs. "Stay with Pel." He headed toward the drawing room.

Hearing footsteps on the steps behind her, she twisted to see Sully coming barefoot down the stairs, clad in only a pair of light blue cotton boxers and a gun in one hand. Bending, he put his free hand under her elbow and helped her up. "You okay?"

"Fine."

The fight spilled out into the foyer. Sully urged her up the stairs.

"But Declan—"

"Can take care of himself," Sully muttered. "And he'll skewer me alive if I let you get hurt. Now go!"

Pelicia let him push her the rest of the way up the stairs but balked when she reached the top. She wrapped her hands around the newel post and refused to budge. "Go back down there and help him," she implored.

Sully shook his head. "I don't want to distract him. He'll be fine."

The intruder punched Declan in the jaw, sending him sprawling onto the foyer floor.

"Yes, I can see he's doing just fine," she whispered and prodded Sully. "Go help him."

Sully sighed and took one step then froze. Pelicia couldn't take her eyes off Declan, either. He was . . . changing. She heard the tearing of his clothes and drew in a deep breath. He rolled to one side, groaning, and the intruder took advantage of his incapacity by fleeing.

Sully muttered a curse and started down the stairs.

"Sully, stop!" Pelicia went down several steps and grabbed his shoulder.

"Make up your mind, would you?" He glanced over his shoulder at her. "Do you want me to help Dec or not?"

"I thought you were going after the other guy."

He frowned. "In my underwear? And barefooted?"

"Declan would."

"Yes, well, Declan can be a bit of a hothead, in case you didn't know it. I know my limitations, and running after someone in my boxers and bare feet is one of them."

Another groan from Declan brought both their attention back to him. The breath snagged in her throat, and she tightened her grip on Sully's shoulder. While they had been arguing, something miraculous and, from her point of view, totally unexpected had happened.

In the pile of Declan's shredded clothing stood a huge dark brown wolf.

Damn the man. When had he become infected and, more important, when had he planned to tell her? She narrowed her eyes. Knowing him, he'd thought long and hard about trying to hide it. Probably thought he could get away with having three-day-long business trips once a month that took him away from her.

"What the hell?" Sully brought his gun arm up and pointed the weapon at the wolf, which slowly turned its head to stare up at them. "Where the fuck did Dec go?"

Pelicia stretched and put her hand on his rigid forearm, gently urging him to lower his gun. "Don't shoot it, Sully. That's Declan."

"What's Declan?"

"The wolf."

When he turned his head to look at her, she raised her shoulders in an I'm-not-kidding shrug. "Apparently he's a werewolf, though he didn't choose to tell me about it."

The wolf whined and, with a clatter of its nails, raced through the still-open front door, no doubt on the trail of the intruder who'd attacked her.

Pelicia stood in silence on the steps, still holding onto Sully's shoulder.

"Declan's a werewolf." His voice was flat, disbelieving.

"It looks that way. Bastard." No one made her want to cuss faster than Declan O'Connell.

Sully started down the stairs. She let go of his shoulder and followed him. While he went straight to close the front door, she turned right and bent to pick up the pile of Declan's ruined clothes. After straightening, she pushed the light switch on the wall, turning on the small, art deco style chandelier in the foyer.

"Declan's a werewolf," Sully said again. His eyes were wide. One corner of his mouth turned down. "Declan's a *werewolf.*" He stared at Pelicia. "My best friend from university is a sodding werewolf."

"Yes." She empathized with his disbelief, though she didn't share it. She'd known from the time she was a little girl that werewolves were real.

So, no skepticism for her. Anger and hurt, that was something else. Because once again Declan O'Connell had chosen to withhold the truth from her.

"I must say, you seem to be taking this rather well. Better than me, in fact." His entire expression reflected his confusion, his brain's struggle to accept what his eyes had seen.

Pelicia sighed. "This isn't new to me, Sully. I know someone else who's a werewolf." She glanced up the stairs. "I'm surprised Neal and Andrew haven't come out to see what's going on."

"Neither one of them are here." Sully came toward her, seemingly unself-conscious with wearing only his underwear. She couldn't help but look and appreciate him for the fine hunk of man flesh he was, though she deliberately kept her gaze off his groin area.

She had enough trouble as it was with just the one man—werewolf!—she had. She wasn't about to add to it.

"How do you know they're not here?"

He shrugged and stopped a few feet away. "I checked their rooms before I went to bed, and they haven't been in since."

"How do you know?" What was he doing, sitting up awake at night?

"I'm a light sleeper." Sully shook his head. "I can't believe . . . Declan's a bloody werewolf!" He scrubbed the back of his neck with one big hand. "It's probably a good thing neither of your other guests *was* here. This would be difficult to explain." He started to say more but stiffened and squinted down the hallway toward the dark kitchen.

Pelicia partly turned to see what he was looking at, but she saw nothing. "What?" she asked in a hushed voice.

He gave a slight shake of his head. "I don't know. There looks like there's something on the kitchen floor. Wait here."

Sully crept down the hallway. Pelicia waited a second or two and then followed him. When she caught up to him he muttered, "What part of 'Wait here' didn't you understand?"

"The part where I wait by myself while the big man with the gun goes off without me," she muttered back, clutching Declan's clothing to her chest. "As long as you're armed, where you go, I go."

His sigh was low and heavy. He stopped in the doorway and checked the room, then reached out and pushed the light switch. Pelicia saw his back stiffen. "Goddamn it." He looked over his shoulder at her, his expression hard. "This time, wait here." When she didn't respond, he said, "I mean it."

Her brows dipped but she gave a nod of agreement. Then she saw what was on the floor. "Oh, my God! Brenna!" Pelicia started to go into the kitchen, and Sully put out one arm to stop her. "Get out of my way, Sully." Her voice shrilled, echoing in the confined space of the hallway. "It's Brenna. I have to get to her."

"I know it's Brenna, love." His voice was soft. "She's dead."

Tears slid down her cheeks. She shook her head sharply. "How can you know that from here? Maybe . . . maybe she's just unconscious."

"There's too much blood, Pel. I'll double check, but I need you to stay here, all right?" He turned and took her by the shoulders. When her gaze stayed plastered to her friend's body, he cupped her chin and made her look at him. In that gentle voice he said, "We don't want to disturb the scene any more than necessary. As a matter of fact, why don't you ring emergency services?"

She swallowed, hard.

"Go on," he murmured.

He was right. Pelicia gave a lingering look at the body of her friend, her heart breaking. Then she went down the hallway and picked up the phone, dialing nine-nine-nine for emergency.

She looked toward the kitchen to see Sully walk carefully over to Brenna's body. Once the operator knew the nature of the call, he transferred her to a Police Community Support Officer in Cornwall. As she gave information to the officer, Sully squatted near Brenna's head and reached out to place two fingers against her neck. After several moments he rose and made his way out of the kitchen.

At the solemn look on his face, a sob broke free and she clapped her hand over her mouth to try to keep the rest of them at bay. She held onto her control long enough to give her address to the officer. She hung up just as Sully reached her. He pulled her against him, one hand at the back of her skull, pressing her face against his chest.

She wrapped her arms around him, clutching his back, and cried.

"I'm sorry, love," she heard him murmur. "I'm so sorry. She's gone."

"This can't be happening." She sobbed into his chest, speech difficult. "Why would anyone want to kill Brenna?" This kind of crime was unheard of on the Isles. Robbery, sure. Even some vandalism now and again, but murder . . . "I don't understand," she whispered.

"A murder like this never makes sense, sweetheart." Sully let her cry another few minutes. "How long until the police get here?"

Pelicia gave a shuddering sigh and wiped tears off her face, grateful for his solid presence. "We only have a couple of constables here on the island—they usually have to take care of traffic tickets and the odd burglary, and during tourist season some drunk and disorderlies. But not murd—" She swallowed back more tears and pulled away from Sully. "Not murder. They'll have to bring a specialized unit over from the Devon and Cornwall Constabulary. It will take a few hours, though I imagine the support officer I spoke to will have called Charlie Tremwith, our local PC. He should be here just as soon as he gets dressed."

Standing there, staring at the floor with tears burning in her eyes, she felt old. And scared. And very much as if her world had just been turned upside down.

Again.

Pelicia tucked her trembling hands into the pockets of her robe and looked up at Sully's face. "I . . . don't know what to tell them when they get here."

His brows lifted. "You can tell them everything that happened, except for the werewolf bit."

No, mustn't tell the cops about the werewolf. At least she and Scully had been the only ones to witness Declan's transformation—even the intruder hadn't seen it.

Sully guided her up the stairs. "Put some clothes on, love," he said in a soft voice. "I'll do the same, then we'll go back downstairs and wait for the police together."

She went into her room and numbly shrugged out of her robe. She took off her nightshirt and got dressed without putting much thought into the process. For the first time since she'd returned to St. Mary's, she wasn't averse to having the police on her doorstep. Someone had killed Brenna.

Pelicia would do whatever was necessary to make sure her killer was found.

Still in wolf form, Declan paused at the end of Garrison Road. A boat engine fired up, and he heard the water slosh as the marine vehicle took off.

Enemy. Lost.

The bastard had gotten away. But it had been the same one who'd fired those shots—the smell of gunpowder lingered in the man's clothing. The sniper had been in her house, trying to hurt Pelicia.

When Declan had first burst into the Nola he'd smelled

blood. His heart had thudded to a stop. Relief and rage had mingled to see a very much alive and apparently unhurt Pelicia struggling with an intruder.

As soon as he'd engaged the attacker, his rage had exploded. Sharp pain had seared his gums as his canines had elongated, his eyes had burned as the wolf struggled to be free. Declan had believed in his own control to the point where he was confident he was stronger than the beast, that when it wasn't a full moon he wouldn't shift.

He'd been wrong.

The transition from human to wolf took an amazingly short time, considering the way bones and sinews had to shorten or lengthen, muscles realigning to match, blood vessels and organs transforming as well. An amazingly short time and an astonishingly painful process.

He'd been aware of Sully's horrified disbelief, though his friend's hands had been steady as he aimed his weapon at the wolf. Pelicia's reaction, on the other hand, had been one of awe quickly followed by anger.

He hadn't wanted her to find out this way. Hell, in the back of his mind he hadn't wanted her to find out at all. Maybe he'd have told her on their fiftieth wedding anniversary when she was too old to run from him. Well, at least, too old to run very fast.

Giving a snuffling snort, he put his nose to the ground and followed the attacker's trail until it ended at the water's edge. It was impossible for him to track the bastard any farther.

With no little trepidation he made his way back to the Nola and tried to prepare himself to face Pelicia and Sully. When he transformed back to human he'd be naked. Wearing his birthday suit to face down an angry lover and friend wasn't high on his list of things to do.

But it was time to face the music.

Naked or not.

He loped back to the Nola, using shrubbery as much as possible to cloak his presence. Wolves weren't indigenous to the Isles, and there was no sense in getting people riled up and started on a wolf hunt. He reached the edge of Pelicia's property and paused, lifting his head to sniff the wind.

Safe.

But . . . he smelled blood.

Before he could proceed farther, a small police car rolled up in front of the Nola and stopped. PC Tremwith got out and walked briskly to the house. He rapped sharply on the front door.

The door opened and Pelicia stood there, looking wan but unhurt. She stood aside and Tremwith entered. As she closed the door Declan saw Sully standing near her.

He couldn't very well walk up to the house stark naked, not with the local police constable there. Besides, now he knew she was safe. And with Sully and Tremwith there, Declan could go on to Phelan's Keep and get a fresh set of clothes.

And brace himself for Pelicia's wrath.

Chapter 11

Hours later, the watcher stood in the shadows and watched while a sheet-draped body was rolled out on a gurney. Rage burned in his gut. He put his attention on the house where Pelicia Cobb stood in the doorway with the London cop behind her, his hands on her shoulders.

He ground his teeth together. He'd made a mistake—he'd thought Brenna was the Cobb woman, had thought he would be able to take her out and finally strike a blow to O'Connell.

Instead she stood there, brave, weeping, sorrowful, and alive. Alive, damn it.

And the lovely Brenna Brown was dead. Killing her had never been part of his plans. Using her, yes. Slaking his carnal thirst with her beautiful body, absolutely. He'd never meant to fall in love with her, but he had.

But killing her?

It had never been part of the plan. She was the best thing that had happened to him in the last twenty years. She hadn't cared about the tremor in his right hand or that he wasn't whole anymore. She had given him strength when he'd needed it the most.

He hadn't been expecting her to be there tonight. When he'd seen a slender blond woman in the dark kitchen, he'd thought it was Pelicia. And he'd struck.

He turned away, resolve hardening his heart. Pelicia Cobb would die, and that Irish bastard would watch and be powerless to stop him.

Chapter 12

Sully stayed by Pelicia's side throughout the investigation, keeping her away from the kitchen when the small police unit took crime scene photos and collected evidence. One of the local constables had assured them this case would take precedence—after all, it was an islander who'd been murdered. He had looked askance at Sully, but at Pelicia's assurances that Sully had been upstairs when she'd been attacked by the intruder, the constable had turned his attention to the two absent guests.

"And you've no idea where they might be?" he asked again, his gaze going from Pelicia to Sully and back again.

"No." She gave a small shrug and folded her arms over her breasts. She looked so lost Sully couldn't help but put one arm around her shoulders and pull her close.

"From what I've seen, Andrew is usually gone when everyone else gets up and doesn't come in until well after we've gone to bed, but he does come back here to sleep at least." He glanced at Pelicia for confirmation, and she nodded. Sully looked at the constable. "I have no idea about Neal. I've only been here a couple of days myself."

The constable made a few more notes and then put away his notebook and pen. His face wore lines of concern. "Pel, if you think of anything else, let me know, all right? And if there's anything I can do for you . . ."

She swallowed. "Thank you, Charlie. I appreciate it."

When they wheeled the gurney with Brenna's sheet-draped body on it down the hallway, Sully turned to block Pelicia's view. He knew she'd seen it, though, because a sob broke from her throat before she buried her face in his shoulder.

This should be Declan here, comforting her, not Sully. It should be Declan's arms around her, his body warming her, his strength bolstering her.

But of course he couldn't be here, because he'd turned into a wolf and run away.

Damn it to hell. His best friend was a bloody werewolf.

Three hours after the police had been summoned Sully followed Pelicia out of the now empty Nola as if he was afraid she'd try to ditch him.

"I'm going with you." His voice rasped low and harsh.

She glanced at him in the dim light of early morning. "Okay," she said slowly. This was the third time he'd told her this, the first two being right after she'd said she was going to confront Declan. She hadn't objected the first time he'd told her he was tagging along when she went to Phelan's Keep, so she wasn't quite sure why he continued to insist he was going.

He grimaced. "Sorry. I keep expecting you to argue with me."

She raised her eyebrows. "He's *your* friend—you have a right to find out what's going on as much as I do."

"He's your friend, too." He shot her a look from beneath his lashes. "Isn't he?"

Once upon a time she would have said yes. But the way she was feeling right now . . . It was like she hardly knew him.

No, that wasn't quite true. She knew him too well—it hadn't surprised her to find out he'd not been honest with her. It had hurt her, angered her, but not surprised her. It was pure Declan in action.

But friends didn't hold secrets—at least big ones—from each other. Especially friends who seemed to want to become more than friendly.

"I don't know," she responded quietly. "I just don't know anymore."

They walked in silence to the wharf. She caught sight of the young man who delivered groceries to the Keep loosening the mooring rope to his boat. "Robbie!"

He looked up and grinned. "Pel! What brings you down here?"

"I'm looking for a ride out to see my dad. Are you heading that way?"

Robbie nodded. "Making my weekly grocery run."

Pelicia tipped her head toward Sully. "Mind if we make the run for you?"

"Not a bit." He helped her into the boat and, once Sully had jumped in, he tossed the rope into the stern. "Can you have her back to me by noon? I have another run this afternoon."

"Sure thing." Considering her mood, she wouldn't need the boat for six hours—she'd probably have it back to him in two.

She and Sully set off across the water and reached the dock at Phelan's Keep in twenty minutes. Once she'd tied the mooring rope, she led the way up the steep stairs to the top of the bluff.

Here she was, yet again, coming to this place but not to visit her father. She sighed. When all of this was over, she and her dad were going to have to spend some quality time together.

She stopped to catch her breath at the top of the bluff and looked back over the ocean. It was beautiful here, with nothing but ocean and little dots of islands.

Sully paused beside her, breathing deeply. "Damn. And here I thought I was in shape."

Even though she was still heartsick about Brenna and angry at Declan, the aggravation in Sully's voice made her grin. "There's nothing like a few dozen steps to show you just how out of shape you are, eh?" Pelicia shook her head. "I always have to stop at the top. Otherwise I end up at the front door blowing air like a bellows."

"You and me both."

After a few minutes, she turned to him. "All right?" At his nod, she walked toward the house, Sully at her side. She lifted the knocker and let it fall.

While waiting for someone to answer the door, she looked again at Sully. "Just what are you going to say to him?"

He gave a shrug. "Hadn't planned on saying anything to him. I'm just going to knock him on his arse."

She pressed her lips together, fighting a grin. How like a guy—no questions, no recriminations, just go out and hit someone.

Of course, O'Connell deserved it, so she wasn't going to argue with Sully's technique.

The door opened. Expecting to see her dad, Pelicia was surprised to see Taite standing there.

"Hey, Pelicia! How good to see you. Come on in." She stood back and let them enter.

Pelicia looked around. "Where's my dad?"

"He's out for his morning constitutional." Taite grinned. "He says it's so he can keep up with me."

Pelicia returned the smile. "He's probably just getting in shape so he can keep up with the babies."

"Whoa there." Taite held up one hand, palm facing outward. "We just got married. Don't be getting me pregnant already."

Pelicia laughed. "Sorry."

Taite shot her "the look" but spoiled it with another grin. Then she looked at Sully, tilting her head slightly to one side. "I'm sorry. Where are my manners?" She held out her hand and shook his. "Hi. I'm Taite Merrick. You look familiar. Do we know each other?"

"I don't think so," he responded with a shake of his head.

"Taite, this is Rory Sullivan, one of Declan and Ryder's friends from college. Sully, this is Ryder's wife."

"Ah. I remember seeing a photo of you boys when you were in college." She sounded so American that Pelicia couldn't help but smile. When Taite glanced toward the study, Pelicia assumed Ryder was ensconced there working on his next novel. Taite went on, "This isn't a good time for visitors—Ryder's closing in on a deadline and his muse isn't cooperating. But I know he'll want to see you, Sully. Let me see if I can pry him away from his computer."

"We really came to see Declan," he said.

Taite paused on her way across the foyer and turned to look at them. "What's he done now?" Resignation was rife in her voice.

She knew him well, too, it seemed.

"He turned into a sodding werewolf. Pardon my language." Sully shrugged. "But that's not something you see every day, is it?"

Pelicia shared a look with Taite but didn't volunteer that the other woman saw something like that on a fairly routine basis, actually.

Taite pursed her lips a moment. "Um, yeah." She shook her head as if warding off an errant thought. "Declan came in about two hours ago. Naked," she added dryly. "He got dressed and went back out. I think he's on the far side of the Keep—he goes there when he needs to sort things out."

"If you'll excuse us." Pelicia turned toward the front door.

"Pel, wait. Please. I'd like to talk to you first." Taite looked at Sully. "If you head straight across the island—there's a goat path of sorts—you'll find Declan. The island's not that big," she said at his wary expression. "Oh, let me get you some water before you go. Can I get you anything, Pel?"

Pel shook her head. "No, thanks. I'm fine."

"Okay. Be right back." Taite rushed off toward the kitchen.

Pelicia and Sully stared at each other in a silence that Sully finally broke. "I expected her to scoff."

"She and Declan have been friends a long time." She wondered how to proceed without telling him about Ryder. But Ryder's . . . condition . . . wasn't her secret to tell. And apparently Taite had felt the same way about Declan's situation, because she certainly hadn't volunteered any information about it.

They lapsed into silence again.

"Maybe I should just pop my head in and say hello to Ryder," Sully said just as Taite came walking back into the foyer.

"Here you go." She handed him a bottle of water with a cheery smile. "Straight across the island, remember. And . . ." She sighed. "Don't be too hard on him. He's only been a werewolf for four months—there are some things he's just not used to yet."

"No kidding." Sully glanced at Pelicia. "Will you be all right?"

"I grew up here, off and on. I'll be fine."

He gave a nod. "Ladies," he drawled and opened the front door. After he closed it behind him, Taite touched Pelicia's arm. "We need to talk." She drew Pelicia into the parlor. They sat down on the mauve Victorian style settee, Taite with one leg curled beneath her, a concerned expression on her lovely face. "First of all," Taite said, "how are you doing? Declan told us about the attack."

"Did he tell you about Brenna?" Pelicia bit her lip against the renewed urge to cry.

"Brenna?"

"My friend Brenna Brown."

Taite frowned. "He didn't say anything about Brenna. What happened?"

In spite of her best efforts, the tears flowed. "She's dead. We found her lying on the kitchen floor." Pelicia swiped at tears trickling down her face. "Sully wouldn't let me go in the room, which I understand, but . . ." She trailed off, shaking her head. A sob broke free, then another.

"Oh, honey." Taite moved closer and put her arm around Pelicia's shoulders. "I'm so, so sorry."

"She was my best friend." Pelicia bowed her head and wiped her face with her fingers again. "I can't help but feel . . ." She looked up, meeting Taite's concerned gaze. "Declan tried to tell me, but I wouldn't listen." Her face grew hot then cold. "Why wouldn't I listen? She's dead because of me."

"No, Pel." Taite took Pelicia's hands in hers and gave them a squeeze. "You can't think that way. This wasn't your fault. It was *his* fault—the one who killed her."

Pelicia took a breath and fought back her tears. Part of her heard and accepted what Taite was saying, but a larger part of her—the part that wept and ached in loss—couldn't believe, *wouldn't* believe that Brenna's death wasn't her fault.

The man who'd shot at her—twice—had come back to finish the job. Either Brenna had surprised him or . . . Dear God. What if . . . Her pulse pounded in her throat and her stomach clenched. What if in the darkness he'd mistaken Brenna for *her?*

With a sharp gasp, she untangled her hands from Taite's and rose to her feet. She'd never even told Brenna that someone had taken shots at her.

Pelicia paced in front of the fireplace, arms hugging herself. God, she'd been such an idiot. So wrapped up in her pathetic pity-party over how Declan had wronged her she'd been unable to see he was right.

And now her friend was dead.

"Pel, please come sit back down. Please," Taite added. Once Pelicia was seated beside her on the settee, she said, "For what it's worth, I don't think Declan realized Brenna was there, that she was dead. I'm sure he would have stayed with you, had he known."

Pelicia shook her head. "He was too busy running after the attacker to pay attention to what was going on with me. As usual." The man focused on his job to the extent he lost sight of everything else. Which was something else they were going to have to talk about at one point or another.

It was all too much. She teared up again. She wiped the moisture from beneath her eyes, fighting to stay in control. If she started crying again, she was afraid she might never stop.

Taite reached to the left and pulled a tissue free from a decorative container. "Here."

"Thank you." Pelicia took the tissue and mopped up her face, then blew her nose.

"Now, what I wanted to talk to you about . . ." Taite met Pelicia's gaze, her eyes dark with concern and holding a hint of unease. "We don't know each other very well, and that's something I hope we can work on. I think we can become very good friends and it's with that in mind that I'm going to butt in where I might not be wanted." She grimaced. "Just stop me if I go too far. I'm told I can be something of a terrier when I'm going after a problem."

"What problem?" Pelicia's brows dipped. Taite was clearly uncomfortable—what in the world was she planning on saying?

Taite drew in a breath and held it a moment before exhaling noisily. Her blue eyes were serious as she held Pelicia's gaze. "Declan loves you. He *really* loves you." When Pelicia started to respond, Taite held up a hand. "I know he can be arrogant at times—okay, all the time," she said when Pelicia snorted. "He's irascible, domineering, and kind of old school when it comes to protectin' the little woman," she said with an exaggerated Irish brogue. "But he means well. And he loves you."

"He has a funny way of showing it." Pelicia shook her head. "How can he love me when he doesn't trust me?"

Taite frowned. "Why would you think he doesn't trust you?"

"You mean beside the fact that he didn't tell me he was planting a spy at the Nola? And that he didn't tell me he'd been bitten by a werewolf?" She shrugged, knowing the gesture and her words were full of sarcasm. But she couldn't stop the hurt from spilling out. "Other than that, you mean?"

Taite stretched one arm along the back of the small sofa. "I think, in all honesty, he didn't believe that his life would be impacted that much. The fact that he can see farther, smell things better, hear more acutely are all bonuses as far as he's concerned. There's just that little thing three days a month." She heaved a sigh. "I can't say I don't understand how you feel. I'd fallen in love with Ryder and we'd already been intimate before I found out what he was. And it wasn't because he told me. Not exactly."

"How did you find out?" Pelicia hadn't heard the story and was curious. Just how similar were she and this American in love with a werewolf?

Well, that was one thing right there they had in common. Not that Pelicia was going to admit it. Besides, love without trust didn't go very far. She might love Declan but she didn't trust him.

She went still at the realization. The very thing she was accusing him of—of not really loving her because he didn't trust her—was the very thing she struggled with.

Giving a mental shake of her head, she knew the situations were completely, absolutely not the same. She had good reason not to trust Declan—the man had lied to her not once, not twice, but three times. She, on the other hand, had never given him cause not to believe in her.

He was just naturally distrustful. How could they have a relationship?

"The werewolf that attacked Declan was sent by Miles, Ryder's cousin. He first attacked Ryder and your dad." Taite hastened to add, "Your dad wasn't bitten, though he was injured. Slightly. Nothing to be worried about and he's completely fine now."

Pelicia blinked. "You are just digging yourself in deeper and deeper, aren't you?"

Taite bit her lower lip. "I can't seem to help myself. I get on a roll." She leaned forward. "I went to Ryder's bathroom to help him get cleaned up and saw the bite marks. I was devastated, thinking that it was my fault, that I had drawn the werewolf to Phelan's Keep—he'd been stalking me. Long story," she said with a wave of one hand. "Anyway, Ryder told me that the bites wouldn't change what he already was."

Pelicia raised her eyebrows. What a way to find out that your lover would get furry once a month.

Taite tipped up her chin at Pelicia's expression. "Yeah. You can imagine how shocked—and scared—I was. I didn't handle the news too well, I'm afraid." She grew pensive for a moment but soon shook off the sadness. "Ryder was just as reticent about telling me as Declan has been in telling you. I think he was afraid you'd completely cut him out of your life if you knew."

"Any cutting isn't going to be because he's a werewolf. It'll be because he's such a bollock-brain."

Taite pressed her lips together as if she fought a grin. She cleared her throat. "Yeah. Well. Regardless that he may or may not be sitting on his brains, it doesn't change the fact that he's madly in love with you. He's talked of nothing else since we got here four months ago." She leaned back against the sofa. "When you refused to see him, after we'd first arrived, he was so frustrated I thought he was going to wear a new trail around this island, all the running he was doing."

"He always did like to run." Pelicia gave a soft growl. "He's still running. From me."

"Maybe so. But only because he's just a poor, simple man."

That startled a laugh out of Pelicia. "Yes, you could have it right there." She stared at Taite. "How long was it before you forgave Ryder?"

Taite shook her head. "There our situations are quite different, Pel. Ryder and I had no prior history. I had no previous hurts to get over. You and Declan have a lot of baggage to get rid of before any healing can begin."

She was right again. And Declan, with his arrogance and secrecy, was making it nearly impossible. But if Taite was telling the truth—and Pelicia had no reason to doubt her—part of Declan's problem was that his anxiety over her continued refusals was making him more rash than normal. He wasn't making clear-headed decisions where she was concerned.

That said something. Actually, it said a lot. He had already admitted he hadn't handled things well two years ago. It would be interesting to hear what he had to say now.

Why hadn't he told her straight away that he was a werewolf? What was he so scared of?

Chapter 13

Declan heard the clomp of footsteps on the packed dirt path and smelled Sully long before his friend came into view. Without turning, he called, "How'd you find me?"

"Ryder's wife." Sully's voice was tight with anger, an anger that Declan was sure had grown as he'd walked across the small island. "She seems nice."

"She is." Declan twisted on the fallen tree he was sitting on and looked up at his friend. The anger he'd heard in Sully's voice glittered in his eyes. "But you didn't track me here to talk about Taite."

"No. I didn't." A muscle flexed in Sully's jaw. "What the bloody hell have you gotten me into, Dec? Werewolves? What the fuck is that?"

"That, my friend, is my new reality." Declan stood and strode to the water's edge. He stared out over the ocean, shading his eyes against the glare of the morning sunlight bouncing off the waves. "Taite was bein' stalked by a were-wolf so I brought her here to Ryder, thinkin' he'd be able to help her, since he's . . . somethin' of an expert. But the other werewolf tracked her—had actually maneuvered the situation so that I'd bring her here. When he tried to take her, we fought." He shrugged, the nonchalant gesture nowhere near what he was feeling. "He won. At least until Ryder caught up with him."

"How'd Ryder manage to beat him if you couldn't?"

Declan turned. From behind Sully he saw Ryder coming down the path. Knowing the other man would hear the conversation, he raised his eyebrows. At Ryder's nod, Declan met Sully's gaze. "Because Ryder's a werewolf as well." He gestured toward the man joining them.

Sully's indrawn breath was sharp. He shifted so that he could see both Declan and Ryder at the same time. Declan noticed he also put about ten feet of space between them.

He didn't think that now would be the right time to tell his friend that both he and Ryder could cover that distance in less than a second.

Sully looked from Ryder to Declan and back again. "What is this, some kind of hair club for men who are over-achievers?"

"If it is," Ryder muttered, "I was born into it. Declan wasn't given a choice."

"Neither of us was given a choice, Ry." Declan folded his arms over his chest. "It's not like you chose to be born into a family with a curse of lycanthropy."

"Wait. What?" Sully narrowed his eyes.

Ryder walked to the water's edge and thrust his hands into the front pockets of his slacks. Water lapped at the tips of his hiking-style boots. "Several generations ago, an Irish witch—called a *cailleach*—placed a curse on my ancestor on his wedding day for being unwilling to marry her daughter. He was twenty-five. At the rising of the next full moon, he turned into a werewolf." He turned to face them. "And so it's been with every succeeding generation, males only. Once we reach our twenty-fifth birthday until the day we die, we are werewolves."

Sully tucked his fingers into the back pockets of his jeans. "So when we were at university together . . ."

"I hadn't yet been affected by the curse." Ryder sighed. Shaking his head, he added, "When my father killed my mother and then himself because he couldn't deal with it anymore, I decided I'd be better off—as would everyone else—if I were alone." He shrugged. "If no one lived with me, there was no opportunity for me to hurt someone." A slight smile tugged one corner of his mouth. "Cobb refused to leave."

"You know, there are a lot of things I might say in complaint about that man," Declan said, "but his loyalty is never in question."

"But you married Taite." Sully sounded as confused as he looked.

"She helped me see that I control my beast, not the other way around." He glanced at Declan. "And so I've been helping Declan to learn this as well."

Sully met Declan's gaze. "Is that *your* story? You been a werewolf all along, too?" Disbelief echoed in his tones, mingled with hurt that he, perhaps, hadn't known them as well as he'd thought he had.

Declan knew how he felt—he'd had the same mix of emotions when he'd discovered Ryder's secret.

"No, not until I was bitten four months ago by the one I fought with—who was sent by Ryder's cousin Miles." He shook his head. "It's a long story. Suffice to say, Miles hates and envies Ryder, and plans on doin' whatever he can to make Ryder suffer. Includin' killin' his friends."

Sully quirked an eyebrow at Ryder. "And you knew all this and married Taite anyway?"

Ryder's jaw tightened. "It wouldn't take much for Miles to find out that Taite had been here, that she and I had fallen in love." His eyes glittered in the sunlight. "She's safer with me than out there on her own where he can get to her."

Sully was silent for a moment. He turned and walked away a few paces, raking one hand through his hair. Pivoting to face them, he demanded, "And you couldn't share any of this with me? You thought it was better that I be in the dark here?" He pointed to Declan. "You should know better. How can I do my job properly when I don't have all the facts?"

Declan looked at Ryder. Neither of them responded— what was there to say? Sully was right, of course, yet blurting out an "I'm a werewolf" hadn't seemed prudent.

Sully propped his hands on his hips. "Fine. I get it. I do." He jabbed a finger at Declan. "When you busted in this morning and chased off the intruder, did you know he'd killed Brenna?"

"What!" Declan moved forward, pausing when Sully took a reflexive step back. "And you're just now tellin' me about it?"

The other man fisted his hands at his sides, looking uncomfortable with his instinctive show of fear. His glare was as fierce as Declan's. "We found her in the kitchen. Her throat had been slit from behind. Aside from that first sharp pain, she probably never even knew what happened."

"And Pelicia?" Declan asked. "How is she?"

"Devastated, as you can imagine." Sully's lips tightened briefly. "And pissed off at you."

"What the hell is goin' on?" Declan walked a few paces away, scrubbing the back of his neck with his palm. "At first I thought Pelicia was the target of this bugger because of her grandfather. Then I decided maybe I was the target after all, that it must be Miles up to his old shenanigans again." He sighed and looked skyward, searching for God knew what among the fluffy clouds. "Now it looks like he must've been after her all along."

"You can't know that for sure," Ryder murmured. "This could be unrelated."

Declan shot him a disbelieving look. "You're kiddin', right? Someone takes shots at us, twice, and now Pel's best friend winds up dead in her kitchen? A best friend who looked a lot like her? Not bloody likely." He started up the path. He had to get to Pelicia.

He couldn't shake the feeling that this was his fault. But he'd deal with that later—for now, he needed to get to his woman and make sure she was all right.

After several minutes of walking at a near trot, Ryder asked, "And just what are you planning on doing, Declan?" He easily kept up with Declan's long strides, his werewolf metabolism keeping him from getting winded.

"Yeah," Sully piped in, his voice labored. "You're not exactly her favorite person right now."

"I'll think of somethin'," Declan muttered. He had to, because he refused to accept anything less than success. If he put his mind to it, he could do anything, and that included winning Pelicia back. Even after the mess he'd made of things.

Again.

"Well, he's going to have to explain himself," Pelicia told Taite. She was through fooling around. Declan O'Connell had better shape up or their relationship—such as it was—was over.

Footsteps sounded in the foyer, coming from the back of

the house, then Declan strode into the drawing room, followed closely by Ryder and Sully.

Declan took one look at her face and hauled her into his arms, one broad hand pressed to the back of her head, holding her close to his chest. "God, Pel. Are you all right?" Without waiting for a response, he murmured, "Of course you're not all right. I'm so sorry, darlin'. I didn't know about Brenna. I'm so sorry," he repeated softly, his voice hoarse and full of regret.

She leaned into him, grateful for his strength, needing the heat of his big body against her cold soul. "You tried to warn me," she whispered, wrapping her arms around his waist. "It's my fault. It's all my fault."

He gripped her shoulders and pushed her back. When she wouldn't look at him, he put one hand beneath her chin and tilted her head up. "Look at me. *Look* at me," he repeated. Once her gaze met his, he said, "None of this was your fault, darlin'. If anyone's to blame, it's me."

Pelicia frowned. How could any of this be his . . . "You mean because of Miles." The mention of Ryder's cousin reminded her she was mad at Declan for not telling her he was a werewolf. Renewed anger at him shoved back her grief. She pushed away from him. "If it was Miles, wouldn't he have killed her by biting her or . . ." Her gaze bounced off of Ryder. "Or by tearing her throat out with his teeth or claws? Her throat was cut by a knife, Declan."

"Aye. That's what Sully said."

And, speaking of werewolves . . .

"You tell me this. Just when were you going to let me know you'd been bitten?" His mouth opened. She forestalled whatever excuse he might be about to spit out. "And don't tell me you didn't think I'd believe you. I grew up here, you know."

"Aye, I know." He sighed. "I thought it would . . . complicate things between us." His gaze met hers, pleading in their dark depths. "I would have told you eventually."

"Like when? On our fiftieth anniversary?" He perked up at that, and she gave herself a mental kick in the rear. No need to get his hopes up by implying they'd ever get married. "Never mind." She held up one hand. "Let me just say that I'm less concerned about the fact that you're a werewolf than I am that you, once again, weren't truthful with me."

He glanced around the room, obviously uncomfortable with discussing this in front of witnesses. "Can we go someplace else and talk about this?"

Pelicia stifled a sigh. If she went somewhere more private, they'd end up having sex. She knew it as surely as she breathed. Already the emotional upheaval she felt was making itself known in a more primal way—and because of Brenna's death, Pelicia was feeling the need to affirm she was still alive.

And there was no better way to prove life than by merging your body with someone else's, to have them steal your breath and give it back, to feel the slide of skin against skin.

"I don't think so." She looked around, too, taking in the faces of their avid audience. Taite stood in the circle of Ryder's arm and both of them wore expressions of concern. Sully, leaning one shoulder indolently against the door frame, seemed amused. Or perhaps bemused. She turned her attention back to Declan. "Besides, there's not much else to say, is there? Same song, second verse. You don't trust me enough to share the truth with me. End of story."

"You're gettin' your metaphors mixed up, darlin'. And it's not about trust—or a lack thereof." He talked loudly

over her sputtered indignation. "It was about you needin'
to know—I didn't think it was the right time."

"And there's the crux of it." Pelicia walked over to him.
"It's always about what *you* think is the right thing to do.
You don't bother to put yourself in the other person's shoes
or question your course of action. And I hate to be the one
to break it to you, O'Connell, but you're not always right."

"I know I'm not always right." He raked a hand through
his hair. "But I'm not always wrong, either. And I will do
what I believe is necessary to protect the ones I love."

Her heart thrilled at his words even as her head pounded.
He was so adept at making her crazy with very little effort,
and he probably wasn't even aware of it. "Oh, just forget
it. I'm going home."

"You need to stay here." Declan grabbed her by the
shoulders. "It's safer."

"I need to talk to Brenna's parents," she responded, shrugging away from his hold. "They'll want to know what
happened." She blinked back ready tears, determined to
hold herself together to get done what needed to be done.
"Besides, I'll have the big, bad cop with me. Won't I,
Sully?"

Sully's brows rose. He glanced at Declan and pursed his
lips, but to her surprise gave a nod. "Yes, you will."

She ignored Declan's glare. If he wanted to throw a
hissy fit, that was fine by her. She wasn't going to hide and
shirk her responsibilities. Brenna's parents would have questions that they'd want to ask, and she wanted to give them
as much closure as she could.

"Let's go." She held up a hand in warning as Declan
started to speak. Looking at Taite and Ryder, she said,
"Please tell my dad I said hi and that I'll ring him later."

"We'll do that." Ryder glanced at Declan. His gaze, when

he met Pelicia's, was serious. "Are you sure you want to leave? You're more than welcome to stay."

She shook her head. "I need to get back—I have a kitchen to clean up . . ." Her voice cracked and she paused, swallowing down tears. God. Brenna.

"Let me come with you and help," Taite said.

"No, really. I'm fine." She wasn't. But she would be. Pelicia gave a small smile—the only kind she could muster—and hugged Taite.

The spontaneity of the gesture seemed to startle the other woman, though she returned the embrace. "Take care of yourself, Pel."

Pelicia nodded. Drawing away, she refused to look back at Declan. "I'll see you later." She walked out of the room and headed toward the front door with Sully following behind. Once there she opened it, then paused. She turned and met Declan's concerned gaze. "From now on, if we're to have any sort of relationship at all, you have to be completely upfront with me. No withholding the truth because I don't need to know. Okay?"

There was a span of silence for a heartbeat or two, and then he nodded. "Okay, darlin'. I promise. No more secrets."

She wanted to believe him. She did. But right now that would take more hope than she had.

Chapter 14

Declan stood on the bluff and watched the small boat pull away from the dock. With his enhanced vision he could clearly make out Pelicia's expression—a mixture of grief for Brenna and lingering anger at him.

The last time he'd let her go when she'd been mad, she'd stayed mad. Two years later he was still trying to get back on her good side. Damned if he'd go through *that* again.

And he needed to make sure she was all right. As soon as he'd heard that Brenna had been killed, his first thought was that the killer had meant to murder Pelicia. If Brenna hadn't been in the house—and God only knew why she was there—the killer might have gone upstairs and found his intended target.

Declan clenched his jaw against the rage boiling in his gut, a rage that tempted the beast out of hiding. His damned inner mutt had better stay leashed—he didn't have time for dog training right now.

He started toward the top of the cliff stairs, calling over his shoulder, "I'm taking your boat."

"You might want to give her some space." Taite's voice rang clear and concerned.

He stopped and faced her and Ryder where they stood on the small portico in front of the house. "I did that once and look where it got me. No." He started down the steps. "This time I'm doing what I should've done then."

The trip to St. Mary's seemed interminable, though in reality it was less than twenty minutes, the way he piloted the boat. Rather than go through the bother of renting another car, he took off on foot from the dock to the Nola. He'd be better able to scope the place out if he could come up on it unseen.

Several houses down from the Nola, he paused, scanning the area, sniffing the air to discover any untoward scents. So far, so good. He eased around the corner of the house and cut through backyards until he reached Pelicia's place. He could tell Pelicia or Sully had started to clean up because the stringent odor of bleach was beginning to cut through the coppery scent of blood that still lingered in the air.

God, he hated that Brenna had gotten caught up in all of this, whatever this was. There was no reason for Miles to kill Brenna—Declan wasn't close to her.

Although Pelicia was, and when Pelicia hurt, Declan hurt.

Was that it? Miles or a flunky he'd sent had killed Brenna to get at Declan through Pelicia?

He closed his eyes. This was giving him a headache. He wished the bastard—whoever it was—would just come at him and get it over with. This running around making shadow plays was driving him crazy.

The wind shifted and a familiar scent filtered through the smell of bleach and blood. Declan stiffened, opening his eyes. It was *him*, the sniper, the man who'd been in Pelicia's house early this morning.

The man who'd murdered Brenna.

Declan whirled. A bullet that would have struck him in the heart instead grazed his upper arm, leaving a stinging trail in its wake. He ducked and rolled, coming up in a crouch a few feet away.

Another bullet went through his left thigh, knocking his leg out from under him. From the muffled sound of the gunfire, Declan knew two things—the rifle had a silencer and the sniper was too far away for Declan to do anything.

Except be a sitting duck. And everyone knew that the sitting kind of ducks were the worst ones to be.

The back door swung open. He looked up to see Sully there, gun drawn. "Sniper. Nine o'clock," Declan said through gritted teeth. Pain streaked up and down his leg, partly from the wound itself and partly from the rapid healing his new metabolism afforded him. "Get back."

Sully glanced in the direction Declan had indicated and gave a snort. "Like I'm going to leave you out here." He tucked his weapon in the holster on his belt and came out into the yard doubled over, making himself as small a target as possible. He grabbed Declan by the hand and hoisted him up, the muscles in his arm bulging with effort. A bullet kicked up the grass near Declan's foot.

With a loud grunt, Sully shoved Declan toward the door. "Get in and get down," he ordered. "Damn it."

A ricochet pinged only a foot or two away, making Sully duck. He barreled in behind Declan and slammed the door, sliding over to crouch behind the cupboards beside Declan. "That last one was close."

"You mean closer than the two that've already hit me?" Declan asked dryly.

Pelicia came into the kitchen from the hallway and stared at the two men. "What the hell's going on?"

"Get down!" Declan started to rise, but his injured leg gave a sharp protest. He fell back with a stifled groan.

Her eyes widened but she dropped to the floor without any argument. "He's back?"

"Aye." He watched as she scrambled across the floor on her hands and knees.

She came around the table. Her gaze fixed on the spot where he knew Brenna's body had lain—there was still a splotch of blood on the floor that Sully hadn't had time to wipe away. Pelicia's throat moved with her hard swallow. Tears filled her eyes but didn't fall as she knelt beside Declan, her gaze tracking over the smear of blood on his arm and leg. "You've been shot."

"I'm all right." When she reached for him, he shook his head. "Pel, I'm fine. It's just a flesh wound—the bullet grazed my arm and went clean through my thigh. Look, the bleeding's already stopped."

"Humor me." She carefully peeled the ripped edges of his shirt away from the wound on his arm and frowned. Reaching up, she grabbed a dish towel from the counter and gently swiped at the blood on his skin. "You've already healed." She looked at him, wonder and a little dismay in her eyes.

"Werewolf metabolism." He sent a sidelong glance to Sully.

The other man shook his head. "I don't want to know." He tilted his head to the side, his attitude one of listening. "I think he's stopped shooting. For now." He got slowly to his feet and peered through the window in the back door. "Why don't you two go upstairs—Dec, you can get cleaned up and Pel . . . Well, you can keep an eye on him." He glanced over, mischief in his eyes. "I'll stay down here and keep watch. And," he said as his levity faded, "get the police out here. Again."

"I'll stay, too." Declan got to his feet, keeping his weight off his left leg.

"Get cleaned up first. I doubt the bastard will try a direct approach—he's too much of a coward." Sully glanced out the back window again. He flipped the lock and then turned. "Go on. Get cleaned up. Then you can help me."

Pelicia slipped one arm around his waist, supporting his weight. He scowled, angry at himself for getting in the way of not one bullet but two, and irritated that he was being weak in front of Pelicia. Bloody hell. He was supposed to be the strong one.

They went slowly down the hallway. Pain flared through his thigh with each step, though it wasn't as acute as before. He limped up the stairs and into Pelicia's bedroom.

She went straight through to the bathroom and pointed to the toilet. "Sit."

He put the lid down and sat.

"Good boy."

Declan scowled. "I'm not a dog."

She looked at him with raised brows. A smirk curled her pretty mouth. "Could've fooled me."

"Ha ha." He watched while she pulled out a bottle of antiseptic and some gauze and tape. Then she turned toward him and hesitated.

He bit back a grin. The only way she'd be able to get at his wounds was for him to undress.

This was going to be fun.

She pursed her lips and looked from his face to his thigh. Even through his pain his cock began to rise to the occasion. Or at least to the promise of an occasion.

A blush stained her cheeks. She jerked her gaze back to his face and shoved the bottle of antiseptic at him. "Here. You can do it yourself. I'm going to see how Sully's getting on."

She left the bathroom so fast he was surprised there weren't burning tread marks left on the wooden floor. "Aye. I can do this myself." He stood and unbuttoned his shirt, yanking it off and peering down at the stripe of reddened flesh along his upper arm. He twisted to look at it in the mirror.

A superficial wound, the bleeding had stopped, the skin and muscle underneath knitted back together. He grabbed a washcloth and wet it, then wiped the drying blood off his arm.

When he leaned over to rinse out the cloth, a twinge of discomfort shot through his left thigh. That wound, at least, hadn't completely healed.

Ryder had told him once that more serious wounds would heal faster if he shifted to wolf—or vice versa if he was wounded while in his wolf form. With a gunman on the loose, he didn't have the time or luxury of being off his game with a leg wound.

Declan reached out and flipped the lock on the bathroom door. With as much speed as possible, he took off his shoes and socks, and shucked his pants and underwear. Taking a breath, he braced himself for the pain a transformation always brought.

With the next heartbeat his bones shifted, lengthening. Muscles and sinew moved with them, screaming a protest. Declan trapped a groan in his throat and dropped to his knees. His breath grew harsh, pain filling his every sense until all he could feel, see and smell was the residue of white-hot agony.

Another heartbeat and his skin felt like it was splitting off his body. Fur erupted along his arms, his legs, his abdomen, almost quicker than his eye could follow. One more heartbeat and his transformation was complete.

He stood on all fours, panting, reeling from the pain the shift to wolf always caused, not looking forward to going through it again so soon. But he needed to be in his human form in order to talk to Pelicia, to make sure she understood that he loved her.

That he'd always loved her.

And so, with a deep sigh, he turned his thoughts inward and focused on reversing the metamorphosis.

When it was done, he collapsed to the floor on his side, wheezing through the lingering pain. With shaking arms he pushed himself upright, then grasped the sink to pull himself to his feet. He looked down and saw the wound on his thigh was gone—only dried blood remained.

He cleaned his leg and got dressed again, grimacing at putting his dirty clothes back on. A thought struck, and he quirked a brow. He'd borrow something of Sully's. They were the same size, and he reckoned his friend wouldn't mind.

But just in case he would, Declan made sure he was extra quiet as he tiptoed down the hallway and eased into Sully's room.

Pelicia paced over to the doorway of the drawing room and glanced up the stairs. "Just how long does it take to slap a bandage on his leg?"

"He's probably playing on your sympathy," Sully ventured.

She looked at him and walked back into the room. "You don't really think . . . He wouldn't."

Sully shrugged. "No, he probably wouldn't. It's not his style."

"You're right about that. More than likely he'll come barreling in here and just try to bowl me over."

Sully grinned. As he looked through the front window, his smile faded. "But I'd feel better if he got his ass down here soon."

"Why? Do you see something?" Pelicia walked toward him, keeping to one side so she wouldn't be directly in front of the window.

"No. But my gut's telling me that something's about to happen, and it's never been wrong." His gaze flicked to her. "You'd be better off upstairs."

She frowned. "I'm not leaving you down here by yourself." She nodded toward his gun. "You have an extra one of those?"

"No." He scowled. "The reason I'm here, Pel, whether you like it or not—whether you *agree* with it or not—is to protect you. So get your ass upstairs. Now."

"But—"

"I mean it. I can't be watching for an intruder and looking out for you, too." He eased away from the window and put an arm around her waist, urging her into the foyer. "Please." His voice was low and urgent. "Go upstairs."

She huffed a sigh and started up the steps. "Fine, but I'm sending Declan down."

"Do that." Sully stayed in the foyer until she reached the top of the stairs. As she walked toward her room, she heard his footsteps heading down the hall to the kitchen. Probably going to check again to make sure the back door was secure.

She shoved open her bedroom door. "Declan, we might

have . . ." He wasn't there. She poked her head around the bathroom door. "Declan . . ."

Not there either.

She turned and walked smack-dab into him. "Bloody hell. Don't do that!"

He finished rolling up the cuff on the right sleeve of the deep red shirt he wore. "Do what, darlin'?"

"Sneak up on me or I'll make you wear a bell." She ignored the flare of heat in his eyes and focused on his clothing. The crimson shirt looked good on him—too good for her peace of mind—and black slacks replaced his torn and bloodied jeans. "Where'd you get those?"

He glanced down at himself.

"Never mind," she said before he could reply. "You need to get downstairs. Sully thinks something's up."

From below them came a shout then a gunshot. Loud thuds and another shot sounded before Declan made it to the bedroom door, Pelicia on his heels. She heard what sounded like the snarling and growling of a dog.

Declan glanced over his shoulder at her. Her heart stuttered at the feral look in his eyes. "There's a wolf down there. You stay here." He ran down the hallway. He was halfway down the stairs before she was even a third of the way down the hall.

God, he was fast. She didn't remember him being that fast before. Pausing at the top of the stairs, she realized it was due to the changes his body had gone through. The werewolf virus or infection, whatever it was, made him faster and stronger than before.

From where she was she could see the front door was wide open. She heard him cursing from outside and took one step down. "Declan?"

"It's clear," he called back, coming through the front door. "The bastard got away, damn it." He headed into the drawing room. "I would've gone after him, but Sully's hurt. Call for help."

Pelicia hurried down the stairs and picked up the receiver on the telephone in the foyer. Once again she punched in the number for emergency services and, keeping one eye on Declan as he knelt beside Sully lying prone on the floor, she hastily explained to the operator that there had been a break-in. "One of my guests has been injured. I don't know how badly—"

"Tell them to hurry," Declan said, his voice harsh.

"Hurry," she obediently told the man on the other end of the phone and hung up. She ran into the drawing room. "What do you need me to do?"

"Gather some towels—we need to get this bleeding stopped." Declan had opened Sully's shirt, baring his torso. Hands slick with blood, he applied pressure to Sully's right side and his right forearm.

Pelicia rushed up the stairs to the linen closet and grabbed an armload of towels. Once she was back downstairs, she dumped the load beside Declan and knelt at Sully's other side. Looking down, she saw the injured man still held the gun in a lax grip. She gently unfolded his fingers and eased the gun away from him, setting it on the floor out of reach.

He was conscious, but barely. "What the hell . . ." He tried to raise his head.

She reached over and put a hand on his shoulder, urging him to stay down. "Be still, Sully. You're hurt."

A set of four long, angry-looking gashes striped across his chest. Another set gouged his abdomen. As he relaxed onto the pillow, Pelicia stroked sweat-soaked hair away from his forehead. She looked at Declan, worry tightening her insides. "This isn't good," she murmured with a glance at the gashes.

"Tell me about it," he muttered back. He lifted his hand from Sully's shoulder. Two curved slashes, looking like quarter moons about two inches apart, carved his skin. "Knife wounds to cover up the bite."

Chapter 15

Declan watched Sully being driven away by the medics. He rotated his shoulders, trying to ease the tight muscles. Blinked to relieve his dry, burning eyes.

They would transport his friend to the airport on the other side of the island, and from there he'd be flown to a trauma center in Penzance, Cornwall. The local hospital here on the island just wasn't equipped to handle the type of injuries Sully had sustained.

Hell. He didn't think the larger hospital in Penzance was ready to deal with someone who'd been bitten by a werewolf, either. Not that they'd realize that. But Sully's injuries had been such that he was in need of an infusion of blood. While the werewolf virus was hard at work and would repair his wounds—most likely by morning—he could still die from blood loss.

If he died, it would be Declan's fault. If he lived, he would live as a werewolf.

And that would be Declan's fault, too.

The outcome was horrendous either way. He just wished it was *him* on his way to the hospital and not Sully.

He could hear Pelicia talking with the police from inside

the house. The unit who'd been out to look over the scene after Brenna's death was still in town, so it had taken them only a few minutes to get to the Nola. He'd already given them his statement, careful to leave any reference to a bite mark out of things. He knew she would do the same, though any observant doctor would more than likely see through the camouflage.

Footsteps sounded behind him. Declan half-turned in the doorway to see Police Constable Tremwith and Pelicia walking toward him.

The policeman put on his hat, adjusting the angle of the brim, and nodded to Declan. "If either of you think of anything else you'd like to add, please call me." He pointed toward the small telephone stand in the foyer. "I've left my card." He paused and then added, "I'll leave a man posted out front, just in case the suspect decides to come back."

He and the sundry police unit members filed out, carrying bags containing collected pieces of evidence—hair, blood, fingerprints—their expressions matter of fact as they exited the house. Declan leaned one shoulder against the door frame and watched them pile into official vehicles and drive away. One lone uniformed officer remained behind, standing at the edge of the front garden.

Declan scrubbed his hand over his face. God, he had to call Ryder—he needed to be prepared for another attack. Cursing under his breath, he yanked his mobile from its holder at his waist and punched in Ryder's number.

Pelicia's soft voice came from behind him. "Sully's going to be all right, isn't he?"

He turned his head and looked at her. "Aye. I hope so." He wasn't sure about anything, except that the attacker was either sent by Miles or was Miles himself. And that the overpowering scent of lemon and citronella had effectively blocked his nasal receptors from determining the attacker's identity. Done on purpose, he knew.

Pelicia sidled up to him. He shifted his phone to his left hand. Lifting his right arm, he laid it across her shoulders, hauling her close to his side.

She wrapped her arm around his waist and leaned her head against his shoulder while he spoke with Ryder.

"Unless the blood loss is too severe," his friend said, "Sully will most likely be completely healed by morning. But he'll need sleep—a lot of it."

"Aye. Just like I did." Declan remembered that from his own transition—sleeping half the day away for a week while his body went through changes on the molecular level. "He's goin' to have a hell of a time explainin' his healed wounds to the medical staff."

"He won't have to explain anything," Ryder said. "All he has to do is play dumb and let the doctors try to explain it."

"Shouldn't be too hard for him to do. Play dumb, I mean." Declan grinned. "He can be as obtuse as the moment requires."

Ryder chuckled. "And you and Pel? You're all right?"

"Aye, we're fine." Declan glanced down at Pelicia, noticing the drawn look on her face. "Listen, Ry, I have to go. I'll call you later."

Ryder murmured, "Watch your back," and ended the call.

Declan tucked his phone away and stood there, staring out at nothing, his gut churning with anger. And guilt. And remorse.

Christ, he'd made a right balls-up of things.

After several moments, Pelicia put her hand on his shoulder. "Come back inside, Declan." When he didn't move, she tugged on his shirt. "Come on."

He let her draw him inside. He stopped in the hallway outside the drawing room and glanced inside at the blood-stained rug. Swallowing back the roiling emotions that crawled their way up his throat, he muttered, "I need to clean that up."

"It can wait." She slid one hand into his and squeezed his fingers gently. "Let's go get a nice cuppa, okay?"

Needing the contact, he kept his hand in hers and followed her into the kitchen. While she filled the kettle and put it on the hot plate, he sat and stared down at his hands a moment, turning the events of the morning over in his head. He glanced at the clock hanging above the kitchen sink.

God above, it was only nine A.M. It felt like it should be much, much later. Which made him wonder aloud, "Where are your other two guests? Neal and Andrew?"

She sighed and turned, leaning against the counter. "I don't know. And I'm worried, frankly. It's not unusual for Andrew to stay out very late—doing whatever it is he does," she said with a shrug. "But he's usually back sometime during the night. I know, because his bed has always been slept in. Neal usually gets an early start, but not *this* early." She glanced at the clock. "Neither one of them was here all night. I just don't know what to think." As she stared at him, her eyes widened. "Do you think . . ." She trailed off, an arrested expression on her face.

"You do realize, darlin', that you didn't finish that sentence out loud, right?"

She gave a slight start. "I was just thinking that Andrew

could be the killer. I mean, I haven't seen him since the day he checked in. What's he been doing all this time? And do you suppose . . . No. It couldn't be."

He sat up a bit straighter in his chair. "What couldn't be?"

"Could he be the one who attacked Sully?" She folded her arms over her chest. "Could he be the werewolf?"

Declan frowned. "I don't think so. Hell, I don't know. I didn't smell werewolf here before this morning, but it's hard to tell anyway, with the citrus and citronella that damned bastard used to disguise his scent." He sighed, wondering how the hell it had all gone so wrong.

"You can't blame yourself." Pelicia pulled up a chair near him. Leaning forward, she placed her hands over his.

He twisted his wrists and linked their fingers together. "Why not?" He looked into her eyes. That there was no censure in those bright blue depths amazed him. "If it's not my fault, whose is it?"

"Miles. Or whoever he put up to this." Her fingers tightened on his. "It's not your fault."

Declan shook his head. "If I hadn't called Sully here, he wouldn't have been hurt. I knew Miles was out there, looking for ways to strike out at Ryder, and yet I brought another of Ryder's friends here, putting him in harm's way."

"You did it to protect me." She reached up and palmed his cheek. "Sully could have said no."

"He didn't have all the facts, you know that." He swallowed, hard. He covered her hand with his. Turning his head, he placed a soft kiss in her palm and then stood up and walked toward the counter. He needed to move around, needed to do something.

But there wasn't anything to do except acknowledge that

he'd been wrong about a lot of things, not the least of which was his insistence on providing only the information he believed people needed to know.

"I'm sorry, Pel." Declan turned and looked at her. "I should have told you about me, about what had happened, from the beginnin'. Not doin' so put you in greater danger." He shook his head. "You're right—I'm a real tosser."

She made a sound of disagreement and rose from her chair. Taking a few steps, she moved in front of him, stopping with only a few inches between them. Her sweet face tipped up toward his. "I was angry when I said that. I didn't really mean it."

He cupped her face between his palms. God, she was so lovely it hurt his heart to look at her. She was bright and beautiful and good. All the things he wasn't. "You had every right to be angry."

He looked down at his hands where they rested against her soft skin. They were hands that had molded explosives and fired a gun, hands that had caressed Pelicia into mindless passion.

They were hands that had been both hard and tender.

Hands that had loved. Hands that had killed.

Pelicia deserved better.

He bent his head and pressed a soft kiss against the corner of her mouth. "I'm sorry," he said again. He moved away from her. "As soon as we get this thing handled, I'll get out of your hair. For good."

Pelicia's breath hitched in her throat. What was he saying? That after all this—after the fighting and the loving, after the heartache and hope—he was just going to walk away?

"You deserve better than me, darlin'." Declan's voice was such a low rasp she had to strain to hear his words. That he didn't face her didn't help, but he seemed reluctant now to look at her. He went on, "Better than someone who gets people killed because he's too determined to do things his way, damn the consequences."

She inhaled, tried to ignore his spicy cologne and warm man scent, and chose her words carefully. Now that he was threatening to do what she'd been telling him to do all along—leave her alone—she realized she didn't want him to. That he could admit he'd been wrong meant a lot. "Do you still feel that way, Declan? Determined to do things your way regardless of the outcome?"

He twisted around to look at her. "No! That's what I'm sayin'. I was wrong, and I'm sorry."

Having him say he was sorry three times in as many minutes was, she was finding, nearly as grating as having him not apologize at all. She didn't want him *this* humble. "I'm glad you're finally willing to admit it, though I'm sorry it . . . took what it did to get you to this point." She went up to him and twined her fingers through Declan's, holding their joined hands between their bodies. "You have no control over what Miles—or whoever it is—chooses to do. And if he's so determined to strike at Ryder this way, he would have eventually gotten Sully. You have to know that." She squeezed his hands.

He stared down at her, dark eyes glittering with so much emotion it brought tears to her eyes. He seemed to struggle for words and finally gave up, dropping his mouth to hers.

His tongue drove between her lips, stroking into her mouth in blatant possession. He brought his broad hands

up to her face and tilted her head, angling her for his pleasure. There wasn't a hint of seduction in his kiss—it was
flat-out desperation.

After a moment he drew away and rested his forehead
against hers. His breath came harsh from between parted
lips. "You're too good for me."

God, she'd never seen him like this—shaken to his core,
doubting himself so much that he was ready to walk away
from her. While his normal arrogance and high-handed
tactics drove her to distraction, *this* broke her heart.

"No, I'm not." She'd held onto her unreasonable anger
for over two years, blaming Declan for something that
wasn't his fault. Her biggest betrayer had been her grandfather, using her to ferry bogus documents to his "clients."
Declan had been doing his job.

That he'd fallen in love with her had complicated things,
but she knew he hadn't planned on using her that way. He
had too much decency in him.

She rose up on her tiptoes and placed her mouth against
his, urging his lips to part. When they did, she slipped her
tongue into his mouth.

He groaned and yanked her closer, one hand at the back
of her head holding her in place, the other hand pressing
against the small of her back. Pelicia collapsed against him
with a sigh, gripping his waist for support. Her nipples
tightened to diamond-hard points, stabbing against the
firm wall of his chest, and her clit began to pulse with carnal hunger.

He devoured her like a starving man, lips and tongue
and teeth bruising in their force. His hands slid from her
face, glided over her breasts, then moved around her to curl
around her buttocks. He hauled her against him, against
the rigid bulge of his erection straining against his jeans.

He took the kiss deeper. The pressure and tension gathered in her pelvis. When he fucked her mouth with his tongue, her pussy clenched in response. Her clit throbbed, her nipples tingled.

She wanted more. She wanted deeper. She wanted . . .

Naked skin sliding against naked skin.

Declan tilted her hips so that the hard ridge of his erection rubbed her clit through her slacks as he pumped slowly against her. Pelicia clutched the strong muscles of his back, fingers digging in, holding him closer. He kissed a path down her throat, lingering over her pulse, a low growl rumbling from deep in his chest. His teeth scraped lightly against her skin then his tongue soothed the slight sting.

Her fingers tightened on his back. "Let's go upstairs," she whispered. "I need to feel alive. I need *you*."

He pulled back and stared down at her. Need darkened his eyes but his expression was uncertain. "Are you sure?"

She curled one palm around his strong jaw and stroked her thumb across his full bottom lip. "I've never been more certain of anything." She moved her hand down and curled her fingers around his hand. "Come on," she urged, pulling him gently along behind her.

The short walk down the hallway and up the steps was punctuated with soft kisses. Once they reached the top of the stairs, Declan leaned down and swept her up into his arms. With a tenderness she'd rarely experienced from him, he carried her to her room. He kicked the door closed behind them and laid her gently on the bed.

He pulled off her shoes, his fingers warm on her ankles. Sitting beside her, he took one of her hands in his and brought it to his mouth. After placing a kiss in her palm, he folded her fingers through his and leaned forward, brushing a strand of hair from her cheek.

"Be sure about this," he murmured. A small smile crinkled the corners of his eyes. "I don't think I'm strong enough to offer to walk away again."

"I don't want you to walk away." Pelicia stroked her fingers down his lean cheek. "You make me crazy—I don't know if I'm coming or going around you." She sat up and wrapped her hands around the back of his head. "But if I get my way, right now I want to be coming." She pulled his mouth down to hers.

Declan seemed to hold back, letting her kiss him, returning the kiss, but gently, softly, as if he was afraid she'd crack if he touched her with the ferocity she craved. When she snaked out her tongue and licked across the seam of his lips, he drew back with a muttered oath. "Tell me you know what you're doin'," he muttered. "Tell me this isn't just a reaction from everythin' that's happened."

"I know what I'm doing." Her emotions *were* topsy-turvy, and she needed him to put her world in focus. "It isn't just a reaction from everything that's happened," she assured him. "Brenna's dead . . ." She blinked back tears. She would mourn her friend properly when all this madness was over. For now, she needed to affirm life—and there was no better way than letting the man she loved become part of her.

And there it was—the thing she'd refused to admit to herself. She still loved Declan. And she was finally ready to start trusting him again, though not without some trepidation.

For now, however, there was this.

Pelicia brought her hands to her blouse and unbuttoned it, shrugging it off and dropping it to the floor beside the bed. Reaching behind her back, she unclasped her bra. Before she let it fall, she pressed a soft kiss against Declan's cheek, his temple, then his lips. "Sully's hurt. But you and I are here, and we're alive. Celebrate that with me." She slowly reclined, drawing her bra away and letting it fall to the floor.

Bracing himself on one forearm, Declan brought his hand up and lightly stroked first one soft breast and then the other. Tingles shot through her straight from her tightening nipples to her pussy. She moaned and shifted against the bed.

When he bent and took one pebbled tip between his lips, she lifted her hands to his head and sifted her fingers through his silky hair. She held on as pleasure cascaded through her.

He kissed a path down her torso. "Let's get this off you," he muttered, fingers flicking open the button of her slacks. She lifted her hips and let him pull both trousers and panties down her legs.

Leaving the material at the foot of the bed, he stared down at her. He slid one big hand slowly up her thigh until it reached the juncture of her legs. Stroking his fingers through her folds, he gathered her cream on his fingers and spread it over her clit.

Pelicia moaned and spread her thighs, opening herself fully to him. His warm breath wafted over her, then he tongued her, taking a slow, long lick from her opening to her swollen pleasure nub. She closed her eyes and fisted her hands in his hair again, holding him close.

"Delicious." Declan swiped the flat of his tongue up her slit and then latched onto her clit. He began to suckle her. As she moaned and pressed against his mouth, he brought his hand up and speared one finger slowly into her drenched sheath.

Pelicia moaned and thrust up to meet his invasion, her hands falling away to clutch at the bedding beneath her.

This was what she wanted, what she needed. Declan's mouth feasting on her, his tongue tugging at her clit.

Her pussy spasmed, and she fought to stave off the orgasm. She wanted this to last, wanted to hold onto this moment. When he added another finger and scissored them inside her, stretching her, preparing her for his thick shaft, she lost the battle. She clenched around his fingers, a low cry leaving her, her body bowing with the climax roaring through her.

"God, you're beautiful."

She barely heard Declan's muttered praise over the thunder of her racing heart. But she felt his mouth leave her clit and she whimpered, wanting more.

Then his tongue replaced his fingers, the pointed tip fluttering around and around her opening, ducking inside to flick against the sensitive inner walls, and she jerked and wailed his name. And it all started up again.

Feeling Pelicia's body beneath his lips, tasting her on his tongue sent Declan's arousal skyrocketing. His cock lengthened and thickened, painfully pressing against the unyielding metal of his zipper. His balls were tight with anticipation.

He wanted this woman like he'd wanted no other.

And as much as he needed to feel her sweet pussy clasping his cock, he needed to show her he wasn't the same man as before. That he could put others ahead of himself.

That he would put her needs before his own.

He moved away from her long enough to toe off his shoes and strip off his clothing. Then he settled fully on top of her, nudging her legs apart, making a place for himself between the sweet cradle of her thighs. Lowering his mouth to hers, he nipped, he sucked, he licked, his tongue sweeping into her mouth. One taste led him to wanting more.

More than just her mouth.

Declan gave a low growl and kissed a path down her throat, lingering at the pulse hammering beneath her soft skin. He raked his teeth over the tendon at the side of her neck, careful not to break the skin, letting her feel just a hint of the wildness that lurked within him.

Pelicia gasped and arched, her groin pressing into his erection. The tight peaks of her breasts rubbed through the hair on his chest, making her gasp.

He bent and latched onto one nipple, drawing on her with slow, strong pulls. He brought up one hand and tweaked the other nipple, twisting and tugging on it with his fingers.

When her hips pumped against him, dragging his erection through her slick folds, he released her breasts and kissed his way down her slender torso. When he reached her sex, he drew back and stared down at her.

God, she was so damned beautiful, all strawberries and cream with her golden hair, her lips and nipples red from his mouth, and her pale, soft skin. Her long torso led to a little tummy and that graceful slit with its sparse shelter of springy hair.

Declan groaned and slid his hands over her inner thighs, up until his thumbs met across her swollen sex. Then he spread her, opening her to his gaze—a gaze riveted to the slick dark pink folds and shadowed opening of her body. He would never tire of seeing her like this.

As the scent of her arousal rose, his nostrils flared. This was his woman. *His mate.* With a hungry growl he bent his head and set his open mouth on her. The first swipe of his tongue through her cleft gave him a tantalizing taste of her spicy-sweet flavor, and made her cry out in passion. When he speared into her channel, her hands came up and clutched his head, her fingers lacing through his hair with a strong grip.

Declan lashed at her sweet pussy with his tongue, plunging into her with fast jabs meant to drive her arousal higher. She moaned and pumped her hips against his mouth, telling him without words that he was succeeding.

He wanted to feel her come, wanted to see her face as she took her pleasure. Sliding his hands under her ass, he lifted her so he could get a better angle. He fucked into her with his tongue, dragging her flavor deep into his mouth, flicking her clit back and forth with the pointed tip of his tongue before thrusting it into her channel once more. All the while he kept his gaze fixed to her face.

"Declan!" Pelicia arched and shuddered, her sheath contracting around his tongue as another orgasm roiled through her. Her eyes squeezed shut, her face darkening with pleasure. He kept the rhythm steady, keeping her arousal ramped high, not letting her come down until she'd careened into yet another climax.

She settled against the mattress, her chest heaving with her heavy breathing. She tugged on his hair and Declan let her draw him up. Crashing his mouth over hers, he thrust his tongue between her lips, letting her taste her own essence. Her lips were soft but her mouth just as ravenous as his. When he finally lifted his head, both of them breathed heavily and her lips were swollen and red.

Now . . . now it was time to get inside her before he exploded. Their last coming together had started out in anger and pent-up frustration. But this time it was done— if not out of love, at least out of mutual respect and the desire to comfort and affirm life—and he wouldn't deny himself any longer.

"Condom?" he managed.

"No." Pelicia stroked one hand down his cheek. "I want to feel you inside me, Declan, just like before. I'm safe, you're safe." Her eyes sparkled with desire. "No latex. Just you."

Declan drew in a sharp breath as his arousal kicked up another notch. He reared up over her and guided his erection to her entrance. As he slowly pressed forward he held her gaze with his. Inch by inch he fed his cock into her clinging sheath until his balls slapped gently against the curve of her buttocks.

Blood roared in his ears. The wolf howled inside, demanding to be set free, but Declan fought it back. He was more than his animal, more than instinct that urged him to pound into her, to take blindly. He would not rut on her like some wild beast.

But, God, she was so tight, so slick. So hot.

Sliding his hands to her back, he lifted her to him and nuzzled her neck, inhaling her scent, searing his lungs and his memory with it. Then he lowered her back to the bed and braced himself on his forearms. He flexed his hips, starting a slow, steady rhythm. She arched against him, her breasts pressing against his chest.

He gently urged her to lie flat on the bed and leaned over her, closing his lips around one turgid nipple. He suckled her, reveling in the warm feel of her in his mouth, the fresh and slightly salty taste of her against his tongue. Releasing her, he tugged the up-thrust peak of her other breast deep into his mouth.

Still Declan kept up the lazy pace, sliding in and out of her with slow, deliberate glides of his hips.

Pelicia tossed her head against the pillow. Her hands went to his shoulders, fingernails digging into his skin. "Faster," she moaned. "Harder."

Sunlight filtering through the gauzy curtains on her windows shafted across her face, lightening her eyes until they glittered like the ocean. He wanted to see them dark with passion, the pupils dilated until only a thin rim of blue remained.

He sped up his tempo. She whimpered, her hips undulating against him, meeting him thrust for thrust. No longer able to temper his lust, Declan reared up and plunged into her. Each stroke made him gasp hoarsely. Her snug inner walls, swollen from her earlier orgasms, held him so tight he had to fight his way past the clinging muscles.

"More!" Pelicia demanded. She gripped him with her thighs, arching against him. Her hands came around to grasp his biceps.

As he hammered into her with a fury he could no longer control, his blood roared in his ears. Hot need coiled in his belly.

Her cries spurred him on. He slammed into her, again and again, and she thrashed below him, crying out his name as she flew apart in his arms. Fire seared his cock. His balls clenched and he gave a shout, jetting his release deep inside her. He hung there, shuddering, grinding his hips against hers as wave after wave of ecstasy pummeled him. Finally he collapsed against her, completely drained.

Chapter 16

A short while later, Declan came to himself enough to move off Pelicia so he wouldn't crush her. Lying on his back, he crooked an arm around her and drew her to his side, gratified at her contented murmur as she rested her head against his shoulder.

God, he loved her. She made him a better man. No, that wasn't quite right. She made him want to be a better man. He didn't want to go back to being without her—he didn't want to go back to what he was.

He opened his mouth to tell her how he felt, but was forestalled by a knock from downstairs. Thinking to ignore it, he said, "Pel, I need to tell you something. It's—" He broke off as the knock came again. He sighed. "Someone's at the door."

She stirred. "I didn't hear any—" She broke off as the knock came again, loud enough this time that she heard it, too. She climbed off the bed with a muttered, "Bloody werewolf hearing."

He frowned, ignoring that little jibe. "Pel, we need to talk."

This time the knock at the door was more of a pounding, either by a fisted hand or a foot.

She paused. "Declan . . ."

More pounding.

Pelicia sighed. "Someone's being persistent, that's for sure. Can this wait, what you need to say?"

"Sure." Declan slid off the bed, bent and picked up his boxers, not bothering to hide his irritation. "Whatever you want."

She sighed. "Don't be that way, Declan. Look, I'm sorry. It's just . . . a lot." She put her bra around her, closing the fasteners and twisting the bra around until the cups were in front. Then she slid her arms through the straps and fit the cups over her breasts. "And you being a werewolf isn't as earth shattering as you admitting you should have handled things differently."

Thinking she was being facetious, he almost gave her a mock laugh. But, realizing she was completely serious, he pressed his lips together and nodded. "Aye," he replied.

What else could he say? He'd been an ass, he'd admitted it, and she'd welcomed him back. He wasn't going to do anything to mess it up this time.

While getting dressed, he watched her do the same and the sight stirred his body to action. Halfhearted at best— hell, it wasn't like he was eighteen anymore—but it still surprised him. He stepped into his pants and pulled them up then stood still a moment, staring down as he pulled up the tab to the zipper.

"Lose something?"

He looked up to see Pelicia, fully clothed with one hand on the doorknob, staring at him with eyebrows raised.

"No. I know exactly where everythin' is," he grumbled good naturedly. It was a nice change, having her playfully teasing him instead of giving him a hard time. "And it's all in perfect workin' condition, too."

"You won't get an argument from me on that one." She grinned and opened the door, dodging his reaching hand. "Don't start something you can't finish, O'Connell. Someone's at the door." She left the room.

Declan swore under his breath. He grabbed his shirt and jogged after her, catching up to her about halfway down the staircase. "Let me check it out first, all right?"

"Okay." She let him precede her. From behind him she muttered, "There is a constable on duty, remember?"

"Aye, I remember," he countered with a glance at her over his shoulder. "And just because he was there thirty minutes ago doesn't mean he's there now."

He cracked open the door. Upon seeing Constable Tremwith, he opened the door all the way and finished buttoning his shirt, leaving the tails hanging outside his slacks. What did the man want now? There were no more dead bodies and no one had taken any more shots at them. "Constable. What can we do for you?"

"You can let me in." Tremwith's gaze traveled down Declan, taking in his obvious hastily dressed body and bare feet with little more than a slightly quirked eyebrow. He looked up again and focused over Declan's shoulder. "Pelicia, may I have a few moments of your time?"

"Sure." Pelicia took a few steps forward. When Declan didn't move, she smacked him lightly on the arm. "Let the man in, Declan."

Without a word, Declan moved to one side.

Tremwith strode inside, taking his hat off and tucking it under one arm. When Pelicia gestured toward the drawing room, he headed that way.

"Can I get you some tea?" she asked as she followed him.

"No, thank you." He waited until she sat down in one of the plump armchairs then he sat on the sofa. "There's no easy way to say this, so I'm just going to come out and say it." He glanced at Declan then put his somber gaze on Pelicia. "I'm sorry to tell you that we found a body washed up on one of the north side beaches earlier. The driver's license found in the wallet identifies the man, and I've just had it confirmed that it was . . ." He paused and leaned forward, hat clasped in his fingers. "I'm sorry to say it's one of your guests, Pelicia. Andrew Montkean."

"Andrew!" Pelicia's lovely face whitened in shock.

Declan went to her side. Sitting on the arm of the chair, he put his arm around her shoulders and pulled her closer. He looked at Tremwith. "Are you sure?"

The constable gave a short nod.

"How . . ." She cleared her throat. "How did he die?"

The constable pressed his lips together as if debating how much to tell her. Then with a small sigh he offered, "He was garroted—strangled with a cord of some sort from behind, the doctor thinks." After setting his cap on the sofa beside him, he pulled a pen and a small notebook from the inside pocket of his uniform jacket. "When was the last time you saw Mr. Montkean, Pelicia?"

She reached up and linked the fingers of her left hand with Declan's where his hand rested on her shoulder. Her skin was cool. "I haven't actually seen him since the day he checked in." At Tremwith's questioning look, she said, "He always came in after everyone else had gone to bed and was gone before dawn the next morning. But his bed always appeared to be slept in, so I just assumed . . ." She glanced up at Declan, a stricken look in her eyes. "You don't suppose . . ." She looked back at the constable. "H-how long has he been dead?"

"Less than a day," Tremwith said. "The doctor thinks not more than twelve to fourteen hours." He looked back and forth between them. "That would be two people—one staying here and one apparently visiting in the middle of the night—who have died in the last twenty-four hours."

Declan scowled. "Thank you for pointin' out the obvious, boyo. Just what is it you're inferrin'?"

"Technically, I'm implying, *you're* inferring." At Declan's deepening scowl, Tremwith muttered, "Sorry." He cleared his throat. "Your history is . . . checkered, isn't it, Mr. O'Connell?"

"You make it sound like I've spent time in prison, which I haven't," he stressed. "Although eighteen years in the Royal Marines sometimes felt like it."

"My point exactly. You were a special operative—you've been trained how to kill."

Declan didn't like where this was going. He had a suspicion the other man was merely feeling him out, not seriously considering him a suspect. Either way, he'd like to tell the bugger to go fuck himself, but that wouldn't go over well, he knew. Plus it would upset Pelicia. As if the conversation already wasn't. He narrowed his eyes. "I sure as hell don't go around tossin' bodies into the ocean or slittin' innocent women's throats."

Pelicia made a choked sound. Her right hand came up to her face, fingers pressing against the bridge of her nose.

He knew she was fighting back tears, and he felt like a louse bringing up such a painful subject in such an indelicate way. He glared at Tremwith even as he murmured, "I'm sorry, darlin'."

She shook her head, her left hand squeezing his for a

moment. She massaged the bridge of her nose and then let her right hand fall to her lap. After taking a deep breath, she seemed to regain her composure. Looking at Tremwith, she said, "Declan didn't kill Andrew, and he certainly didn't kill Brenna."

The constable appeared to accept that, at least for the moment. "What about your other missing guest?" He glanced down at his notepad. "Neal White?"

"Technically," Declan responded, unable to resist throwing some of Tremwith's snark back at him, "there's only one missin' guest, since you've already found Montkean."

"Declan, don't be such a smartass," Pelicia muttered, letting go of his hand. Before he could protest the loss of her touch, she leaned into his side, clearly taking comfort from his nearness.

"Smart's the only kind of ass I know how to be, you know that, darlin'."

She gave a snort but otherwise ignored him. "Charlie, what are you thinking? That Neal killed Andrew and Brenna?" Her voice thickened at her friend's name, but she held her composure.

"Until I can rule him out, yes, he's a . . . person of interest." Tremwith glanced at Declan as if to say he hadn't ruled Declan out yet, either, then put his gaze back on Pelicia. "Has he acted suspiciously that you've seen?"

"No." She shook her head. "He's been coming here pretty much since I opened the place. He's working on a coffee table book and comes here to photograph the islands." She glanced up at Declan. "I can't believe he'd hurt Brenna, let alone kill her." She looked at Tremwith. "He seemed to really care for her."

"Care for her in what way?"

She hesitated, no doubt not wanting to cast her friend in a negative light.

"They were shagging each other," Declan offered.

Pelicia shot him a look.

He shrugged. "There's no way to dress it up, darlin'. Unless you think they were in love?"

She sighed and shook her head.

Declan looked at the constable. "They were fuck buddies. Friends with benefits," he added when Pelicia glared at him again.

"And his relationship with Montkean?"

"I wasn't aware they had one," she said. "Andrew was never around. I mean, I suppose they could have bumped into one another at some point, but Neal didn't talk about Andrew at all."

"And Andrew?" Tremwith scribbled a note on his pad.

Her brows dipped. "I don't understand."

"Did he talk about Neal?"

Her frown deepened. "No. Charlie, I just said, Andrew was never around." She heaved another sigh. "I just can't see how it could be Neal."

"Well, we'll be wanting to talk with him, especially since he was intimate with the first victim." He looked at Declan again, his eyebrows slightly raised.

"And it wasn't Declan, either." She stood up and paced toward the fireplace, turning to stand with her back against the wall next to it. She folded her arms over her chest, looking forlorn and worried. "Declan wouldn't have hurt Bren . . ." She trailed off, biting her lip.

Standing, Declan went to her and pulled her into his arms, pressing her face gently against his chest. He stared at Tremwith. "Do you have all you need, Constable?"

"No. I'd like to speak to you, Mr. O'Connell. In private, if I may."

Pelicia pulled away from Declan and looked at the constable. Her face was pale but she remained composed. "About what?"

"That's between Mr. O'Connell and myself. For the moment." Tremwith scooped up his hat and got to his feet. "Mr. O'Connell?" As if thinking his words may have been too abrupt, he sent a smile Pelicia's way and a softly spoken, "Perhaps I might have that cup of tea, then?"

She glanced from one man to the other. Declan could see she wanted to stay, to find out what the two were going to discuss, but knew she realized the constable wouldn't talk in front of her. She sighed. "Of course," she murmured and walked out of the drawing room.

Declan turned his attention back to the constable. "What is it?"

The man's troubled gaze met his. "I didn't want to say this in front of Pelicia, though I know she's not stupid and may have already pieced it together. Or will before too much longer." He paused and rubbed the back of his neck. "I'm thinking that Brenna Brown was killed by mistake. Unless she was living a secret life, no one had any major grudges against her." He shook his head. "Whoever murdered her thought he was killing Pelicia."

Declan drew a deep breath and held it a moment before exhaling. "Aye. I'd thought so, too." He'd seen the look in Pelicia's eyes that told him she felt guilt over her friend's death. "So does Pel."

Tremwith nodded. He turned his cap around and around in his hands. "If this Neal White returns, watch yourself."

"He's a bloody photographer." Declan frowned. "You aren't seriously considering him as a suspect?"

The constable's heavy eyebrows rose. "And if he's not a suspect, who does that leave?"

The man had a point. "Well, it wasn't me."

Tremwith gave another nod. "I didn't really think it was, to be truthful. I just wanted to see your reaction."

Just as Declan had thought. "My reaction is that it was unnecessary and all it did was further upset Pel."

"I'm sorry about that." Tremwith put his hat on, fidgeting with it until the brim was just the way he wanted it. "I'm just doing my job."

Declan sighed. "Aye. I know." He walked with the man to the front door and opened it, resting one hand on the doorknob. "Let me know if there's anything else you need. And I'll let you know if we see White."

"Thank you." The constable touched the brim of his hat with two fingers. "Tell Pelicia I said thanks for the tea, but I had to leave. I don't think she'll mind." He gave a small smile then nodded toward the officer at the far side of the front garden. "I'll leave Kenny here. Another lad will replace him for the overnight shift."

Declan nodded. "Thanks." Another set of eyes would be welcome, especially since Sully was out of the picture. For now.

Pelicia stood by the sink and stared through the window at the back garden. How had her life turned so upside down in such a short time? Declan had barreled back into her life, she'd basically gotten an offer to go back to a job in London, her best friend had been murdered in *her* house and another man seriously wounded, and Andrew . . . She shook her head.

God, some days it just didn't pay to get out of bed.

Movement from outside caught her eye. She leaned forward and gasped to see Neal standing at the edge of the garden. Without thinking, she went to the back door and opened it. She went outside and walked over to him. "What are you doing out here?" she asked. Not waiting for a response, she said starkly, "Brenna's dead. Did you know that?"

A look of what appeared to be genuine shock lit his features. "What? How . . ." He spread his hands. "How did it happen?"

He seemed upset, but she couldn't shake the suspicion that Tremwith had planted. Could Neal really be a murderer? He seemed so . . . harmless.

"You really didn't know?" she asked, watching him carefully.

He frowned, shaking his head. "I stayed out last night to do some after-dark shots. When I started to come in this morning I saw . . . at least, I *thought* I saw a fucking wolf in your house." He shoved his hands into the front pocket of his khakis. "It freaked me out, and I took off. I've been trying to calm down ever since."

Pelicia wanted to believe him. But somehow she thought it would take more than a wolf to make him wander around for hours trying to calm down.

"I . . . loved her, you know?" Neal's eyes held a sheen of moisture. "Oh, not the ever-after kind of love—I wasn't looking to marry her or anything like that. But she . . ." He broke off. His chin trembled as he fought for composure. "She was a good sort."

"Yes, she was."

"How did she die?"

"She was murdered. In my kitchen." Pelicia walked slowly toward the back door, and Neal followed, though at a slower pace. When she was even with the door, she glanced over her shoulder. Declan and Tremwith stood by the opened front door. The constable had his hat on, so it looked like he was getting ready to leave. Turning back to Neal, she said, "Had Brenna come to see you? Is that why she was here?"

"God, I don't know." He heaved a trembling sigh. "If she was here for me, she must have been trying to surprise me. I wasn't expecting her."

She glanced over her shoulder again. Then, meeting Neal's gaze, she murmured, "Constable Tremwith will want to talk to you."

Neal shook his head and backed up a few steps. "No."

She frowned. "Neal, he's investigating Brenna's murder. You *have* to talk to him. Tell him what you know. It might help him find out who did this to her."

"I can't tell him anything that would help." When Pelicia made a disgusted sound in her throat and turned toward the house, he grabbed her upper right arm in a rough grip. "Where're you going?"

She gazed at him in disbelief. His eyes, normally full of light, were dark, flinty with resolve. His fingers dug into her arm. "Neal, let go of me." When he tightened his grip, she said, "You're hurting me." Her heart lurched in fear. If he had already killed, what would stop him from killing her now? Even with Declan's newfound abilities, he was too far away to do anything.

Something flickered in Neal's eyes. His grip tightened

even more, dragging a cry of pain from her. He cursed, his gaze going over her shoulder. Then he let go of her and turned, running through the back garden of the house next door before disappearing around the corner to be lost from sight.

The back door opened behind her. She turned to see Declan, his face hard with anger. Tremwith was right behind him.

"Pelicia?" Declan strode up to her. "I heard you yell. What happened?" Before she could respond, his nostrils flared. "Fuck! He was here. The bastard who attacked you— that damned sniper. He was just here. Did you see him?"

She stared at him wide-eyed. "It . . . was Neal."

"And you just stood here talkin' to him instead of callin' for one of us?"

"Which way did he go?" Tremwith asked. When Pelicia pointed a shaky finger in the direction Neal had fled, the constable turned his head and spoke into the radio on his shoulder, recalling the police unit back to the scene. He shot a look at both of them and with a terse, "Stay here," he pulled his gun and started off in search of the suspect.

Declan stalked to the edge of the garden and then turned back to her. "Jaysus, Pelicia. What the hell were you thinkin'?"

"I . . ." She shrugged. She hadn't been thinking, not until she was already outside with him and he'd started acting so strangely. By then it had been too late.

"Well, what did he have to say? Where's he been? What's he been doin'?"

"He said he came back this morning and saw, well, you. When you were in wolf form, I mean. He said the wolf scared him so much that he ran and has been trying to calm down ever since." She bit the inside of her lip when Declan shot her a glance.

"And you bought that?" His voice echoed his look of disbelief.

"Declan, I just cannot believe he's a murderer." Pelicia crossed her arms, knowing her posture was defensive and not caring. She'd known she'd been stupid to go out into the garden with Neal—she didn't need Declan pointing it out to her. "I mean, I know you've recognized the scent— and I trust you on this—but I've known the man for two years. He just doesn't seem . . ." She shook her head. "And why kill Brenna, for God's sake? He said he loved her."

"You're talkin' as if you think Brenna was killed deliberately, when I know that you know in all probability she was killed by mistake." He sighed and walked back to her, cupping her elbows in his broad palms. "You have to know that, Pel," he said, his voice soft, the hands on her arms warm and strong. "Whoever did it thought it was you."

"But why?" She searched his gaze, bewilderment swirling through her. "Why would someone be after me?"

"Because of me. With Sully's attack, I think it's Ryder's cousin, back for another try. And since you're important to me, that makes you a target, too." He looked up to see Constable Tremwith pushing his way back through the short hedgerow on the edge of Pelicia's property. "What is it?" Declan asked, tensing.

The police constable shook his head. "I lost him." He was breathing heavily. "I'm going to meet up with the unit, but we'll leave a man stationed out front, as before." He paused and stared at Declan, no doubt reading the tension that rode him. The constable looked from Declan to Pelicia and back again. "Perhaps we'd best post a man here in the back garden as well."

Pelicia opened her mouth to voice an instinctive protest— she valued her privacy and to have the police mucking about wasn't going to do anything for her reputation, either— but then she reminded herself that her friend and one of her lodgers were dead. There was no question that a police presence was necessary. "Yes, I think perhaps you should."

Chapter 17

He waited until the cops had cleared out and then made his way closer to the Nola. Twice as he lay in his sniper's camouflage in the tall grasses policemen had walked past him, one no more than a half-meter away. But he was patient and knew how to remain absolutely still. He'd had years of training—and experience—and could blend into his surroundings.

Hitching up his trousers, he hunkered down behind a bush at the corner of the house across the street and assessed the situation. One uniformed bobby out front in his vehicle and, as he watched, another peered around the corner of the house from the back garden. So, two constables standing guard. As if they could stop him.

He snorted. Two country policemen, with no experience dealing with someone like him . . . Hell. It was going to be like shooting fish in a barrel.

By removing that fop Andrew, he'd already ensured that O'Connell and Pelicia would be alone in the house. Now all he had to do was take care of these two coppers—loaned out from the mainland contingent—and he could put his final plan in motion.

He pushed back the surge of anger he felt over Brenna. Yet another thing in his life that had gone wrong and, as far as he was concerned, it was O'Connell's fault. The bastard would pay dearly for everything, including that.

Looking down, he double-checked the contents of his backpack one more time. Satisfied that he had everything, he shoved his arms through the straps and settled the pack onto his back.

He started to rise to his feet and then stopped, his attention caught by a low, skulking shadow at the edge of the front garden. It looked like a big dog. When it moved away from the house, crossing into a patch of sunlight, he caught his breath.

It was that bloody wolf again.

He hadn't been kidding when he'd told Pelicia that he'd seen a wolf before. From the scuttlebutt in town he'd discovered that her other guest, the man who'd turned out to be a policeman from London, had been attacked by the thing.

That was fine by him—one more person out of the way. And it had saved him the trouble.

But it still made the hair on the back of his neck stand on end. There was something . . . unnatural about the animal. He'd heed his instincts and wait until the thing was gone.

Three houses down the street, the wolf paused, looking back toward the Nola. Looking, it seemed, straight at *him*. He held himself still, hardly breathing.

He could face down an enemy without breaking a sweat, could site a human target through his sniper's scope and pull the trigger without flinching. But this thing made him pause, made the perspiration break out along his spine, under his arms.

Finally the animal turned away and trotted off.

He watched it until it was swallowed by the tall grasses where the road ended. Then he turned his sights back onto the bed and breakfast.

Now came the fun part. Reaching up, he messed his hair. He unzipped his jacket. Pulling out his knife, he ripped through the facing, then ripped the zipper partway. He replaced the knife in the scabbard at the small of his back. "Show time."

Pasting a panicked expression on his face, he ran up to the police car.

The copper saw him coming and rolled down the window about an inch. "What is it, sir?"

"Oh, God. Ohgodohgod." He panted, laying it on thick. "I just saw . . ." He trailed off and gagged. "Oh, God. You have to come. I think she's dead."

Alarm spread over the constable's face. He pushed open the door. Before the man could step out, he yanked his knife free and sliced across the policeman's throat.

Deep enough to sever the man's vocal chords so he couldn't cry out. Deep enough that he'd bleed to death in a matter of minutes.

He felt no remorse as he shoved the body onto the floor of the backseat and quietly closed the door.

He felt nothing. He was doing a job, nothing more, nothing less.

Stepping carefully, he crept around the side of the bed and breakfast and paused to peer around the corner into the back garden.

The constable on guard was at the opposite side of the

small yard, too far away for him to sneak up on the man. So, he'd wait. Wait for the prey to come to him.

Then he'd strike out at O'Connell. Hit him where it would hurt the most.

And O'Connell would finally understand what it felt like to be filled by the same rage that consumed *him*.

Chapter 18

Declan eased down onto the mattress and exhaled heavily. "What a day."

Pelicia rolled to her side and draped an arm across his stomach.

He brought one hand up and rubbed his palm gently over her forearm. God, it felt good to have her back in his bed. It felt good to think she might be back to stay.

She yawned, her breath blowing warmly against his skin. "So much has happened. Brenna, Sully, and now Andrew . . . And to think that Neal could have something to do with it all . . ." She shook her head. "It's just *too* much."

"I know, darlin'." He shifted and wrapped his arms around her, pulling her closer. "Neal may have had somethin' to do with Brenna and Andrew, but he wasn't involved in the attack on Sully. That was someone completely different."

She rose up on her elbow and stared down at him. "What do you mean?"

"Whoever attacked Sully is a werewolf." He tucked a heavy strand of blond hair behind her ear. "Neal's not." At her questioning look, he said, "I'd have smelled it."

The skin between her fine brows crinkled. "Werewolves have a smell? I've not heard that before." She shook her head. "Of course, I haven't been around Ryder during the full moon—he forbade it."

"Hmm." Declan reached up and smoothed her frown lines with his thumb. "I suppose it's kind of like . . . sage. But with somethin' a bit darker underneath."

She nodded. "I've always smelled sage over on Phelan's Keep, but I just assumed there was sage growing." A small smile curled her full lips. "I never realized it was Ryder." She sobered, her eyes widening. "But if it wasn't Neal who attacked Sully, who was it?"

"I don't know." And that bothered him. What bothered him more was that there seemed to be two bad guys at work here—the werewolf, no doubt sent by Miles, and whoever it was that had been taking pot shots at Pelicia.

Or at him. He still wasn't sure about that.

Pelicia yawned again and lay down, resting her head on his shoulder once more. "I can't believe how tired I am. We should be trying to figure this out, but I just can't think straight." Her yawn was wide enough to make her jaw crack.

Declan ran his fingers through her hair. He was exhausted as well, though determined to stay awake. Just in case. "There are two constables on duty outside," he murmured, more to put her at ease than in any real belief they would provide safety. That sniper was skilled enough to take them out from a distance, though of course the sound of the bullets firing would alert Declan and Pelicia. And they should be safe enough until nightfall, at any rate.

But because it was the first night of a full moon, he'd turn into a wolf once the moon was up. He'd deal with that when the time came. For now, at least, he could provide some level of comfort to Pelicia. "Get some rest, darlin'. I'll be right here."

He glanced at the bedside table and noted the time readout on the digital alarm clock. Five P.M. Just a little over an hour before the sun set and the full moon called to the beast within him.

The even sound of Pelicia's breathing told him she'd succumbed to slumber. He held her, thanking God and the Fates that she was back in his arms. He was determined to keep her there—he wanted to watch this woman grow old, wanted to grow old with her.

He stroked his hand down her back and curled it over her hip. She shifted, throwing one leg over his thigh, her knee nestling against the juncture of his thighs. Even as tired as he was, his flesh stirred at the innocent, unknowing touch. If she weren't so exhausted he'd be tempted to roll over and ask her to help him take care of things.

But she needed her rest. He needed rest, too.

Later. Right now . . . no rest for the wicked.

Pelicia murmured in her sleep, and he tightened his arm around her. He would keep her safe. There was no other option.

A sound like the creaking of a stair or loose floorboard from out in the hallway caught his attention. He stiffened. Easing his arm from around Pelicia, he sat up. Still asleep, she grumbled under her breath but settled against the pillow.

Declan slowed his breathing and listened, hard. After

several minutes of hearing nothing else, he relaxed. The Nola was an old house—a couple of centuries old—and doubtless made quite a few settling noises at night.

He leaned against the headboard and stared across the room at the bookshelf on the wall opposite the big bed. With his heightened vision he could make out the title of every book she had there. Fiction books—horror, mystery, science fiction, and romance—lined the shelves beneath a row of nonfiction books that ranged from biographies to self-help.

Another creak sounded from the hallway. He straightened, swinging his legs over the edge of the mattress.

"Whazzit?" Pelicia's sleepy voice came from behind him.

"I'm not sure. Maybe nothin'." He kept his voice low. The faintest smell of gunpowder wafted to his nose. His eyes widened. "Goddamnit."

At that moment the door cracked open and a small canister was fired into the room. Declan caught a glimpse of muzzle fire and surged to his feet. Pelicia yelled. He heard the rustle of bedclothes and gave a quick glance over his shoulder to see her on her knees on the mattress.

The door slammed shut as a hissing noise started from the canister. He couldn't smell anything, and there was no visible sign of gas, but his throat started to burn and his vision blurred. He managed to stagger forward a few steps before crashing to the floor. Blackness crept over him, and he knew no more.

He came to consciousness to find someone kneeling beside him. Declan smelled the salt air of the ocean, heard waves crashing nearby, and realized that he'd been moved. His hands were bound behind his back with what felt like standard issue restraint cable.

A subtle floral perfume and the sound of soft breathing told him that Pelicia was nearby, and she was alive. He also smelled the acrid stench of hate emanating from the man next to him and the lingering odor of expended gunpowder.

It was the sniper. The bastard who'd fired at Pelicia. The one who'd been trying to take him out.

Well, boyo, not if I have anything to say about it.

Without warning, Declan kicked out, catching the man in the upper thigh and knocking him on his ass.

The intruder was back on his feet in a heartbeat and kicked Declan in the jaw. Declan's head snapped back and stars swam in his blackening vision before he fought it off and managed to roll to the side to avoid another blow.

He wasn't able to block the next kick, and it disoriented him long enough for the man to bind his ankles together with another length of flexible restraint. As Declan started to struggle, the man moved around behind him.

Declan heard the *snick* of a gun's safety being flicked. He stilled. The tip of a gun barrel pressed against the back of his head.

"I'd think about your next move there, laddie."

He knew that voice. But from where?

He glanced quickly at his surroundings, gauging the lay of the land and trying to find whatever advantages he could. From the position of the sun he could tell he'd been out at least an hour. Moon's rise wouldn't be far off now.

And then we'll just see what's what.

Mindful of the pistol pressed against his skull, he kept his head still while he quickly gazed around the area. He was at the entrance to a stone barrow—one of the many Stone Age burial chambers that dotted the islands. Pelicia, still unconscious, lay inside the chamber, her legs bent, wrists bound in front of her. He smelled no blood so he could only assume she was unhurt. With his enhanced hearing he could hear her breathing, slow and even.

For the moment, at least, she was all right.

"Now, you just stay put, O'Connell, while I see to Pelicia."

The man stepped away from him, keeping his gaze on Declan while he walked around him toward the entrance of the barrow.

As he came into Declan's line of sight, Declan's breath caught in his throat. "Addison?" he asked with a confused frown. It was Fletcher Addison, a member of his special ops team back in his Royal Marine days. A man who'd always seemed to have something to prove—whether to Declan or himself he'd never been sure. But the younger man had been reckless, and in the end that recklessness had nearly killed them all. It had cost Addison more than anyone else.

Declan remembered the man's agonized cries, the stench of burning flesh, the coppery scent of blood—and that had been before he'd become a werewolf and better able to pick different smells from the air.

He'd lost track of Addison after he'd been released from hospital. If he were honest with himself, he hadn't tried very hard to find him—the man was a loose cannon and one Declan had been relieved to get away from.

The former lieutenant grinned now as he put his fingers

against Pelicia's neck. "Aye. You didn't have a clue, did you, Mr. Hotshot?" The vaguest hint of a Scottish burr came through his speech, though it was blunted. "Which just goes to show that I'm better than you. Even after what you did to me." His grin was full of malicious glee. "And don't be thinking anyone will be coming to your rescue. Those two coppers from Penzance didn't stand a chance against someone like me. And, just to be sure I wouldn't be interrupted, I've moved us all to a more . . . isolated spot."

Declan shook his head. Two more people dead because of this madman.

Addison hunkered down and glanced inside the dim chamber. The huge capstones on the top of the structure meant the small enclosure—less than two meters high and perhaps three meters deep—had very little light. Once the sun went down it would be nearly pitch black inside.

"She's still out," Addison said, "as she should be. That gas should've kept both of you out for at least a couple of hours. That's what the Russian I bought it from told me, though he might have been lying," he mumbled. Looking back at Declan, his gaze glittered with the same hatred that caused a stink in Declan's nostrils. "Because otherwise, why did you wake up so soon?"

'Cause I'm a werewolf Declan wanted to snarl. *One that's gonna rip your soddin' face off, you bastard.* But that was his secret for now—and perhaps their only way out. Yet it was another positive aspect to this whole werewolf thing, one he wouldn't change if it meant he could better protect Pelicia. He gave a careless shrug in response to Addison's question and asked one of his own. "Just what is it you think I did to you?"

"What is it I think . . ." Addison cast him an incredulous glare. "Because of you I lost part of my right leg, I have continuous tremors in my right hand, and I'm damned lucky I didn't lose the vision in my right eye. You bloody well cost me my livelihood, you bastard."

Declan knew his former special ops teammate spoke of the explosion that ended his military career, an accident that could have cost the man his life.

An accident that would have been prevented if Addison had listened to him. "I told you that you had too much C-4, Lieutenant," he said, keeping his voice low and calm. "You didn't have anythin' to prove to anyone. You still don't."

Keeping his gun trained on Declan, Addison reached out and picked up a backpack resting against the entrance to the burial chamber. Going onto his knees, he crawled into the chamber. He dropped the backpack next to Pelicia and, with one hand, reached inside the bag.

As Addison pulled his hand out of the backpack, Declan's eyes widened at what the other man held. Three sticks of dynamite wrapped together with black tape. Declan called upon his wolf's vision and focused more closely on the device—three separate wires connected the dynamite to a timer. There was also a smaller black box next to the timer that made Declan frown.

A timer and a remote control? Kind of overkill.

"I liked the look of dynamite better than C-4," Addison murmured, running his index finger along the side of one of the red-papered sticks. "It's somehow more . . . elegant, don't you think?"

Not responding, Declan struggled against the strong nylon cord binding his wrists and, though he thought he felt a little give to them, they held firm, keeping him effectively hobbled. He briefly considered transforming to his wolf form, but even the three seconds or so that the change would take would leave Pelicia vulnerable.

He had to wait for a better opportunity, and he had to talk Addison out of whatever he was planning with that bomb. "What're you thinkin' there, boyo?"

Addison looked at him and without a word bent over Pelicia and held the homemade device against her chest. Pulling her upright and then forward, he braced her against his body as he threaded the straps beneath her arms and fastened them behind her back. Another strap went between her legs to fasten behind her back as well.

Declan fought back a howl of rage. The bastard was touching Pelicia with no sexual intent, but he had his hands on Declan's mate just the same. He'd better pray that he killed Declan, because if Pelicia died and Declan somehow managed to live, he would hunt. The bastard. Down.

"It should be obvious what I'm thinking, O'Connell." Addison gently settled her against the granite wall of the chamber and stroked hair away from her cheek, tucking it behind her ear. Her head lolled forward, chin resting against her chest.

Declan saw a look of regret flicker across Addison's face as he leaned away from her. He reached into the backpack and pulled out a large flashlight. Flicking it on, he set it on the ground, the light streaming upward toward the capstone ceiling. Then he crawled back to the entrance and placed another flashlight there. He straightened, staring at Declan. "You took something from me. Now I'm going to take something from you."

Declan swallowed. He'd been here before, in this place where he could either allow emotion to overtake him or battle it. If it was something that could distract him, he'd clear his mind of it. But this . . . this was something that could fuel his anger. And that he could use.

But first he had to talk Addison down. "Pelicia has nothin' to do with this. Whatever *this* is. It's me you want—leave her out of it."

"Oh, I had planned to. At first. I was just going to use her to get to you." Addison sat down, leaning his back against the rough granite behind him, and rested his left hand—the hand holding the gun—on his knee, keeping the weapon trained on Declan. "But when I was here four months ago and saw how desperate you were to win her back, I realized she was the key."

Declan ground his jaw. "The key to what?"

"To my plan. I kept you guessing by shooting at you, didn't I?" Addison grinned, clearly impressed with his own cleverness. "You didn't know which end was up. But now I'll tell you." He pointed toward Pelicia. "I'm going to watch your face as you come to realize there's nothing you can do to keep her from dying. I'm going to savor it—enjoy every nuance of your anguish and guilt."

Declan kept twisting his wrists, putting strain against the flexible binding, but even with his enhanced werewolf strength he couldn't get the cable to give. He needed to keep the man talking so he had time to figure out what to do.

The one thing that could not—*would not*—happen was that harm would come to Pelicia. Declan would die protecting her from this man. This . . .

Enemy.

"What happened to you, Addison? The man I knew would never countenance the killin' of an innocent."

Addison surged to his feet, his face red with anger. "The man you knew is dead. You killed him."

"I tried to stop you." Declan wriggled his hands, testing the strength of the restraint around his wrists. The damned corded fiber continued to hold firm.

A muscle flexed in the other man's jaw. "You were trying to make me feel stupid, like you always did." When Declan started to argue, Addison slashed his hand through the air. "Just shut up. You're making my head pound." He glanced at Pelicia. "I wanted to do this from the moment I first came here two years ago." His gaze locked on Declan's. "But you were stubborn and didn't come around to see her. I was beginning to think I'd have to rethink my plans."

"Sorry to have spoiled things for you."

"You didn't spoil anything, O'Connell. As it turns out, my plans were merely . . . delayed." He took a deep breath, visibly making himself relax. "Anyway, anticipation makes the wait worthwhile." He holstered his gun and reached into a front pocket of his jacket. When he withdrew his hand, he held a black rectangular plastic box roughly the size of his palm.

It was the detonator to the bomb now strapped around Pelicia's chest.

"Now," Addison said, sitting down and resting his back against the rough granite of the barrow entrance, "we'll just wait for Pelicia to wake up, and we can get the show on the road, as the Americans say."

Declan's heart pounded. Rage beat at him like a living, breathing thing, twisting his gut and setting fire to his blood. The wolf began to stir, called forth by his rage and the soon-to-rise full moon. A howl fought to be set free from a throat tight with fear.

Not for himself—anything Addison wanted to dish out Declan was more than ready to face. But Pelicia . . . She was an innocent in all of this. He had to make Addison see that.

And he had to make his move carefully. The maniac could set the bomb off at any moment.

"Listen, Addison." He paused, gentling his voice. "Fletcher." Declan tamped down the beast and met Addison's gaze with what he hoped was a calm look. That was the expression he strove for, at any rate. "Talk to me. I mean, why now? Why not five years ago? Or even ten? The accident was almost fifteen years ago, mate."

"Don't call me 'mate.' I'm not your *mate,* your chum, or your pal." He brought up his right hand and held it out in front of him. The fingers held a distinct tremble. "See that? I had to retrain myself to use my left hand. I also had a lot of years of therapy, O'Connell, to regain the use of my hand, to get used to my prosthetic leg, to listen to shrinks tell me I needed to let go of my anger and hatred so I could fully heal." He gave a short bark of laughter. "As if I would ever fully heal with half of my leg gone."

He drew a deep breath and held it before exhaling noisily. "Then I couldn't find you, once you'd moved to the States. So I figured . . ." He lifted his shoulders in a slight shrug. "I'd start coming here. I knew the way you felt about Pelicia back in our RM days—even if you didn't. God, you talked about her so much it was sickening. I knew eventually you'd come nosing around, trying to get her into your bed." His lips twisted. "One thing I learned during all those hours and hours and hours of endless therapy was patience. And you know what they say—revenge is a dish best served cold."

Pelicia moaned, her head lifting slightly as she fought the effects of the gas and tried to wake up.

"Easy there, love," Addison murmured. Once again on his knees, he moved a bit closer to her.

Declan saw the affection the other man tried to hide. "You like her, don't you? Look at her. She's an innocent. You can't do this."

"You think I can't?" Addison's jaw tightened. "Who do you think killed Brenna?"

Declan's eyes widened. Of course it had been Addison who'd killed Pelicia's friend. "Why? Because she found out who you really are?"

"Because I thought she was *her,*" he bellowed, jabbing a finger toward Pelicia. "I didn't expect Brenna to be in the house, and in the dark I mistook her for Pelicia." His lips thinned, and he breathed in through his nose, obviously trying to regain control of his fractured emotions. "That's another thing you have to pay for."

"Me?" Declan frowned. "How in the hell is that *my* fault?"

Addison made a rough sound deep in his throat. "How can you ask that? It's because of you that I'm here. Like this." He thrust out his right hand again, letting Declan see the ever-present trembling. Then Addison rapped his knuckles against the calf of his right leg. The sound of hard plastic being knocked against was muffled by the man's pants, but it made noise the way a real leg never would. "You really had to ask, didn't you. You arrogant son of a bitch."

Pelicia groaned and lifted her head fully, opening her eyes and blinking. "Declan?"

"Right here, darlin'." He kept his voice soothing when all he wanted to do was let loose and rage. But that would get him nowhere fast. "Just stay calm, and you'll be all right."

"Oh, aye. Lie to the lass, why don't you?"

Pelicia looked toward Addison, her lovely face scrunching with confusion. "Neal?"

Declan bit back a growl at his own thickness as he realized just who Addison was. Neal White, one of Pelicia's house guests. A guest who'd been staying with her off and on for two fucking years.

"Now you see, don't you?" Addison grinned. "'The two most powerful warriors are patience and time.' You used to tell me that, remember?"

"I can't take credit for it," Declan muttered, casting his mind about for a way to get out of this. Time was running out—in a matter of minutes the sun would set, the full moon would rise, and the wolf would be set free. He needed to neutralize Addison before that happened. "Leo Tolstoy said it first."

"I . . . I don't understand." Pelicia looked from one man to the other, her blue eyes wide and dark with fear in the miniscule light from the flashlight. She took in her surroundings and gasped. "Why are we at a barrow? Why am I tied up? *What the bloody hell is going on here?*"

"What's going on, my dear, is that you have a bomb strapped to your chest that's set to go off in just over two hours. As soon as I think O'Connell's suffered enough, I'm going to leave and listen to the explosion from a distance. And in case you get any ideas . . ." He waved the remote. "I don't *have* to wait an hour." He heaved a theatrical sigh. "As much as I'd love to see the look on your face, Dec, really I would, I have no desire to die here myself."

In the gathering dusk, Pelicia's face went white.

"Pity, that." Declan tried to clear his mind of everything else except for one task—morphing his hands into werewolf claws so he could try to cut through the bindings. He had no idea if the claws would be sharp enough, but he had to try.

Pelicia's life depended on it.

Chapter 19

"You can't be serious, Neal." Pelicia stared at the blond-haired man she'd begun to think of as a friend. He was dressed in camouflage gear—jacket with an olive-green T-shirt underneath, cargo pants, and military-style boots. He wore a holstered gun strapped to one thigh. Not exactly the image of the carefree photojournalist she'd come to know.

Nor was it the look of someone who'd seemed so concerned about her, about how well she was doing in her efforts to run a bed and breakfast.

When he briefly turned to one side, his jacket flapped behind him, and she saw a knife in its scabbard secured to his belt and a mobile phone next to it.

"Tell me you're not serious." She looked down at her chest. What appeared to be three sticks of dynamite—she'd only ever seen dynamite on the telly, for God's sake—were taped together with two small black boxes attached, one of which was a digital timer. Three wires—one blue, one red, and one yellow-and-white striped—led from one box to the next and then to the dynamite. It didn't look like a real bomb, but what did she know? She'd never seen a real live bomb up close—and you couldn't get any closer than this. She swallowed and closed her eyes. She was very much afraid it was all too real.

Deadly real.

Pulse throbbing in her throat, she raised her gaze once more to Neal. *God, please tell me you're joking.* "Neal—"

"My name's not Neal. It's Fletcher. Fletcher Addison." The expression on his face made it seem as if he hated her. Her heart stuttered with fear. He scowled. "You really want to know just how serious I am? Ask O'Connell."

She looked at Declan, sitting at the entrance to the barrow.

His face was dark with anger. His eyes glittered with feral intensity, though his voice was soft as he said, "He's serious, darlin'. He blames me for an accident that happened a lotta years ago."

"Maybe a lot of years ago to you, laddie. Not all that many to me."

Pelicia's breath came hard and fast between parted lips. She felt light-headed and concentrated on slowing her breathing. *Don't pass out,* she commanded herself. *Just because you've a bomb strapped to your chest and you're sitting in a burial chamber is no reason to panic.*

Bloody hell. If ever there *was* a time to panic, now would be it.

"Stay calm, Pel." Declan snagged her gaze with his. "Don't be afraid."

"Easy for you to say," she muttered. Her voice quavered. "You're not the one with a bomb strapped to your chest."

"No, I'm not, because Addison here is a coward hidin' behind a woman." Declan stared at the other man, his eyes holding so much rage that Pelicia was surprised he hadn't already lost control and transformed into his wolf.

But then Declan had always been a man with great self-control.

"*He's* the one who's afraid, darlin'."

Addison gave a low growl. "You don't know what fear is, you son of a bitch."

"False Evidence Appearing Real," Declan responded. "It's something that was drilled into all of us early on in our training," he said with a glance toward Pelicia.

She held her breath. Maybe if he reminded Addison of those days, of the camaraderie they shared, the goals and mind-sets they'd had in common, he could get him to let them go.

"Remember that, Fletch?" Declan's voice was softly cajoling. It seemed he had the same idea as she.

"Aye, I remember." The other man stared at the dirt floor of the barrow, his face reflecting his conflicting emotions. Just when she thought he might be softening, he turned. "I also remember that the accident was your fault." He crawled out of the barrow toward Declan. "Maybe if I give you an idea of the pain I still experience, you'll understand what I mean."

Without any further warning, he yanked the knife from its scabbard and plunged it into Declan's right thigh, just above his knee.

Declan jerked. The muscles in his jaw and neck went rigid, and she knew he held back a yell. Nonetheless, a low groan came from behind his clenched teeth. His eyes lightened, turning tawny.

Pelicia caught her breath. The wolf struggled to break free. Shadows lengthened across his face, dimming the light in those eerie eyes. Her eyes widened as she realized something else.

The sun was setting, and tonight was the first night of the full moon.

Whether he wanted it or not, Declan was about to go furry.

Neal . . . no, *Fletcher* didn't stand a chance.

And while she didn't feel any particular loyalty to the man who'd strapped a bomb to her chest, she was pretty sure she didn't want to watch someone get ripped to shreds by an enraged werewolf.

"Fletcher, please. I thought we were friends." She cast a pleading gaze toward him, hoping to appeal to whatever sense of morality he might have. "This isn't right. You know this isn't right."

"Shut up." With a glare, he pulled the knife free from Declan's leg and pointed it at her. Declan's blood glistened along the edge, dripped off the tip. "It's your own damned fault for taking up with *him.*" The knife slashed toward Declan again, slicing across his upper left arm.

Declan grunted in pain, grimacing. He flexed his arms then, with another grunt, his hands swung around, reaching for Addison. He dodged the other man's swipe at him with the knife and wrapped one hand around Addison's left wrist.

Pelicia gasped. Somehow he'd been able to free his hands from his bindings. Then she saw that the hand wrapped around Addison's wrist was long-fingered and furry, tipped with two-inch claws.

He'd partially transformed. She hadn't known he could do that. From the brief look of surprise on his face, she guessed he hadn't either.

He raked the claws of his free hand across the binding around his ankles and freed his feet.

"What the—" Addison's voice cracked as he looked at Declan's hand. His frightened gaze lifted to Declan's face. "What the hell are you?"

"Your worst nightmare, boyo." Declan twisted his hand. Bones crunched. Addison screamed and jerked away from Declan. With his uninjured hand—but not unimpaired, for Pelicia saw the way it trembled—he pulled out his gun.

She heard the snick of the safety being clicked off and shouted, "Declan, watch out!"

Addison pulled the trigger.

The bullet sliced a path across Declan's face, leaving a bloody gash on his cheek. As he reached for Addison the man fired another shot that went wild, the pinging ricochet echoing in the still air.

Pelicia squeaked, the only sound that could break free from her fear-tightened throat. When she saw the gun swinging her way, her eyes widened. She tried to scoot sideways, to go deeper into the barrow, but realized she would still be at risk, sitting up as she was. She needed to be as small a target as possible. Seeing no other choice, she jerked to the side, tipping herself over. She landed on her side with a grunt.

"Pelicia!" Declan sounded panicked.

"I'm all right," she hurried to assure him. "Just trying to get out of the way."

"Good girl," she heard him mutter. Then in a louder voice he snarled, "Come on, Addison. Let's see what you're really made of."

Pelicia craned her neck to watch the two men. Declan started toward Addison again, and the man danced out of reach. He holstered his gun and then held up the detonator.

"Ah-ah." Cradling his broken wrist in front of him, he moved away from the barrow. "I'll set this off."

"And blow yourself up, too? I don't think so." Declan took a step forward.

"I mean it." He held the detonator higher and thumbed open the small safety cover. "You take one more step, and we all die." He pointed one finger, still holding the detonator in that shaking hand. "And in case you have any ideas about taking the bomb off her, I've rigged it. You try to take the harness off without disconnecting the correct wire, the bomb blows. You cut the wrong wire trying to disable the bomb, it blows."

Pelicia could see Addison's face, could see he meant what he said. In order to take his revenge against Declan he was prepared to die.

Almost faster than she could follow, Declan dove toward him. He wrapped one hand around Addison's, and Pelicia closed her eyes, expecting to be blown to bits at any second. She heard a crunching sound and Addison's high-pitched scream, and opened her eyes to see him sitting on the ground, the detonator by his feet. The flashlight at the entrance to the barrow had gotten knocked over in the struggle. The beam shone directly on Addison. From the way his fingers were bent, she realized Declan had broken most—if not all—of them.

Declan snatched up the detonator and flipped the safety cover over the switch, then drew back his arm and threw the small black box as hard as he could. Chest heaving, he stared at Addison. "Give me one reason, boyo. Just one reason I shouldn't kill you." His voice was guttural, sounding forced and not quite human.

"You'd better kill me, you son of a bitch. If you don't, I'll be back. You can count on that." His gaze cut to Pelicia where she lay on her side in the narrow rock chamber. "I am sorry, Pel. I didn't start out with this plan in mind." He shrugged. "I was only staying with you to look out for O'Connell." Without warning, he kicked one leg out at Declan.

Declan jumped back, avoiding the strike.

With a grimace of pain, Addison reached for his gun, pulling it out and aiming it toward Declan. "I still have at least one good finger that I can use to pull the trigger, O'Connell."

Declan stood still, hands clenched at his sides.

Addison shook his head. He met her gaze, his own sorrowful. "Looks like I've made a right balls-up of this, eh?"

Was he sorry for what he'd done? Or merely sorry that it hadn't worked out as he'd planned?

"Nea . . . Fletcher," she corrected. She struggled to sit upright again and, as she did so, made sure she moved a little closer to the entrance to the barrow. The closer she was to Declan, the easier it would be for him to help her. "It's not too late. Tell us how to disable the bomb."

Addison's breath began to rasp and a lone tear tracked down one lean cheek. "I loved Brenna. I wasn't lying when I told you that."

Declan turned. Pelicia saw a line of sweat beading on his forehead, one droplet sliding down the side of his face. He swiped at it with blunt-edged fingers. "Tell me how to disarm this bomb, boyo, or—"

"Or what? You'll kill me?" Addison shook his head and waggled the gun. "I don't think so."

Declan might be in the mood to threaten, but Pelicia wasn't above pleading. "Fletcher, please!" She stared at him, blinking back tears. "If you ever felt anything for me, please . . ."

He stared at her. His lips twisted. "I . . . Oh, God, Pelicia. I'm sorry. I'm . . ." He rolled his shoulders in a forward hunch. "Sorry." He sighed and licked his lips. "It's the blue wire. Cut the blue wire to disable the bomb and the booby trap."

It was getting too dark. She twisted to the side and grabbed the flashlight beside her, pointing the beam away from her to the entrance of the barrow. She trained it on Declan. When he lifted his gaze to hers, she gasped and instinctively pressed against the cool granite behind her.

His eyes were completely tawny now, the wildness of the wolf shining clearly. Even as she watched, his facial features shifted, his nose and the surrounding area elongating, his teeth sliding into sharp fangs.

"Declan!" Pelicia glanced up at the sky and gasped. The moon, big and full, was rising over the ocean. She couldn't believe she hadn't realized the sun had set.

But all her attention had been focused on what was happening between Declan and Addison, even with darkness falling.

"I can't . . ." He groaned and doubled over, crumpling to the floor. "I can't . . . stop it."

She watched with wide eyes as his clothing ripped, torn by the body transforming beneath them. His shoes split along the soles. He gave another groan. She heard bones cracking and winced at the pain she imagined he must be feeling.

Then it was over, and a large dark brown wolf rose to its feet, mouth slightly open in a slow pant.

Fear surged within her. She'd never seen Ryder transform, had never been face-to-face with a werewolf in its wolf form before. Was Declan still in there somewhere? Or was this a monster before her, ready to tear into her?

Licking her lips, she looked at the wolf in front of her. He really was beautiful, standing at least as high as her waist, his paws huge, big, barrel chest and—at least she hoped it wasn't her own wishful thinking—intelligence gazing from its golden eyes.

The sound of a gunshot made her jump. Declan yelped and turned toward Addison. Blood trailed down the wolf's right flank.

Pelicia looked at the madman who'd pretended to be her friend.

"What the hell is that?" Addison's hand shook, making the gun waver up and down. When Declan's lips pulled back in a snarl, the man gave a shout of fear and fired again.

The shot went wild, striking the granite barrow only a few inches from Pelicia's head. She screamed. Closing her eyes, she fell to her side to once again try to stay out of the path of bullets.

She heard another shot and then Addison's loud yell abruptly cut off. She looked to see the wolf had his jaws clamped around the man's throat, lips drawn back over gleaming teeth covered in blood, nose wrinkled as he bore down in a death grip.

Addison struggled weakly. Pressing the gun against the wolf's rib cage, he pulled the trigger. Then again.

Declan's yelp slid into in a deep growl. He shook his head, making Addison's head flop back and forth. After only a few seconds, Addison dropped his hand and went still.

The wolf stayed where he was, still gripping the man's throat, his growl low and menacing, for several more moments. Then he raised his head and, lifting his blood-covered muzzle to the sky, let loose a howl that made the hair on the back of Pelicia's neck stand on end.

When the howl ended, that massive head swung her way.

Keeping one eye on the bomb strapped to her boobs and another on the very big wolf that now stood at the entrance to the barrow, Pelicia struggled to a sitting position. "Um, Declan?" She cleared her throat. "Um . . . nice doggy?"

His eyebrows twitched above those expressive eyes in what she would have sworn was a frown. He chuffed a sigh and then yipped a couple of times.

She chanced a look at Addison. Blood covered his throat, glistening in the bright light of the full moon.

Part of her felt sorry for him, tried to understand the despair and hatred that had driven him to this, but another part of her—a very large part—was glad he was dead. He'd killed at least four people. Even if he'd killed just Brenna, his death in exchange wouldn't have been enough. She'd prefer he spend the rest of his miserable life in the deepest, darkest hole available.

But if this was all she'd get, she'd take it.

Declan swished his tail back and forth and walked forward.

Pelicia took a breath and forced herself to stay still, though she wanted to skitter away from him. As if sensing her fear, he slowed and came to a stop a little over a meter away. His tongue swiped along his lips, washing away most of the remaining blood.

She just hoped he wasn't still hungry. Or whatever. . . .

When it appeared that he was going to stay put, she looked down at her chest. "He said to cut the blue wire," she murmured to herself. "But I don't trust him. Just because he thought his plan might not work after all . . ."

She looked up at Declan. That eerie intelligence still shone in his eyes, making her believe that Declan was still there, that he hadn't been completely overtaken by animal instinct. Whether he could understand her was something else. "Well, it doesn't mean he was telling the truth, right?"

He whined.

"So, if it's not the blue wire, which one would it be?"

The wolf whined again.

Her knight in shining armor was looking a bit tarnished. Actually, a bit furry. Well, to be completely accurate, *very* furry. She sighed. "I've said it before, O'Connell—your timing sucks."

He barked.

"God, Declan. What am I supposed to do?" She maneuvered her legs around until she could get on her knees. She picked up the flashlight and, watching him closely, started crawling toward the entrance of the burial chamber, slow going while holding the flashlight in her bound hands. "I need to see where we are."

He woofed and backed up several steps, giving her room to scuttle out of the barrow.

Once outside the confined space, she slowly got to her feet, carefully stretching the kinks out of her back. Then she looked around, trying to figure out where exactly they were. Toward the south she could make out the lights from Hugh Town and realized they were on one of the smaller uninhabited islands that dotted the ocean around the larger isles.

And time was running out.

She took a deep breath and held it, staring at Addison's body. She had to get his mobile so she could call the police and get someone out here who could take this damned bomb off her.

She didn't want to touch him. She'd never touched a corpse in her life and she wasn't crazy about doing so now.

But she needed that phone.

Or . . . she could cut the wire herself with that big knife.

She walked over to Addison and knelt by his side. Reaching out, she pulled the knife free from its scabbard and then glanced at Declan. "He said the blue wire, right?"

Declan whined and shook his head.

"I'll take that as a no." As much as she wanted to sit here and scream until she was hoarse, she needed to stay calm. Once the bomb was safely away from her, *then* she'd scream herself silly. "Okay. Let me think a minute."

He barked. Walking over to her, he bent and nosed the mobile phone attached to Addison's belt. When she made no move to take it, he barked again, louder this time.

"All right, I get it. You want me to make a phone call. Just . . . be quiet and let me think, Cujo."

He backed off a few steps and sat down, watching her with those alert amber eyes.

Pelicia stared at the phone. If she called for help—which she realized was the prudent thing to do—police would swarm the place within half an hour. She glanced down at the timer on the bomb. That would give the police less than an hour to diffuse the bomb.

And if they didn't have a bomb expert in the group from the mainland, she'd be screwed.

But if they came now, they'd either find a large wolf with her—which would be quite difficult to explain—or they'd find her alone and wonder where Declan was. Plus there was the fact that when he shifted back to human form he'd be completely naked—and how the bloody hell would they explain *that?*

Of course, she could claim that the wolf . . . no, the big dog had attacked Addison in order to keep him from shooting her. Which wasn't a lie. But, still, she wanted to protect Declan.

Which left . . . the bomb.

"All right." She stared at Declan. He tipped his head to one side, studying her. It was all so surreal—she fought back the feeling that she was ready to zone out, though being a zombie would fit right in with having a werewolf at her side. She wiped at the sweat on her upper lip. "Let's play canine charades, shall we?"

He chuffed and moved forward, alertness portrayed in the tilt of his ears and the lolling tongue.

"Oh, God." She set the flashlight on the ground, the beam shining upward, and brought her hands up to her face. She rubbed the bridge of her nose. "Someone please wake me up. Anytime now."

Declan yipped, a high-pitched we-don't-have-time-for-this bark.

She looked at him. "Okay, okay. Pushy werewolf," she muttered. "Whether you're on two feet or four, you're still a bossy pain in the ass."

The sigh that came from deep in his chest was long suffering. The look that he sent her . . . not so much.

"So, let's do it this way." She looked into his eyes and reminded herself that this was Declan. The man she loved. The man who loved her. The man who would lay down his life for her. He might not be as protective of her heart, but she'd never doubted his determination to keep her safe from physical harm. "One bark for yes, two for no. Okay?"

He barked once.

Yes.

Pelicia blew out a breath and looked down at the bomb and its three wires. "All right, then." She brought her gaze back to Declan. "Should I cut the blue wire?"

Two barks.

Okay. That was a no.

She glanced down at the wires. "How about the red one?"

Two barks.

"So, that leaves the striped one." Pelicia hooked a finger under the yellow-and-white wire and was about to work the tip of the knife under it when Declan barked again.

Twice.

Chapter 20

"What do you mean, *no?* Declan, there are only three wires here. If I'm not supposed to cut the blue wire or the red wire, that only leaves the striped one."

Declan heard the frustration and fear in Pelicia's voice and wished he could say something to alleviate both. But he was stuck as a damned wolf until morning. He glanced back at Addison.

The man's eyes had glazed over, sightless now. The stench of death was strong in Declan's nostrils, though he knew he could discern it only because of his enhanced sense of smell. The primitive beast inside him reacted.

Enemy. Dead.

Good.

Addison had not only had a background in demolitions, like Declan, but he had also been devious—even before the accident had twisted his psyche. Declan didn't trust that it might be as simple as cutting one wire.

He looked at Pelicia. Her face was pale, shiny with sweat. Her pupils were so dilated he could hardly see the color of her irises. But his intrepid woman was holding onto her courage, even managing to make jokes.

That they were at his expense didn't matter. As long as she stayed calm, she could poke fun at him all she wanted.

He huffed a sigh. This wasn't right. She needed to call the police and get that damned thing off her instead of him trying to bark his way through instructions.

The killer might be dead, but the danger was by no means over.

He stood and padded over to the body again, nudged the phone at Addison's waist with his nose. She had to call the police. That was the only option left open.

He'd figure out how to explain . . . Hell. To "out" himself as a werewolf was to potentially reveal Ryder as well. He sat down and leaned on one haunch. Pelicia was staring at him, her brows furrowed, lips pursed. Wrists tied in front of her, bomb strapped to her chest.

Rage bloomed anew. Damn Addison. The bastard was lucky he could only die once.

Sorry, Ryder. If he could, Declan would keep Ryder's secret. But he couldn't let Pelicia sit there with that fucking bomb on her chest.

He bent and tried to pull the phone from its holder with his teeth. Giving a low growl of frustration when he couldn't get a good enough grip, he sat back and looked at Pelicia.

She sighed and yanked the mobile from the holder. "Ew, Declan. God. Dog slime all over the phone . . ." She swiped the phone against her jeans as well as she could with her wrists bound the way they were, making a face the whole time.

He chuffed at her. Now was not the time for her to be whining.

If anyone was going to do any whining around here, it was going to be him. And he did so now, trying to push her to make the call.

"Declan, how am I going to explain about all this? You're a wolf." She gave a pointed glance to one of his big paws. "I don't think I can convince them that you just happened to show up when I needed some help."

Declan frowned at her sarcasm, but acknowledged her point. At the same time, though, he didn't see another choice. It would be better for a demolitions expert who was in human form to deactivate that bomb.

He whined and nudged the hand holding the phone.

Pelicia heaved a sigh and closed her eyes. "Okay. You're right." She opened her eyes and stared down at him. "You need to get out of here. I'll have an easier time making up a story about why you're not here than explaining the big, bad wolf sitting at my feet. I think."

He was not going to leave her alone with that thing strapped to her chest. And so the big, bad wolf sat down, his tail curled over the tops of her toes.

"Very funny," she muttered.

He woofed at her. *Phone.*

She sighed again. "Yes. Right." With her thumb she punched in the emergency number and then brought the phone to her ear. Her explanation was terse. "Yes, I'll stay on the line," she said to the person on the other end of the line. "But please hurry. There's not much time left."

Over the next several minutes, minutes that felt like hours, Declan stayed by her side as the support officer talked to her, trying to keep her calm. Finally low male voices drifted to Declan's ears, coming from the shore. He bounded to his feet and turned toward the sound, ears twitching forward to listen more carefully.

He recognized one man's voice—Tremwith, the local police constable. Declan's nostrils flared as he took in the variety of scents.

The acrid smell of fear.

The crisp odor of determination.

The tang of gunpowder.

Light flickered as men moved up from the beach with flashlights lighting their way.

He gave a sharp bark, then glanced at Pelicia and sat back down. Guess she'd *have* to explain to the police unit about to barge into view how it was she'd come to have a wolf sitting at her feet.

"They're here," she said into the phone. She disconnected the call. "It's okay," she said in a loud voice. "He's dead."

The team of men in full riot gear moved slowly into their line of sight. Tremwith brought up the rear, a bullet-proof vest fastened over his uniform shirt. He glanced at Addison and then looked at Pelicia, eyes widening. "You all right?"

"Well, except for this little bomb here, yes."

"Oh, God. Pelicia, how the hell did you get yourself into this mess?"

"It wasn't easy," she muttered.

When Tremwith's gaze slid to Declan, his eyebrows shot up. "That's a—"

"Can we please," she interrupted, "talk about my . . . dog later?"

"Ah. Yes. Right." The police constable brought his gaze back to Pelicia. He moved closer, keeping a wary eye on Declan. Looking over his shoulder, he told the other men, "There's about fifty minutes left on the timer." He looked at Pelicia again. "When neither of the men we'd posted called in at their appointed check-in times, we knew something was wrong." He shook his head. "But I never suspected *this*."

She pressed her lips together and stared at Addison. "I'm sorry. I think he killed them."

A muscle flexed in the constable's jaw as he turned to look at the dead man. "Pity he can only die once."

A sentiment Declan completely shared.

Tremwith moved over to Addison and crouched beside the body. He looked again at Pelicia. "God Almighty. His throat looks to be completely ripped out." He gave a pointed glance at Declan. "He do that?"

She nodded. "Addison was threatening to shoot me. He'd already come close to doing so a couple of times. He . . . the dog . . . attacked him, trying to protect me."

"Uh-huh." The constable pointed one finger at Declan. "Looks more like a wolf to me, not a dog."

Declan turned his head to look at Pelicia, curious to hear her explanation.

She pressed her lips together a moment and glanced at Declan. "Actually, he's a . . . hybrid, not a full-bred wolf."

"He's damned big."

"Yes." She cleared her throat and tipped her chin toward the bomb. "Do you think someone could get this off me?"

Declan swung his head back toward Tremwith.

"Oh, aye." He gestured toward one of the men. "Bowers, raise Support on the radio. Let them know the situation. We're going to need a bomb unit."

"Yes, sir." The man walked a few feet away, head tilted to one side as he spoke into the comm unit on his shoulder.

Keeping an eye on the wolf, Tremwith stood and slowly moved closer. He looked at the timer and blew out a breath. His smile looked forced. "We've still forty-five minutes to go. Plenty of time."

"Still, I'd really like someone to get this off me. Now."

"We'll need to wait on that just a bit longer." Tremwith went down on one knee beside her. He pulled out a small penknife and sawed through the flexible cable around her wrists. As soon as the binding fell free, she started rubbing her wrists, wincing at the soreness left from the cord cutting into her skin.

"How long has that thing been strapped to you?" Tremwith flipped the knife blade back into the handle and put the penknife back into his pocket.

She blew out a sigh that fluttered her bangs. "I'm not sure. He"—she gestured toward Addison with her chin—"knocked us, um, I mean, me out with some kind of gas. When I came to, well, here I am." She looked down at the bomb then back up at Tremwith. "It's been at least two hours, maybe closer to three." She grimaced. "I'd really like to get it off me. Sooner rather than later."

"As soon as we get an expert on the radio. Just hold on a bit longer." The constable looked at Declan. "And where did *he* come from? I didn't think you had a dog."

She cleared her throat. "Him? Ah, he's, um . . ." She trailed off. Declan could see her thinking by the way she bit her lower lip. Her eyes widened suddenly and a small smile tipped one corner of her mouth. "He's my dad's. I'm dog-sitting for a couple of days."

Declan chuffed in a canine laugh—the only kind he could do at the moment. William Cobb would not appreciate it when he found out he was the proud owner of a werewolf—even if it was only a story to explain the wolf's presence here.

"And O'Connell?" Tremwith made an exaggerated show of looking around the area. "Where's he?"

Pelicia bit her lip again. "I think . . . maybe Addison did something to him. Otherwise you know he'd be here."

"Hmm."

At that moment, Bowers walked back over to them, a mobile phone in one hand. "Sir, I've Support on the line. They can get a bomb squad here in roughly five hours."

"Five hours?" Pelicia's voice rose in dismay. "I don't have five hours. I have . . ." She looked down at the timer. "Forty-two minutes! Please. Get this *off* me."

Tremwith stood. "They can't get here any sooner than that?"

Bowers shook his head. His gaze, when he looked at Pelicia, was full of sympathy. "They do have an explosives expert standing by." He held out a multifunction tool, a small pair of scissors already unfolded from the handle.

"What? *I'm* doing this?" Tremwith slowly reached out and took the tool and the phone from the other officer.

Bowers shrugged. "You *are* the officer in charge, sir." He then pulled another phone out of his pocket. "I've been asked to snap a few pictures of the device and transmit them to Support." He looked at the bomb. "I've some experience with homemade devices like this. As I told Support, it looks to be fairly straightforward." His gaze cut back to Tremwith and a sheepish grin tugged at his mouth. "For what that's worth."

"Fairly straightforward my barmy Aunt Nell's ass." He shook his head and muttered, "Bloody 'ell." Tremwith gestured toward Pelicia with a sigh. "Take the photos." He looked at her and then at Declan as Bowers moved closer.

Bowers stopped a meter away, his gaze fixed on Declan.

Declan could smell the man's anxiety, an anxiety that

bordered on fear. Big strong policeman had a phobia of dogs, it seemed. Declan couldn't contain his grin, even knowing it showed off his pearly whites and made the man even more nervous.

"Ah, sir . . ."

"Pel, could you call off the mutt?" Tremwith raised his eyebrows in question.

Mutt? Declan lost his canine smile. *Who the hell was he calling a mutt?*

"It's all right. He's very protective of me, but he's not dangerous."

Well, he wasn't as long as no one threatened her.

She snapped her fingers. "Come here, boy," she called, her voice cajoling and, in spite of the danger, holding a note of suppressed humor.

Declan wasn't so amused. Just wait until he was back on two feet again, then they'd see how easily she could order him around.

Who was he kidding? If she was amenable, he'd let her order him around for the rest of his life.

He gave a huff, stood and padded in front of her to sit at her left side, keeping his gaze fixed on Tremwith and Bowers.

The men had better not muck this up, or all four of them were dead.

Bowers snapped a few photos, then stepped back and punched in a number on the phone's keypad. "There," he murmured. "The pictures have been sent." He grimaced. "Good luck, sir."

Tremwith started to crouch in front of Pelicia but paused and looked over his shoulder at Bowers and the other officers standing clustered a few meters away. "The rest of you clear out. All the way out—back to the beach. Just in case I end up making a wrong move . . ."

He waited until the men's movements could no longer be heard. Turning back toward Pelicia, he asked, "Are you ready?"

"Just do it, Charlie."

He nodded and brought the mobile to his ear. "All right. Let's get this done, then." He listened for a few seconds. Flicking his gaze over the homemade bomb, he began describing it.

When he got to the part about the wires, Pelicia interrupted him. "He said to cut the blue one, but I think he was lying."

Tremwith repeated what she said into the phone. He listened to the person on the other end again then held the phone toward Pelicia. "Take this for a minute. He wants me to look at the harness he's strapped you up with."

He pressed the phone against Pelicia's palm. She curled her fingers around it and watched as he carefully moved around to her right, looking at the harness, carefully lifting one edge to peer underneath the black strap. "Hold on. What's this?"

Declan stood to see better and watched while the constable gently pulled a piece of black tape loose. Declan gave a growl of warning.

"Shit." Tremwith let go of the strap and sat back on his heels, staring over at Declan. "Easy, boy. I'm just following directions." The constable took the mobile from Pelicia. "I see the blue wire and the striped wire," he said into the phone. He listened to the man on the other end of the line and then gave a nod. "Right. Red then striped. Be right back with you. I hope." He pressed the phone into Pelicia's hand again.

"That doesn't sound very confidence inspiring, Charlie." She ran her tongue over her lips.

"Sorry. I've just . . . Well, I've never done anything quite like this before. I'm a bit nervous." He swallowed. Transferring the tool to his left hand, he rubbed his right palm down the leg of his trousers. Then he took up the tool in his right hand again and leaned in toward the bomb.

A snip of the red wire and then the yellow-and-white one, and it was all over.

They both heaved a sigh of relief, though Pelicia was sure hers was louder than Tremwith's. She leaned forward, letting him unfasten the harness and pull it off her. He radioed for assistance. As soon as he moved away from her to hand the bomb off to another officer who'd responded to the call, she stood and wrapped her arms around herself. God, now that the danger was over, she was ready to fall to pieces, she could feel it.

The only thing that was holding her together was the thought that she couldn't fail Declan now. She had to make sure nothing happened to him while he was in his wolf form. Were they to want to cart him away for some reason . . .

God, he could wake up at sunrise naked and stuffed into a dog crate.

He'd never forgive her for the indignity.

But the picture in her mind brought a near-hysterical giggle from her throat, which she stifled by pressing her lips together.

"Hey, it's all right now." Tremwith put one arm around her, squeezing her against him in a hug. "You're all right."

"I know." And then the tears came—tears of relief, tears of anguish, tears of emotional pain long suppressed. She collapsed to the ground, wrapping her arms around Declan and burying her face in the thick fur along the back of his neck.

Dimly over her sobs she heard Declan whining. He stood there, leaning against her, giving comfort in the only way open to him, and she took it even while she wished he could put his arms around her and murmur soothing nonsense in her ear.

After several minutes she pulled away and swiped her hands over her cheeks. She sniffed and put one finger beneath her nose.

"Here." The constable handed her a white handkerchief.

She took it with a muttered "Thanks" and mopped her face. She blew her nose and stared down at the crumpled linen.

"That's all right," he murmured. "You keep it." He paused a moment, his gaze searching hers. "Do you feel up to coming to the station to make a full report?"

She shook her head. "Not now, Charlie." She closed her eyes, suddenly so weary she felt light-headed. She swayed slightly. When Tremwith's hand wrapped around her upper arm, she opened her eyes. "I just want to go home. To my dad."

He nodded. "I understand. As long as you promise to come and see us tomorrow?"

She nodded.

She'd just survived the closest brush to death she ever wanted—at least, not until she was a really, really old woman—and all she wanted to do was run home to daddy.

Tremwith put a hand at the small of her back to help her over a rough patch of ground. As they reached the beach, she saw two boats, motors idling.

Motioning another officer over, the constable said, "Take Ms. Cobb over to Phelan's Keep, would you?"

The officer nodded. Holding out his hand, he helped Pelicia into the boat. Declan sloshed through the water and jumped in on his own, giving himself a shake to dislodge the water in his fur.

"Oh, Pel," Tremwith said, "we'll start a search for O'Connell. I'll phone you when we've found him."

She stopped so abruptly the officer bumped into her as he was climbing in behind her. Turning, she stared at Tremwith. She knew she should act as if she were mightily concerned for Declan, but it was hard, knowing he was fine and standing by her left knee. She threaded her fingers through the thick ruff of fur along the back of his neck and stared at the constable.

He apparently misread her silence. "I'm sure he's all right," he hastened to assure her, his voice soothing. "You go on and spend time with your dad."

Pelicia nodded without speaking and turned toward the bunk seat at the back of the small craft. She wanted to be wrapped up in her father's arms, his voice telling her everything would be all right, comforting her like when she was a little girl. As well, she needed to update them all on the situation—whoever had attacked Sully was still out there.

Her father and Taite were waiting for her on the pier. As the officer pulled up next to the wooden dock, Cobb said, "PC Tremwith phoned to let us know you were coming." He reached out and helped her onto the dock and wrapped her up in a blanket, then held her in a tight hug. "Darling, are you all right?"

She fought back ready tears. Even though she was a couple of inches taller than her father, she felt small and vulnerable, and this hug from him was exactly what she needed at the moment. "I'm okay. I'll be okay," she amended.

"What the hell . . ." Taite's voice trailed off.

Pelicia remembered Declan and pulled out of her father's embrace. "Oh, I had to bring your dog back with me," she said for benefit of the policeman, trying to convey with her eyes that Taite and her dad should play along. "I couldn't leave him at the Nola all alone."

Her father, bless his heart, picked up on the subterfuge right away. He pulled her into a one-armed hug and turned her toward the beach. "Of course you couldn't, darling. It's good to see . . . him."

"Thank you for bringing Pelicia home," she heard Taite say.

"Sure thing. And Ms. Cobb?"

Pelicia stopped and looked at the young officer.

"We'll let you know as soon as we find Mr. O'Connell. In the meantime, try not to worry."

She pressed her lips together and nodded. It was harder than she'd thought it would be, lying to the police. But it wasn't as if she could tell them not to bother. Hopefully Declan could come up with a plausible explanation as to what had happened.

What had *allegedly* happened.

She should probably get used to this. It most likely wouldn't be the last time she had to lie to someone to protect Declan's secret.

With everything they'd been through together, she was *not* about to let him walk away from her again.

Chapter 21

In the dim light of dawn, Declan made his way back to Ryder's house, wincing when his bare foot came down on a particularly sharp stone. Why the tough pads of the wolf didn't translate to tougher soles in his human form didn't make sense.

Just another part of the magic, he supposed.

He glanced down and grimaced at the hard-on he sported.

Yet another part of the freaking magic. It was always like this after he shifted—ready for sex.

Ready to mate.

God. He had to get back to Pelicia. Once they'd reached the island and the policeman had left, Ryder—also in his wolf form—had been waiting for Declan. The two of them had run around the island in the bright moonlight, exhilarated at the freedom the wolf provided. Just before dawn Ryder had made his way back to the house.

Declan had wanted to wait until he was able to transform to human before he saw Pelicia again. Now, as yet another sharp rock gouged the bottom of his foot, he thought perhaps Ryder had had the right idea.

When he reached the edge of the sculptured lawn, the back door opened and Pelicia stepped outside, leaving the door open behind her. Her fresh scent was the finest perfume to him. She was dressed in a red sundress and held a large cream-colored blanket.

He took it from her and wrapped it around his shoulders, holding it together in front of him to cover his nudity.

Not that he cared about walking around naked, but he supposed Pelicia would. Not to mention Taite.

"Thanks, darlin'," he murmured and bent his head to kiss her. She threw her arms around his neck and held on tightly, her kiss telling him much more than words could.

She was happy he was back.

She remained unsettled from the events of the night and needed his comfort.

She still loved him.

His wolf perked up, primal satisfaction rushing through him at the knowledge he hadn't lost her. He let loose a growl and let go of the blanket to cup her head between his palms.

The blanket fell to the ground.

He thrust his tongue between her lips, claiming her, being claimed, groaning when she lightly sucked on it. Her fingers twined in the hair at the nape of his neck before sliding to his shoulders in a tight grip.

Declan lifted his mouth from hers and buried his face in the curve of her neck, holding her tight against him. God, she felt so good in his arms, so right. He would never let her go.

"Don't let me go," she whispered, her arms holding him just as tightly. "Don't ever let me go."

"Never again," he promised.

She sighed and leaned into him. "Is it over?" Her fingers tightened on the muscles of his back.

"Aye." He straightened and loosened his grip, clasping his hands at the small of her back. "I just have to come up with a plausible excuse for not bein' with you while you were bein' terrorized by a madman."

He rocked his hips forward, pressing his erection into the cleft of her thighs. He needed to fuck her, claim her. Needed to know without a doubt that she was his.

That he was hers.

Familiar scents wafted to his sensitive nose. He looked over her shoulder to see Ryder and Taite standing in the doorway. Ryder stared at Declan with an amused tilt on his lips while Taite looked somewhere over his left shoulder.

"I have an idea about that excuse," Ryder said, humor lacing his deep voice. His gaze was knowing, but satiated, which told Declan two things.

One, his friend knew about his current state of arousal and, two, Ryder's arousal had already been dealt with by his wife.

Next time, he'd definitely follow Ryder's lead and get back to Pelicia before he shifted back to human. That way, when he did, there'd be no wasted time.

Ryder's grin widened. "But you might want to pick up that blanket first."

"Yes, please," Taite added, her voice pert but with an underlying hint of embarrassment. "Seeing Ryder naked after he shifts is one thing. Seeing you . . ." She met his gaze and shrugged. "I love ya, buddy, but not *that* much."

Declan laughed and bent, retrieving the blanket. Once he'd wrapped it around himself, he cocked an eyebrow at Ryder. "So what's this grand idea of yours?"

"Why don't you come back inside?" Taite stepped away from the door.

Ryder followed, taking her hand in his and tucking it in the crook of his elbow. Once Pelicia and Declan were both inside, the door closed behind them, Ryder said, "We can say that Addison lured you away from the Nola, managed to get the drop on you and left you stranded on one of the uninhabited smaller islands, then went back to the bed and breakfast to take care of Pelicia."

"And just how is it I ended up here instead of back at the Nola?"

Ryder gave an unconcerned shrug. "One of us can run you over to an island and leave you there but we'll make sure it's on the tourist route so you'll be able to catch someone's attention." He quirked an eyebrow. "You know the simpler you keep it the more apt they are to believe you, however unbelievable the story seems to be."

Declan sighed. It seemed he wasn't going to be able to get Pelicia in bed just yet. His erection wilted.

Ryder cleared his throat. "You know, Declan, you might want to go upstairs and get, ah, cleaned up." He pressed his lips together, clearly fighting a grin. "I know how . . . dirty I felt when I came home this morning. In an effort to conserve water I had Taite take a shower with me."

Taite smacked her husband on the arm. "You can just be quiet."

Ryder laughed and put an arm around her waist, pulling her against him in an affectionate hug.

Seeing their closeness made Declan's arousal surge once again. He bumped his hip against Pelicia's and, when she looked at him, jerked his chin toward the kitchen door.

She pressed her lips together but couldn't contain the

grin. "All right, then. We're going to go upstairs now so Declan can, ah, get cleaned up."

Taite shook her head. "See what you started," she muttered to her husband.

"What *I* started?" Ryder tried—unsuccessfully—to appear suitably grim. "I'll phone the police in ten . . ."

Declan shot him a look.

"Thirty minutes," he amended with a grin. "That should give you time to get cleaned up, especially if Pelicia helps."

"That's what I'm thinking." Pelicia grinned at Declan's start of surprise.

He'd expected her to be embarrassed that Ryder and Taite knew that they were about to go at each other like bunny rabbits hyped up on steroids. But, seeing the sparkle in her eyes—a sparkle that was a combination of humor and passion—he realized that she wasn't embarrassed.

Didn't need to tell him twice.

Without another word he walked out of the kitchen.

He heard Pelicia's low murmur of "See you later," then she called out, "Hey! Wait for me."

Declan paused in the hallway until she reached him. They walked into the foyer and turned to go up the stairs, where they were met by her father. He looked from Pelicia to Declan and back again. His face as stern as Declan had ever seen it, the little man said, "If you hurt her again, werewolf or no, you'll answer to me."

"Dad!" Pelicia's cheeks went red.

Declan stared down at William Cobb, a little surprised that the wolf in him didn't rise up in a snarl. Perhaps because Cobb wasn't trying to usurp Declan's alpha position with his mate; rather, he was trying to protect the woman Declan loved.

"I have no intention of hurtin' her," he responded. "And every intention of lovin' her for the rest of my life."

Cobb searched his gaze for a long moment then gave a small nod. He moved to one side to allow them to go up the stairs.

Pelicia paused beside her father and pressed a kiss on his cheek. "I love you," she whispered.

"I love you, too, darling." He patted her shoulder. "Go on with you." His smile held a hint of sadness that made Declan wonder a moment, but as soon as Pelicia turned back to him with such love in her eyes—love for *him*—his only remaining thought was to get her upstairs and in bed without any further delay.

He met Cobb's gaze and tipped his chin down in acknowledgment. "Come on, darlin'," he said to Pelicia. "We're on the clock here."

The climb up the stairs to the second floor heightened his anticipation. By the time they reached his room, his arousal was in full force again.

He let Pelicia enter the room before him. He closed the door and let the blanket drop to the floor. Walking up to her, he brought her hands to his mouth and pressed a kiss in each palm. Then he framed her face with his hands and slanted his mouth over hers.

Pelicia leaned into him and moaned, her tongue twining with his. With a groan that rumbled from deep in his gut, Declan went to one knee and slipped first one of her shoes and then the other from her slender feet. Standing, he reached behind her and unzipped her dress. She slipped the straps off her shoulders and the dress pooled at her feet, leaving her clad in a pair of lacy black panties . . . and nothing else.

God. She was beautiful. Her breasts were full, slightly

uptilted, with nipples already hard. He swept her up into his arms and took the few steps to the big bed. Bracing himself with one knee on the mattress, he gently laid her down.

Before he knew what she was about, she put her hands on his chest and pushed him over. "It seems to me," she murmured, her eyes a deep, dark blue sparkling with arousal, "that you're the one who needs taking care of."

She placed her hands on his knees and nudged his legs apart, moving between his thighs. Her soft palms slid with excruciating slowness up his thighs, making his muscles bunch and spasm as those soft fingers came closer and closer toward treasured territory.

Blood surged into his cock. He twitched with the need to grab her, take her.

Claim his mate.

Clenching his fists at his sides, Declan forced himself to remain still. If she wanted to take care of him, who was he to say no?

An imp of pure sexual mischief sparked in her eyes as she bypassed his erection and slid her hands over his abdomen. She nuzzled his sac with her nose while she lightly raked her nails across his skin. When her tongue darted out in a quick lick, he grunted and surged against her.

"Ah, darlin'?"

Her second lick was a long, slow stroke that brought his hips arching off the bed.

"This doesn't feel like you're takin' care of me, Pel." His words came out in a low growl of need. "It feels more like—"

She drew one of his balls into the wet heat of her mouth.

"Torture," he groaned.

She switched to his other testicle, laving it with her tongue while her hands stroked up his chest, fingers rubbing against his hard nipples.

"God, Pel, you're killin' me here."

"I've only just begun."

Her breath puffed against his moist skin, making his balls draw up tight against his body. His cock throbbed, the skin stretched taut across the tip.

"Just remember," he managed to say, using what little brain cells he still had working. "Payback can be a real bitch."

"Oh, I certainly hope so." She peeped up at him from under her lashes. Sliding her hands down, she ran her fingers lightly through the trail of dark hair that swirled down his abdomen and didn't stop until she reached the thicket that surrounded his cock. He couldn't stop the groan that rumbled from his chest.

She was beautiful. He could smell her arousal and it heightened his own. He opened his mouth and closed it again without speaking. He loved her—he always had. But he wasn't sure about her feelings anymore.

He was sure he didn't want to get shot down again.

He was also sure that he wasn't ready to ruin this moment by saying something that would make her withdraw from him. Sex could be a conduit to more—they'd seemed to reach some sort of understanding, but had that been because of the danger they'd faced?

Could it last now that they were safe?

He knew he wanted her forever.

But what did she want?

She took his shaft in a firm grip and closed her mouth over the head of his cock, her tongue swiping up the drop of fluid seeping from the tip. He flexed his fingers, curling them around the bedding at his sides.

Later. They'd talk later.

Big hands came up and grasped her head. Long fingers threaded through her hair. "Yes. Christ, Pel. Suck me."

Gripping his erection in one hand, Pelicia palmed his balls, rolling them in her fingers. She stroked his cock with her fingers as she took as much of him as she could into her mouth.

"Take it, darlin'." He pushed her hair out of her face. She looked at him, seeing his eyes glowing wolf-amber but she wasn't afraid. It was arousal that turned his eyes gold and tightened his jaw. His head fell back, giving her a perfect view of the strong column of his neck.

God, this was one beautiful man. And he was hers.

Or, at least, he had been. He could be again if she was brave enough. He had said he loved her, and it was clear to her that she still loved him. But was it enough?

He groaned and pumped his hips, pushing more of his cock into her mouth. She was doing this to him, making him crazy with lust. She flushed with heated arousal, her pussy swelling and pulsing with need.

Later. She'd think about where they went from here later. Right now, she needed to focus—the feel of him, so hard, so thick. Life pulsing under her tongue.

She licked her way around the head to the sensitive underside. Nibbling gently, she moved along the heavy shaft until she reached the base, where she promptly drew one of his tight balls once again into her mouth.

He gave a shout and arched against her. Swirling her tongue around the hair-roughened skin, she gently suckled him while lightly squeezing his shaft with one hand. The other rested against one of his heavy thighs. She could feel his muscles trembling, and it was an incredible rush that she could bring this strong man to the brink of sexual insanity.

It made her so hot she was ready to come just from touching him.

She moved to the other testicle and gave it the same tender treatment, moaning around him as his hips pumped beneath her. He tasted of salt and vinegar. She whimpered with her own need.

Pelicia rose up on one elbow and stared down at him. His eyes were squeezed shut, his breath coming fast and hard from flared nostrils as he fought to hold onto his control.

This would never do. She didn't want him in control—she wanted him wild with passion.

"Release the hounds," she murmured and brought her lips back to his cock.

When that hot mouth closed over him again, Declan knew he wouldn't last much longer. And he wanted to be inside her when he came. With a deep growl, he lifted her away from him, depositing her on her back on the mattress next to him as he came down on top of her. He sipped from her lips then trailed his mouth over her chin and down her slender throat.

When he reached the sensitive spot where neck met shoulder, she sighed and tilted her head, giving him better access. He lingered, his cock jerking as she shifted and gasped under him.

Impatient need riding him, Declan moved down to her breasts and took one nipple into his mouth. He suckled her, gentle at first, then harder, his cheeks hollowing as he feasted on her.

Her hands came up and grasped his head, fingers curling through his hair. He switched to the other breast and brought his hand to the nipple he'd abandoned. Pinching and rolling and tugging, he kept it hard while his mouth and tongue worked the other one.

"Declan, please," Pelicia moaned, her hips moving restlessly under him.

"Oh, I plan to please you, darlin'. That's what this is all about," he muttered against flesh wet from his mouth. He kissed a path down her belly, feeling her shiver. Moving between her legs, he swept her panties off her and stared at her pussy. Her folds were swollen and slick, her cream coating the plump lips.

His fingers trembled slightly as he parted her sex. With a groan, he leaned in and swiped the flat of his tongue up her slit from her opening to her clit. He tongued through her folds, flicking now and again against the swollen pleasure nub, before finally settling in for a leisurely suckle.

He speared one finger into her sheath, and she shivered and moaned. When he added another finger and began thrusting into her, she drew her knees up farther and let her legs fall open, widening herself to his touch. Her hips began to meet his thrusting hand.

Declan redoubled his efforts and soon she cried out and arched. Her sheath clenched around his fingers, her hands tightened in his hair. Cream gushed into his palm. He moaned around her clit.

As her climax eased, he gentled his touch, dipping his tongue into the well of her body, tasting the sweet-salty flavor of her arousal.

"Declan, I want you. Now."

He surged over her, catching her mouth with his, letting her taste herself on his lips. With a last, lingering kiss, he rolled to his back and motioned to his erection. "Ride me," he husked.

He didn't need to tell her twice. Pelicia threw her leg over him. He put his hands on her hips to help her as she eased down onto his shaft. When the curve of her ass rested against him, she paused, letting her body adjust to the thick invasion. He felt so big, filled her so completely.

Bracing her palms against his wide chest, she began to rise and fall, faster and faster, the drag of his cock sending shock waves from her core to her clit.

His face was hard and dark with need, amber eyes glittering as he brought his hands up to cup her breasts, rubbing his thumbs over the hard tips. Her breath hitched as her arousal spiraled tighter and tighter. One last slide down and it broke over her, arching her back, making her cry out in a raw voice.

Declan stiffened and shouted with his own release, his fingers digging into her hips. After a few moments, Pelicia collapsed against him.

His big hands roamed her back. She snuggled her face into the crook of his neck.

His sigh was heavy against the top of her head. "I hope I'm not gonna ruin things by sayin' this, but . . . I love you, Pelicia." His fingers curled around the back of her neck, the tips lightly massaging the base of her head. "And I am so sorry for how I treated you, what I put you through."

She rose up until she could look into his face. His eyes were dark and serious, and in their depths lurked a fear she'd never expected to see.

If she wanted to get even with him, now was the time.

But that wasn't what she wanted—it had never been about that. She'd come to accept that a while ago.

It was about love.

About loving him.

About him loving her.

She traced the line of his lower lip with her index finger. "I love you, too. You have to know that," she whispered. "There was more to this"—she gestured vaguely at their bodies—"than just sex."

His eyes went liquid, shocking her from saying more.

"You must love me," he murmured, "to put up with my shit." He reached up and cupped her face. "I'm sorry it took me so long to come 'round."

She swallowed back the jangle of emotions clogging her throat. She'd never seen Declan this vulnerable. That his feelings ran so deep had never been a question—he'd just never before let her see it. It was something she'd always wished for and now that she had it, and could see how uncomfortable it made him, she didn't want to prolong his emotional distress.

Time to lighten things up a bit.

"Yeah, well," she drawled, "I guess in addition to putting up with your shit I have to also put up with your slowness."

As his lips tilted in a grin, her heart lifted. She laughed.

"Aye, I guess you do. But, seriously, thank you." He rubbed his palm up and down her slender arm.

"For what?"

"For trustin' me." When she rose up until she could look at his face, he met her gaze. Emotion thickened his voice. "For givin' me another chance."

She stared at him a moment. Drawing a deep breath, she held it, pressing her lips together. Then she sighed. "Don't muck it up this time."

It obviously wasn't what he'd expected her to say and it surprised a short bark of laughter from him. "I'll do my best, darlin'.'" He pressed his lips softly to her. "I'll do my very best."

"I know you will."

They shared another gentle kiss.

"So . . . what now?" Pelicia stared down into his eyes, feeling uncertainty flare again. It was obvious to her that she wouldn't be taking her friend up on her offer of a place to stay in London, but did that mean that she and Declan stayed here in the Isles of Scilly and ran a bed and breakfast together? Somehow she just didn't see him in the role of innkeeper.

He reached up and stroked his fingers down her cheek. "Is your passport up to date?" He slid his hand to her neck, resting it where neck met shoulder as if he needed that physical contact.

Her breath caught in her throat. "Yes," she responded slowly, searching his gaze with hers. Exactly what was he asking?

He licked his lips, looking nervous. Another first—she'd never seen him without that sometimes infuriating self-confidence before. "I want you to come back to America with me."

She swallowed, plagued by her own nervousness now. Go to the States? Just pick up and . . . what? Leave everyone and everything familiar? Leave all the memories of her grandfather's betrayal that were attached to them?

"Go with you to America as . . . what? Your live-in girl-friend?" If he wasn't ready to commit, she wasn't ready to draw up stakes and move halfway across the world.

Gentleness softened his eyes. "As my wife." He slid his hand around to cup her nape. "I love you, Pelicia. I want to spend the rest of my life with you." That hint of uncertainty darkened his eyes again. "Can you put up with me turnin' furry once a month?"

Her heart thumped so hard she thought she might go into cardiac arrest. He wanted to marry her? "I can put up with your furriness," she responded, holding his gaze. "As long as you can respect my need to know what's going on. No more secrets."

"Agreed." He drew her down and they shared a sweet, soft kiss that brought tears to her eyes.

Before things could progress any further, a knock sounded on the door, and from the hallway Ryder, his voice muffled by the closed door, said, "I've phoned the police. They're due to arrive any moment."

"Guess that means we should go downstairs." Declan pressed a kiss to Pelicia's shoulder. "But first, just so we're clear . . ." He sat up and looked down at her. "You *are* comin' back with me, right?"

She smiled. "Right."

His grin chased away the last of his uncertainty. With a yell of triumph, he rolled out of bed. He went to the dresser and grabbed a pair of clean jeans, underwear, and a T-shirt.

Pelicia slid off the mattress and stepped into her underwear, then picked up the rest of her clothes.

As he pulled on his clothing, he watched her getting dressed, grinning when she arched a brow at him.

"Enjoying the view?" she asked.

"Always."

She sat on the bedside chair and put on her shoes. When she stood again, he took her hand, and they went downstairs together. They had just walked into the parlor when someone knocked on the front door. She and Declan stood in the doorway of the small room as Ryder crossed the foyer.

"Here goes," Ryder said and opened the front door.

Instead of the local constable, Sully pushed his way into the house and glared at Declan with eyes the color of rich, primal amber. "What the hell have you gotten me into, you son of a bitch?"

Don't miss Shannon McKenna's latest, TASTING FEAR, out now from Brava . . .

Liam sounded exhausted. Fed up. She didn't blame him a bit. She was a piece of work. Her mind raced, to come up with a plausible lie. Letting him see how small she felt would just embarrass them both.

She shook her head. "Nothing," she whispered.

He let out a sigh, and leaned back, leaning his head against the back of the couch. Covering his eyes with his hands.

That was when she noticed the condition of his hand. His knuckles were torn and raw, encrusted with blood. God, she hadn't even given a thought for his injuries, his trauma, his shock. She'd just zoned out, floated in her bubble, leaned on him. As if he were an oak.

But he wasn't an oak. He was a man. He'd fought like a demon for her, and risked his life, and gotten hurt, and she was so freaked out and self-absorbed, she hadn't even noticed. She was mortified.

"Liam. Your hand," she fussed, getting up. "Let me get some disinfectant, and some—"

"It's OK," he muttered. "Forget about it."

"Like hell! You're bleeding!" She bustled around, muttering and scolding to hide her own discomfiture, gathering gauze and cotton balls and antibiotic ointment. He let her fuss, a martyred look on his face. After she'd finished taping his hand, she looked at his battered face and grabbed a handful of his polo. "What about the rest of you?"

"Just some bruises," he hedged.

"Where?" she persisted, tugging at his shirt. "Show me."

He wrenched the fabric out of her hand. "If I take off my clothes now, it's not going to be to show you my bruises," he said.

She blinked, swallowed, tried to breathe. Reorganized her mind. There it was. Finally verbalized. No more glossing over it, running away.

"After all this?" Her voice was timid. "You still want to . . . now?"

"Fuck, yes." His tone was savage. "I've wanted it since I laid eyes on you. It's gotten worse ever since. And combat adrenaline gives a guy a hard-on like a railroad spike, even if there weren't a beautiful woman in my face, driving me fucking nuts. Which puts me in a bad place, Nancy. I know the timing sucks for you. The timing's been piss poor since we met, but it never gets any better. It just keeps getting worse."

"Hey. It's OK." She patted his back with a shy, nervous hand. He was usually so calm, so controlled. It unnerved her to see him agitated.

He didn't seem to hear her. "And the worse it gets, the worse I want it," he went on, his voice harsh. "Which makes me feel like a jerk, and a user, and an asshole. Promising to protect you—"

"You did protect me," she reminded him.

"Yeah, and I told you it wasn't an exchange. You don't

owe me sex. You don't owe me anything. And that really fucks me up. Because I can't even remove myself from the situation. I'm scared to death to leave you alone. And that puts me between a rock and a hard place."

She put her finger over his mouth. "Wow," she murmured. "I had no idea you could get worked into such a state. Mr. Super-mellow Liam let's-contemplate-the-beauty-of-the-flower Knightly."

His explosive snort of derision cut her off. She shushed him again, enjoying the feel of his lips beneath her finger. "You're not a jerk or a user," she said gently. "You were magnificent. Thank you. Again."

He looked away. There was a brief, embarrassed pause. "That's very generous of you," he said, trying to flex the wounded hand. "But I'm not fishing for compliments."

"I never thought that you were." She placed her own hand below his, and rested them both gently on his thigh. Her fingers dug into the thick muscle of his quadriceps, through the dirty, bloodstained denim of his jeans. Beneath the fabric, he was so hot. So strong and solid.

She moved her hand up, slowly but surely, stroking higher towards his groin. His breath caught, and then stopped entirely as her fingers brushed the turgid bulge of his penis beneath the fabric.

Here went nothing. "I think I know what you mean, about the hard place," she whispered, swirling her finger-tips over it. Wow. A lot of him. That thick broad, hard stalk just went on and on. "Or was this what you meant when you were referring to the rock?"

His face was a mask of tension, neck muscles clenched, tendons standing out. "You don't have to do this," he said, his voice strangled.

Aw. So sweet. Her fingers closed around him, squeezing. He groaned, and a shudder jarred his body. "I can't seem to stop," she said.

"Watch out, Nancy," he said hoarsely. "If you start something now, there's no stopping it."

She stroked him again, deeper, tighter, a slow caress that wrung a keening gasp from his throat. "I know," she said. "I know."

He reached out, a little awkwardly, clasping his arms around her shoulders, staring into her eyes as if expecting her to bolt.

He pulled her close, enfolding her in his warmth, his power.

Suddenly, they were kissing. She had no idea who had kissed who. The kiss was desperate, achingly sweet. Not a power struggle, not a matter of talent or skill, just a hunger to get as close as two humans could be. He held her like he was afraid she'd be torn away from him.

And Katherine Garbera returns with a great new series,
The Savage Seven. Check out the first book,
THE MERCENARY, out now from Brava . . .

"You've got kind eyes," she said.

"Kind eyes?"

"You're the kind of person who cares about strangers."

"Not really," he said.

She shivered. Was she putting her trust in the wrong man? The image of him coming into the hallway and rescuing her from Burati played in her mind. He was the only man she trusted.

"Sit down and get comfortable," he said. "I'm going to ask you a bunch of questions. I'll record everything you say."

"Okay."

"Before we get started, do you have the stuff you took from Lambert?"

"Yes. I left it upstairs. Should I go get it?" she asked.

"Yes, please."

She left the room but couldn't make herself go upstairs. It was dark and . . . suck it up, she thought. Was she really going to stand here like some kind of wimp? Kirk wasn't going to let anyone into the house or upstairs while she was there.

She took a deep breath and ran up the stairs two at a time. She held on to the railing and then ran flat out to the room she'd been given. She'd left the lights on and she entered the room quietly. She took the pile of things from the dresser and then ran back downstairs.

She hadn't had a chance to look at them and she hoped there was something incriminating in the information. Despite the fact that she was having a hard time believing the man who wooed her in London would want to kill her. Even though she'd seen him with the gun and he'd sent her bodyguard after her. She wondered if she'd simply misinterpreted things.

Kirk still sat where she'd left him. He'd turned on an overhead light now but had left his shirt off. She could see his skin better and realized he had a lot of scars on his back.

"What happened?"

"When?" he asked turning to glance over his shoulder at her.

She walked over and put her hand on his back and moved her fingers lightly over his skin, tracing the scars that covered his back.

"Fire," he said. Standing up, he walked over to his T-shirt and pulled it on.

"You didn't have to put your shirt on," she said.

"Yes, I did."

"I'm sorry if I made you uncomfortable," she said. She had liked touching him. Had been wondering how he'd feel since the moment he'd come to her rescue. Well, to be honest, she hadn't thought of that until they'd been in the car together and she'd started feeling safe.

Her fascination had to stem from the fact that he wasn't like any other man she knew.

"I'm not uncomfortable," he said. "I just don't think it's a good idea for you to touch me."

"Why not?" she asked, because she thought after the way he'd touched her that he was interested in her. Oh, man, what if she was reaching for him because she needed the distraction? The distraction from her memories of today, from the betrayal that Ray had inflicted on her.

"You've just been through a traumatic event and you aren't yourself."

"What makes you sure?"

"I've been a woman's adrenaline lover before."

"What a rude thing to say," she said. She wasn't going to pretend that she hadn't been looking at him in a sexual way, but it was more than that. The attraction she felt for him stemmed from . . . she didn't know what it stemmed from.

"Just calling it like I see it," he said. He walked back over to her and tipped her head up toward his. "I don't want you to regret anything, Olivia."

There it was again—the way he touched her. "I can live with the consequences of my actions."

"Can you?"

"Yes," she said. Then to prove that she could, she went up on tiptoe and kissed him.

Upcoming courses include PRIDE AND PASSION
by Sylvia Day. Turn the page for a preview!

"What type of individual would you consider ideal to play this role of suitor, protector, investigator?" Jasper asked finally.

Eliza's head tilted slightly as she pondered her answer. "He should be quiet, even-tempered, and a proficient dancer."

"How do dullness and the ability to dance signify in catching a possible murderer?" he queried, scowling.

"I did not say 'dull,' Mr. Bond. Kindly do not put words into my mouth. In order to be seen as a true threat for my attentions, he should be someone that everyone would believe I would be attracted to."

"You are not attracted to handsome men?"

"Mr. Bond, I dislike being rude. However, you leave me no choice. The point of fact is that you clearly are not marriage material."

"I am quite relieved to hear a female recognize that," he drawled.

"How could anyone doubt it?" She made a sweeping gesture with her hand. "I can more easily picture you in a swordfight or fisticuffs than I can see you enjoying an afternoon of croquet or after dinner chess. I am an intellectual, sir. And while I do not mean to say that you are lacking in mental acuity, you are obviously built for more physically strenuous pursuits."

"I see."

"Why, anyone would take one look at you and ascertain that you are not like the others at all! It would be evident straightaway that I would never consider a man such as you with even remote seriousness. Quite frankly, sir, you are not my type of male."

A slow smile began in his dark eyes, then moved downward to curve his lips. It was arresting. Slightly wicked. Troublesome.

Eliza did not like trouble overmuch.

He glanced at her uncle, the earl. "Please forgive me, my lord, but I must speak bluntly in regards to this subject. Most especially because this is a matter of life and death."

"Quite right," Melville agreed. "Straight to the point, I always say. Time is too precious to waste on inanities."

"Agreed." Jasper glanced back at Eliza, his mischievous smile widening. "Miss Martin, forgive me, but I must point out that your inexperience is limiting your understanding of the situation."

"Inexperience with what?"

"Men. More precisely, fortune hunting men."

"I would have you know," she retorted, bristling, "that in my six years on the marriage market I have had more than enough experience with gentlemen in want of funds."

"Then why," he drawled, "do you not know that they are successful for reasons far removed from social suitability?"

Eliza blinked. "I beg your pardon?"

"Women do not marry fortune hunters because they can dance and sit quietly. They marry them for their appearance and physical prowess—two attributes you have already established that I have."

"I do not see—"

"Clearly, you do not, so I shall explain." His smile continued to grow. "Fortune hunters who flourish do not strive to satisfy a woman's intellectual needs. Those can be met through friends and acquaintances. They do not seek to provide the type of companionship one enjoys in social settings or with a game table between them. Again, there are others who can do so."

"Mr. Bond—"

"No, they strive to satisfying the only position that is theirs alone, a position that some men make no effort to excel in. So rare is the skill, that many a woman will disregard other considerations in favor of it."

She growled softly. "Will you get to the point, please?"

"Fornication," his lordship said, before returning to mumbling to himself.

Eliza shot to her feet. "I beg your pardon?"

As courtesy dictated, both her uncle and Jasper rose along with her.

"I prefer to call it 'seduction,'" Jasper said, his eyes laughing.

"I call it ridiculous," she rejoined, hands on her hips. "In the grand scheme of life, do you collect how little time a person spends abed when compared to other activities?"

His gaze dropped to her hips. The smile became a full-blown grin. "That truly depends on who else is occupying said bed."

"Dear heavens." Eliza shivered at the look Jasper was giving her now. It was certainly *not* a bug-under-the-glass look. No, it was more triumphant. Challenged. Anticipatory. For some unknown, godforsaken reason she had managed to prod the man's damnable masculine pride into action. "While I acknowledge that a man's brain might traverse such channels of thought, I cannot see a woman's doing so."

"But is it not men whom you wish to affect with this scheme?"

She bit her lower lip. Clever, clever man. He knew quite well that she had no idea how men's minds worked. She had no notion of whether he was correct, or simply tenacious about securing work.

"Give me a sennight," he offered. "One week to prove both my point and competency. If at the end you do not agree with one or the other, I will accept no payment for services rendered."